IN THE MOOD FOR LOVE

HARPER BLISS

Copyright © 2012 to 2015 by Harper Bliss
All the stories in this book have been previously published as standalone titles and some have appeared in the anthologies A Hotter State, Endless Summer and Can't Get Enough, all published by Ladylit Publishing.

Cover design by Caroline Manchoulas
Published by Ladylit Publishing – a division of Q.P.S. Projects Limited - Hong Kong
ISBN-13 978-988-79123-8-5

Contents

I Still Remember

HER HAIR IS STYLED DIFFERENTLY NOW, but her eyes are still the same dark-chocolate brown. They stare at me with the same amazement that buzzes through my unsuspecting bones. Amy Waters. Twenty years ago I loved her with an intensity I didn't understand. I never told her, but looking at her now, at the way the edges of her mouth quirk up, suppressing that distinct pout I dreamed of for months on end, I realise she must have known.

"I have the name Jane Smith here in my appointment book." Amy's eyes quiz me. Or maybe they mock me for the dreariness of my chosen alias. I never was really good at reading her. Too much emotion in the way.

"People tend to freak out when I book under my real name."

"And they don't when you show up?" She bites her lip. There are many reasons why this situation could unsettle her. None can be as nerve-racking as unexpectedly standing eye-to-eye with the girl—a woman now—I silently adored in high school.

"Sure, but then at least I'm present to manage the fuss." I

look different in real life than I do on TV. Some call it dressing down, but I'm never more comfortable than in jeans and t-shirt. On the air, my face is covered in layers of make-up and the top half of my body—the only part visible—is styled down to a tee by Jake and Andrew, *The Morning News with Elise Frost*'s wardrobe managers. Sans make-up and in leisure wear, I hardly ever get recognised. This time it's different though. Amy and I, we have history. And I had no way of knowing she owned The Body Spa.

"How long are you in town for?" Is that a tinge of accusation in her tone? Of course, it's my fault we lost touch. We had laid out our plans. That's what best friends do in high school. They think it will be the two of them forever, think that ten years down the line they'll be bridesmaids at each other's wedding. Only, I always knew my future didn't hold the kind of wedding Amy started planning for herself as soon as she turned twelve.

"For the weekend. It's dad's sixtieth." I shuffle my weight around as I try to identify the tumbling feeling in my stomach. So much has changed since we last saw each other a few days after our high school graduation. I barely even thought of Amy the past few years. We're grown-ups now, and as good as strangers. Still, all that was left unsaid between us seems to rush through my mind now.

"How is Ralph?" Amy's voice is still a well of calmness. It always was, even when she leafed through bridal magazines at the age of sixteen and dreamed out loud about marrying Brett. I wonder what happened to her dreams. Does she have the two suburb-required children? Good heavens, did she marry Brett?

I shrug off Amy's question because I don't want to discuss my father. This small talk seems so inappropriate, so lukewarm, so out of sync with my memories of her. "How are you, Amy?" I ask, painting on a smile.

She wears a black spaghetti strap tank top, showing off spectacular collarbones. Her dark curls are pinned up into a bun, but she always had a mane that couldn't be tamed and a few stray ones frame her face. She looks tanned and healthy.

"Twice married, twice divorced." She wiggles her fingers as if she's proud of the fact they hold no rings. "You?"

I can't help but think of Celia and how we left things back in New York. She moved out more than three months ago but the bed still feels empty without her. And didn't I just ask Amy how *she* was doing? I didn't even hint at inquiring about her marital status, but here she is, offering up the information freely, as if it sums up her entire life since we lost touch.

"My love life's a bit of a disaster, but I can't complain about the rest." I smile apologetically. I don't know why I always do that when I refer to my career and how it has skyrocketed over the last few years.

"I watch the news every morning. It was so strange at first, you know. That you were this girl I played hooky with…" She pauses for a moment. "Shared my first cigarette with." The gentle lines on her face crinkle into a melancholic expression before she sends me a wide smile. The Amy smile. The one that always got me. "And gosh, you come across so well on the screen, Eli—" She hesitates again. "Do you still go by Eli?"

No one has called me Eli since Amy. Eli expired the day I left town—and Amy. I shake my head and grin, because I can't help myself.

"Ahum." A girl in white slacks who I hadn't even noticed before clears her throat. I suspect she's my designated massage therapist.

"If you don't mind, Sarita," Amy addresses her. "I'll be taking care of Ms Smith myself."

"Sure." Sarita turns on her heels and leaves the reception area.

"I hope that's all right," Amy is quick to say.

My pulse quickens at the thought of Amy's hands on my body. "Of course." I give her my camera smile—the one that hides everything.

"Please, follow me." She moves from behind the reception counter and leads me to a door on the right. As teenagers, we were always about the same height, but she seems so much taller now. She wears a pair of black linen trousers that flow around her long legs. We walk into a waiting area with low couches and soothing music. "Would you like some tea first?"

"Sure." I nod eagerly. One part of me can't wait to get on Amy's massage table, but at the same time my heart hammers frantically in my chest. I watch her as she pours two cups of tea from a pot next to the kettle. Her movements are graceful and easy, just like I remember.

We'd been swimming in a small pond behind Amy's house. It was cordoned off from their garden by a bunch of pine trees and, as the afternoon progressed, the sun dipped away behind the trees, leaving us with early evening shadows. We were wet from the water and the sky was the colour of summer: blue streaked with soft yellows and dashes of pink I never understood. The colours that would forever remind me of Amy.

It was the height of my crush on her, a few weeks before we'd leave high school forever. All my energy went into trying to keep my eyes off her as she adjusted her bathing suit while we let the last of the heat dry our skin. I tried so hard not to look at her that all I did was stare in the distance.

"What's wrong, Eli?" Amy playfully pinched me in the

side, catching me by surprise. I swathed her hand away as if it were a vile mosquito, quickly regretting my impulsive reaction. To mask the turmoil ripping me apart inside, I shot her a quick grin before rolling on top of her and pinning her arms above her head.

I stared down at her, every cell in my body tingling. Her dark eyes smiled up at me and a surge of something I couldn't control swelled inside my gut. I closed my eyes for a second and saw what was going to happen next. I was going to lean down and kiss her. I saw myself do it on the back of my eyelids. I could almost taste her lips and smell beyond the heady mixture of sun and lotion on her skin.

When I opened my eyes, it seemed as if hours had passed, but it was still the same Amy squirming below me on the grass. It was the same pond giving away its summery sparkle to the falling darkness. Amy's eyes were still the same mocha brown and her hair the same shock of wild curls, but I had changed. I'd never come so close and suddenly I realised it was the closest I would ever get.

"Eli?" Amy's voice never really suited her until now. It was always the voice of a grown woman with endless legs, strong hands, and pronounced collarbones.

"Sorry. Miles away." I take the cup of tea she hands me and, awkward as I feel, sip from it immediately. The tea is scalding hot and I burn the tip of my tongue but I don't say anything.

Amy looks at me over the rim of her cup while she, wisely, blows on it to cool the liquid. Her eyes radiate a softness I don't recognise. But we are different people now, even though I feel myself slipping into my teenage skin again—and adoring Amy silently. Me, of the endless chatter on TV, the never-ending banter I've made a career of. A few minutes with Amy and I'm sixteen again.

"Why don't we get on with it." She places her cup on a small table next to the chair she sits in, one leg folded over the other. She looks at me, her eyes almost watery now, and in that one glance I see it. In that instant, I realise she always knew. "I give a mean massage, even if I do say so myself." She erases the moment with a quip and a smile and I don't know what to think.

The words *massage* and *Amy* seem to flash in my mind in big red letters. My brain can't process the two of them together, as if it has neatly shelved any physicality away from the memory of Amy.

This morning when I drove past The Body Spa in my rental car, it just looked like a good place to book a massage. Now, it seems to have become a feverish dream location from puberty. A throwback to a time in my life I remember fondly, but don't revisit very often.

"Sure." I get up and we stand shoulder to shoulder, just like years ago in gym class.

"This way." Was that a tremble in Amy's voice?

Our arms brush together and, despite being fully dressed, it still has an instant impact on the flow of blood in my veins.

"It's only a massage," I tell myself. I treat myself to one every weekend. Usually, I nod off about halfway through to wake up invigorated after. Usually, the person administering the massage is Raj, a man with golden hands whom I'm not attracted to in the slightest.

The situation is quite different today, because, no matter how I twist or turn it—no matter how many years have passed—Amy is still that dark-haired girl who walked to school with me every single day of our senior year. She's a woman now, but twenty years ago, my heart beat in my throat every time she waited for me at the corner of the street. Emotions I deemed erased by life a long time ago, seep back inside my brain as we walk to the therapy room.

And I know what comes next. I'm a massage aficionado and, usually, I don't even think twice about it. It's second nature to me and massages are simply not a clothed activity.

"You can undress over there." Amy points to a door. "You'll find a towel. Please take everything off."

She might as well have planted a kiss on my lips, that's how flushed I suddenly feel.

Amy's tone is professional though, as is her demeanour. She adjusts the volume of the music in the room. "Do you mind if I put on something a bit unconventional for a place like this?"

I shake my head as she locks her iPhone in the dock without waiting for my reply. I already know what she has in mind.

Legs shaking, I head for the locker room. I close the door and lean my head against it for a brief moment. From the other side of the wood I hear the first notes of 'Round Here'. Amy and I listened to it endlessly the year we turned sixteen. No song could ever be more ours.

Nostalgia washes over me as I slowly undress. I scan myself in the mirror on the wall. A TV job has made me vain enough to hire a personal trainer. For all its shallowness, I take great pleasure in spotting a hint of tricep when I watch myself back on screen. I run a finger over my arm, but can't begin to imagine what it will feel like when it will be Amy's finger. I know that I somehow need to steel myself for what's to come. But it's just me and a towel in a dressing room. And a slew of ragged memories.

I wrap myself in the plush cotton of the towel. It's wide enough to cover me from the top of my breasts to under my knees and long enough to fit snugly around my body. I take a deep breath before stepping back into the therapy room.

Amy waits for me with a big smile, Adam Duritz's voice humming in the background. I may have dreamed of a situation like this twenty years ago—Adam's warm voice and me about to get naked for an eager Amy—but if I did, I forced myself to forget long ago. My brain is busy taking it all in. I'm also nervous and, truth be told, quite turned-on by the sentimental strangeness of it all.

"Please, get comfortable on the table while I wash my hands." Amy turns away from me to give me the privacy I need to settle on the table. I climb on and lie down on my belly while covering my backside with the towel. My face finds the hole at the head of the table and I try to at least pretend I'm relaxed.

My field of vision is limited to a basket of flowers on the floor below me. I can only rely on sound now.

"I prefer not to talk during a session as I feel it hinders relaxation." Amy's words float above my head. I'm fully aware of the nakedness of my skin and I wonder how she sees it. I wonder how this makes her feel. Her footsteps approach. She has taken off her shoes and she's barefoot. She adjusts the towel briefly and the air that flows underneath is enough to instigate a mad pitter-patter in my chest.

Her hands are so close, almost as close as I dreamed they would be when we were teenagers.

All my memories of Amy seem to be bathed in the warm colours of summer. We'd ridden our bikes to a record store a few miles away, a CD-sized plastic bag dangling from both of our handlebars. When we arrived at our spot by the pond in her backyard, she tore the wrapper off the case. The album cover was orange, on it the title *August & Everything After* seemingly scribbled in handwriting. We'd only heard 'Mr. Jones' and 'Round Here' on the radio and had no idea this record would become the soundtrack to our friendship, the notes rousing nostalgia from my soul forever after.

Amy pried the in-lay from the case and unearthed a pen from her bag. Without explanation, she wrote something on the back of the booklet and handed it to me.

It read: 'Amy + Eli Forever'.

She grabbed my copy from my hands and repeated the process, marking both our CDs with what looked like a couple's inscription.

Maybe I should have said something then.

Amy starts the massage by lightly running her fingertips over my entire body. The motion is quick and over in a flash, but my skin breaks out in goosebumps nonetheless. I need to use all my energy to hold back a sigh. The next thing I feel is the drizzle of warm oil on my back and shoulders. She rubs it on my skin before applying any pressure. I melt into the table the way the lotion does on my skin.

Gradually, her fingers dig deeper into my flesh. Her thumbs press into the muscles surrounding my neck and I think I must be in heaven.

I love a good massage and I treat myself to one as much as I can, but this is something entirely different. I can feel my nipples poke into the soft towel covering the table already and my breath does not come with the relaxed huff-and-puff that I know from massages administered by Raj.

When we were teens, Amy and I spent the majority of our time together, but our relationship wasn't a tactile one. Neither one of us were big on hugs and impulsive displays of affection. We expressed our friendship by always being there and nodding our heads to the drum beat of the Counting Crows. God knows what would have happened if Amy were a hugger.

Amy's fingers wander along my spine and seem to dent my skin permanently. The difference between being touched intimately by someone you care for as opposed to someone whose hands you've simply come to admire is striking. Every touch of her hands on my skin—and I seem to count a hundred per second, but my brain lost processing power a while ago—releases a current of energy in my flesh. I know it's sexual and the pureness of my first bouts of teenage lust bubbles to the surface. Nothing happened between Amy and me then, and I have no reason to assume it will now, but I am Eli again. Beneath Amy's hands, there's no sign of the national TV news anchor. There is only the memory of those very first seeds of longing, innocent but oh so present. Then and now.

She stretches her body over mine to reach the small of my back, an area dubbed by Raj as 'my problem zone'. I sit in a chair most of the day. That's how glamorous my life is.

It's as if Amy can sense it—years of experience must have done that to her fingers—and she pushes deeper to undo the knots in my muscles. And I simply can't help but wonder what those fingers must feel like inside. What it would do to me if they slipped. I shut down the thought as quickly as I can, because I can't go there. Although it seems like the perfect place for it, this is no time for thoughts like that. The towel beneath me feels fairly absorbent, but I fear I may slide off in a puddle of my own wetness if I go down that route.

Her fingers knead the flesh of my back and shoulders. Up and down they roam for minutes on end and—despite myself and the feverish thoughts crashing through my brain —I'm about to reach that state of zen-like calm, of shutting off the world and just returning to myself. But then it happens. Her finger brushes against the side of my breast, which protrudes a bit as I lay on my belly.

Amy doesn't apologise, she simply continues, but it feels as if my life has just changed considerably. As if the world has shifted and new possibilities have been born. This happens all the time during massage therapy, of course. The number of times Raj has accidentally brushed his fingers along my breast equals the number of times I haven't cared an iota about it. But the furtive skating of Amy's finger along my skin there feels more like a promise. An opening. Maybe a declaration.

Both of her pinkies glide along on either side now, and I never before realised how sensitive my skin is there. Maybe this is just the way she does her job. Or maybe she has a few buried emotions rising to the surface as well.

Every time her fingers dip a little too low, a flash of heat tumbles through my bones, all the way from my spine to my toes. Goosebumps have made way for hot flashes and then—oh no—an involuntary moan escapes me. I snap my mouth shut as soon as it happens, but it's too late. I've given myself away. I lay there dying a little bit, my face pressed into a hole, my eyes fixed on Amy's toes. Her nails are painted a deep red and—I may be losing my mind by now—it's the most beautiful colour I've ever seen.

But Amy is a true professional and she pretends nothing happened. She must have heard though, her ears are not that far removed from my over-enthusiastic mouth and the volume of the music is high enough to make a point, but low enough to easily fade into the background when not given any attention.

She moves her field of action more to the middle of my back again, with long kneading motions of her hands. She covers a lot of ground and drags the heel of her hand all the way down to the curve of my ass, her fingers slipping briefly underneath the edge of the towel. This expansive movement also causes her belly to sweep against the top of my head every time she stretches forward, which does not help with the hot flashes I seem to be experiencing at regular intervals now. So much so, in fact, that I can't distinguish the flashes anymore from the fire that has started simmering beneath my skin. How long can I hold off the inevitable explosion?

I never officially told Amy I'm a lesbian. She probably read about it in a gossip magazine when it went public a few years ago. Maybe this is her revenge. But we were sixteen back then, and while the knowledge of something being different was always very present within me, I hardly had a clue myself. Twenty years ago the word *lesbian* was not one you heard often. I knew I had a mad crush on Amy and sometimes I simply believed that it was completely normal but just not outspoken, while other times the sheer strength of my feelings for her obliterated any notion of it being different. All I knew was that I loved her and that, in the end, she could never love me the same way.

After a last soft caress of my back, Amy pads to the middle of the table. Without saying a word, she removes the towel. At first, I think she's just adjusting it—that touching me underneath it has made it slip—but she doesn't put it back. That's something Raj never does.

The conditioned air of the room breezes across the skin of my buttocks and a new onslaught of lust rips through me. If this is revenge, or a test, I don't stand a chance. But I don't move and let Amy carry on wordlessly. Adam Duritz launches into 'Anna Begins' and I still know the lyrics by heart so I try to focus on those instead. They're complicated and quick so that works for about thirty seconds, until Amy drizzles oil on the back of my thighs and then, all the way up the burning cheeks of my bum.

Whatever happened to a simple neck massage, I wonder, when her fingers hit my skin. They're soft and warm and I melt again. But this time, after the brushing of her fingers against my breasts and the exposing of my butt, I melt differently, as if the wetness of my centre has spread throughout my body and has liquified every bone beneath my skin.

When her fingers dip a little too low the first time, I have no doubt she knows exactly what she's doing. She still applies pressure to the muscles in my thighs, but it's as if I can sense her focus shifting. She doesn't pay nearly as much attention to the outside of my legs as to the inside, but every time she's on the verge of touching me really inappropriately, she pulls back.

I can hear her inhale and exhale quickly over the music and I try to determine if this is the breath of a woman performing a massage or foreplay.

Then, just when I think I'm about to dissolve in a puddle of my own wetness, her hands move to my calves. Every single one of the cells between my belly button and my knees throbs wildly. A sensation I could probably cope with if this was a stranger venturing into the territory of a massage with a happy ending, but this is Amy Waters, the girl I wrote bad poetry for in high school. The girl who once told me that the two lone freckles on the left of my nose were the cutest thing she ever saw, after which I spent at least two sleepless nights thinking up ways to grow more.

Amy's nails trail along my ankles, but they don't stay there very long. Up they come again, and the closer they get to the massive erogenous zone every inch of skin within an arm's length distance of my bum has become, the more moisture I can feel trickle out of me. Can she see? The room is dimly lit and my face—with cheeks as flushed as a blazing fire—is safely hidden in the hole of the table, but is my excitement visible to her at all?

The answer comes in the shape of her finger tracking the line where my butt becomes thigh. I know enough about massages to realise this is not standard procedure in respected establishments. When her bold finger meets the wetness spreading from between my legs, it doesn't waver. Instead, it dives lower and lingers there, barely moving. Instinctively, I find myself spreading wider. I didn't mean to, but if I try to close my legs now it could be perceived as disapproval and I don't want this to stop.

Amy takes advantage of the better access I offer her and now traces the tip of her finger along my pussy lips. Up and down it goes, skimming my lips, which are swollen and soaked and ready to be parted. Has she ever even touched a woman like this?

Her fingertips continue to play with my pussy non-intrusively, almost tickling, but it's enough to send wave after wave of smouldering heat through my blood. I'm afraid to make a noise that will break the spell she's under. I'm afraid to face the consequences of having her stop now she's gone this far.

Her fingers start probing deeper, sliding between my folds and I inadvertently press myself against them, meeting her lazy strokes. It feels as if my entire body has transformed into a slithering mass of want. I'm close to abandon, close to asking her to please fuck me, when her fingers retreat.

My heart thunders so furiously beneath my rib cage I fear my torso might pulse upwards with every beat.

"Turn around, please," she says as if this is the normal midway point of any massage therapy session. But there's a strain in her voice, a slight tremor informing me she might just be as turned on as I am.

And I want nothing more than to flip over, but then I have to face her. How can I meet her gaze after she has touched me like that? But I'm not the one who started it. I only came here for a massage.

I free my head from the hole and push myself up slowly. Before looking up, I try to swallow away the nerves bunching up in my throat. There are a lot of things I want to say, but I don't want to ruin the moment by speaking.

Amy is fumbling with something at the sink when I finally turn around. She has her back to me and, silently, I lie down and wait for her.

"Close your eyes," she whispers as she approaches.

I do as I'm told.

The process of sprinkling oil on my skin is repeated. A drop crashes down on my erect nipple and I can sense Amy's hesitation before her fingers descend on my flesh and spread the lotion. She stands at the head of the table, her belly close to my scalp again, and I can hear her sharp intake of breath as her fingertip brushes my nipple.

It's different lying on my back, all exposed like that. I try to keep still as Amy's fingers knead my breasts, but it's impossible. She's watching me now. She's seeing the emotions running across my face and the way my skin crinkles into goosebumps as she touches me. I only came to town to celebrate my dad's birthday and I had no way of preparing for this level of intimacy. I decide there and then I have two choices. Shut off my brain and enjoy the physical bliss Amy's hands provide—no matter the emotional fall-out later. Or do as I did years ago. Work myself into a frenzy over how she makes me feel, decide I can't deal with it anymore, and leave.

But this is now, and Amy's hands have already ventured much further than I ever dreamed they would. She's the one who slipped her fingers between my legs and whose nails are now tracing circles around my nipples.

"Oh god," I groan as she pinches my nipple and leaves me with no choice at all.

"Don't move," she says, her voice hoarse and throaty above my head.

And I stay still but I have to open my eyes. I have to see her. Just as our gazes lock, her hands squeeze my breasts.

I could cry for the teenager I was once was. A young body filled to the brim with an inexplicable burgeoning lust for Amy. If time is supposed to heal all wounds, what is it doing now? Coming home is always a fleeting exercise in dredging up the past, no matter who you see or don't see. But then you leave and forget about it all over again, a bit more with every departure. How will I ever leave this behind?

Amy's eyes seem to tell me everything I need to know—in this moment, anyway. Because what really happened to us are the things that didn't happen. The conversation we never had. The feelings I never shared. If this is her way of saying we're okay, then I'm fine with that.

She gives my breasts one last gentle squeeze before abandoning them. Her left hand trails downward along my chest as she walks to the side of the table. She leans her hip against it and I follow her with my eyes. Her face is tanned, but I can easily spot the blush below her cheekbones.

She searches for my eyes again, and arches up her eyebrows a fraction, as if asking for permission. It's a little late for that, I think to myself, but I know what she means. The time for foreplay has ended.

I want what's going to happen next so much, my body breaks out into a shiver. She puts her hand on my belly to calm me down, but it hardly has the required effect. Her fingers already point south, to that moist mess of a pussy of mine.

Shouldn't it have been the other way around, I wonder? Should I not have been the one seducing her? But this role reversal—if you will—turns me on more than the prospect of Amy's fingers inside of me.

It reminds me of hot summer nights alone in my bed. I left the curtains open to see the last of the light fade away, while I dreamed of Amy's face before she kissed me and told me it was all real.

It can't be more real now. Amy's one hand travels lower, while her other one stays on my belly, driving her nails into my skin. I spread wider, because it's all I ever wanted to do for Amy.

Her eyes are on mine when the first fingertip enters me. Something shimmers in the chocolate brown of them. As her finger slips all the way in, I realise it's lust. The same lust shaking my bones.

It's more shock than anything else rattling through me as Amy starts to fuck me slowly, almost leisurely. A hint of a smile plays on her lips, as if this was the only possible outcome of us running into each other the way we have.

All the years of friendship we shared flash through my mind in that moment. The time I almost kissed her. The day we took dozens of pictures at a photo booth, my face drawn into a serious frown in all of them because Amy was sitting on my lap.

But Amy has her finger inside of me and, as she slides it back, I feel the tip of another one getting ready to slip in. And yes, this is sex—unmistakably so—but it's also much more than that. My pelvis bucks upward to meet Amy's thrusts. Her gaze doesn't waver and I feel moisture build behind my eyes. Because this is too much. The essence of what is happening right now has been with me as a fantasy for more than twenty years.

In the silence between two Counting Crows songs, I can make out the sucking noise Amy's fingers produce between my legs. It stokes the fire in my belly even more, and when her other hand starts to travel south as well, her fingers tickling the trimmed hair down there, I'm about to spontaneously combust.

I know she's going for my clit and I know that when she reaches it, I'll be lost. The moment will pass forever. Confusion, nostalgia and years of pent-up lust descend from my mind into my blood.

Amy thrusts deep with the two fingers of her left hand as her right index finger brushes the side of my clit. My muscles contract at the touch of her finger against my swollen bud. I want to pull her close and kiss her, but Amy is calling the shots, and I don't want to break the spell she's under.

She finds a rhythm with her hands. A deep stroke with one hand, while the fingers of the other circle my clit. It's more than enough to send me on my way to the deliverance I've been waiting for what feels like forever.

Amy in her mum's high heels. Amy in boxer shorts and a tank top at her cousin's sleep over. Amy by the pond, careless and with the promise of everything shimmering in the darkness of her eyes. Amy right here, right now. Eyes blazing and fingers on fire inside of me. Her muscles working underneath her skin as she takes me.

I throw my head back because her glance is too much for me to take in that moment when my body surrenders. It all crashes through me, lightning quick fireballs reaching the end of my fingers and my toes at the same time. The walls of my pussy clamping tightly around her fingers. The pleasure that shoots up inside of me through her hands, which are, in the end, mere extensions of her eyes and what I've seen pool in them. I had to wait twenty years and maybe that's why it feels so good, life-changing even, but definitely shattering the world as I know it for a brief instant.

Amy doesn't slide her fingers out of me immediately. She leaves them inside to linger for a few seconds as I find her eyes again. I know that mine are filled with tears of release and a slew of other emotions I don't have the presence of mind to identify.

"Jesus," I say, because, at times like this, it always seems like the only appropriate thing to say.

Amy looks at me in disbelief, her eyes wide and her lips slightly parted. As if she's just slipped back into her skin after an out-of-body experience. Gently, her fingers leave me and I have as much a clue of what to say as she has.

Mute, she stares at her hands and I know, despite being the one naked on a massage table, I have to step in.

My muscles are weak and soft from the massage and the climax, but I pull myself together. "Hey," I say, while I push myself up. I shoot her a reassuring smile. "You really do give a mean massage."

She seems to snap out of her trance and starts looking around the room. I hope for the towel she took off me at the beginning of our session. I'm not sure if it's possible to feel more naked than I am, but I do.

Thankfully, Amy locates the towel on a chair behind her and, instead of simply handing it to me, she steps toward me and wraps it around my bare skin.

"I wish I knew what to say," she whispers in my ear as her arms fold around me.

For all the intimacy we just shared, this unexpected hug touches me more than Amy's fingers inside of me.

In response, I curl my arms around her waist and hold her. I realise this is the first time I've intently touched her this way.

"Whatever it was you wanted to say, you've said it loud and clear." My cheek is pressed against Amy's chest and I can hear her heart hammer away at a ridiculous pace.

I can't help myself, because the next thing I know, my fingers snake down her back, finding the hem of her tank top, wanting desperately to feel the skin underneath.

She gives me one last squeeze before freeing herself from our hug. She doesn't pull completely away though, and in the motion, my fingers wander to her sides. I look up at her and I can't shake the feeling there's something more going on here than two old friends reconnecting in an unexpectedly physical way.

"Eli, I…" she starts. Her fingers play with the white towel that's slung around my body. "I really don't know what came over me."

"I'm not complaining." I slip off the table so I can stand tall and face her properly. The towel starts sliding down, but Amy catches it and fastens it with a tight fold above my breasts.

Again, it's an intimate gesture. There's only one way I know how to acknowledge it. My hands are back on her waist and I pull her close. The short, ragged puffs of her breath travel across my cheeks. Slowly, I slant my head to the side and lean in for that kiss I should have gone for years ago.

Amy doesn't display any signs of hesitation as our lips meet. I figure it's a little late for doubts after her fingers brought me to orgasm mere minutes ago.

My fingers travel the length of her arms, all the way to her face, where I cup her chin. The towel slips off me anyway—and Amy lets it—but I'm past caring. I'm ready to be naked with Amy again.

Amy's nails trail along the skin of my back as our tongues dance with one another. The kiss seems to freeze time and I have no idea how long we've been at it when we finally break apart.

"We should talk," Amy says, but her breath comes out in chopped puffs and her body language doesn't exactly signal a talking mood.

But I probably need this conversation more than Amy, and I'm dying to hear what she has to say, so I nod before ducking down to grab the towel again.

"That thing obviously does not want to stay on your body," she jokes. "I can see why."

For an instant, I'm flabbergasted, and a flush rises to my

cheeks. While I'm still grappling to come up with a response, Amy moves in again and pecks me on my burning cheek. "There's a shower through there." She points to a door behind me. "Take your time. I'll wait for you at reception."

I grab my belongings from the dressing room and head for the shower, all the while wondering if I'm not trapped in a dream. I don't want to wash away the oil Amy rubbed into my skin, but as I do and my hands caress the spots she just did, my mind already wanders to the next step. I'm not leaving town until I've touched Amy the way she has touched me.

After I've put myself together as best as I can, smelling of lavender and satisfaction, I find my way to the reception area. My legs are still a bit shaky and my cheek still tingles where Amy kissed it last. I half-expect reception to not be there and wake up in my old bedroom in my parents' house, sweaty from a passionate dream. But there's Amy, leaning against the reception desk, one ankle crossed over the other. She looks so different from when I first walked in. A lot has changed since then.

"I presume you have a party to go to tonight." Amy's voice is playful, almost seductive.

I remember the reason why I'm in town and all the prying questions on my relationship status I have to look forward to. "Yes. Oh, joy." I check my watch. "But it only starts at seven."

Amy draws her lips into a pensive pout. "Let me check with the boss if I can take the rest of the day off." She tucks her chin in and looks at her own chest. "Great. She agrees." She sends me a wide smile and I'm sixteen again.

We exit The Body Spa together and I wait for her initiative as we stand around on the parking lot in front.

"Did you know I live in my parents' old house now?"

Due to the fact I appear on TV five times a week, Amy

probably has a lot more superficial knowledge of me than I of her. I realise I know nothing about her life. "Really?" But, oh gosh, the memories that place holds.

"Yep. Do you still know the way?"

I nod. I could never forget. "See you there in ten minutes."

I step into my rental and notice my hand is shaking when I put the key in the ignition. I'm going to Amy Waters's house. It's the only thought occupying my mind as I drive the route I could take blindfolded—still, after all these years.

I used to ride my bike to Amy's house. An old beat-up BMX I inherited from my older brother. I'd attach cards from a deck to the spokes with clothespins and pretend it was the scooter my parents would never allow me to have.

The Waters house is still in the same spot in the same street, but that's about all that still resembles the memory I have of it. The bricks are no longer red and the roof is flat instead of slated.

I sit staring at the sleek, whitewashed walls of the rectangular shape in front of me, when a knock on my car window wakes me from my daze.

"Coming?" Amy's arched-up eyebrows ask—just like they've always done.

I get out of the car and, apparently, I can't hide the look of bewilderment on my face.

"If this surprises you, wait until you see the inside," Amy teases. But I'm not really interested in the inside of her house —not for now, anyway. I want to go round the back and see if the pond is still there. That pond where we passed hours of our youth just lying around and dreaming out loud of the kind of life I knew I would never lead.

Amy catches my glance and it's as if she can read my mind. "Come on." She curls her fingers around my wrist and drags me to the path circling around the house. "You can admire my flair for interior design later."

My pace quickens as we approach the backyard. To my surprise, not a lot has changed. The pine trees are still there, and so is the pond. I can see its surface flicker through the spaces between the trees.

A rush of tears pricks behind my eyes. I have to breathe in deeply to stop them from crashing through.

"I've spent a fortune redoing the house, but this is still my favourite spot." Amy stands behind me and her voice sounds exactly the same as then, except, everything is different now. I turn around to face her.

"Did you know?" I ask, the words coming out a bit shaken.

Her face mellows into a soft expression foreign to me. Is this how she looked at her husbands when they proposed? How did she regard them when the divorces came through? But I'm no different, not having had a romantic relationship last longer than a few years. I broke my record with Celia, who, in the end, I also successfully managed to chase away. I blame the job. Presenting the morning news doesn't make for a lot of date nights. Or maybe the right woman simply hasn't come along yet.

"How could I not?" Her fingers intertwine with mine. "You were my best friend, Eli. Of course I knew."

My heart beats in my throat. Why did I never say anything? What if our years of friendship turned out to be one big missed opportunity? What if it could have been so much more than me sneaking glances and pining for her secretly?

In my teenage mind, Amy was the cruel one for, suppos- edly, never being able to return my affections. But in the end, I was the one who left without looking back.

This baggage hangs heavy in the air between us, thick like the remnants of summer clouding the late afternoon.

"I'm sorry for leaving like that." The words tumble out of me like a confession, like something that should have been said ages ago.

"Hey," she yanks my arms up by the wrists and places my hands on her hips, "I always told myself you simply loved me too much to stay." Amy was always the brave, hopeful one. But when she puts it like that, my defences against the tears burning behind my eyes crumble.

"Gosh." Tears stream down my cheeks and I can't wipe them away because Amy is holding my wrists.

"You're here now." Amy leans in and presses her lips against my cheek.

It's the simple truth. I'm here, by Amy's pond and she just kissed me again. I'm no longer Eli the lovesick teenager. I'm Elise Frost, the morning news anchor who caused a riot on a lesbian website when she dared to exchange her signature glasses for a new model.

"I am." Amy's been running this show long enough. Unafraid of whatever happens next, I loosen my wrists from her grip. I bring my hands to her cheeks and draw her near. When our lips meet, the past falls away and I easily shake off whatever's left of my teenage self. We're two grown women and this couldn't be more perfect.

While our lips meet again and again, I trace my fingertips over the skin of her arms until they find the hem of her tank top. I don't just want to get underneath, I want it off of her. I hoist it over her chest and break the kiss to pull the top over her head. I've ogled those collarbones long enough. As gorgeous as they are, I need more.

Heat travels through me at high speed and I do hope there will be time for slow caresses and endless gazing into each other's eyes later, because I can't stop myself now. My actions border on the edge of frantic when I pull the straps of her bra down and scoop a soft breast out of its cup. Feeling its weight in my hand brings me pause, though, and I stop to worship it. My lips are drawn to the dark brown of Amy's nipple and when I taste it, I taste her. I taste afternoons riding our bikes along the high street, looking for excitement. I taste the sun that slanted across the tops of the pine trees when we sunbathed in this very spot. I taste our history.

Amy's hands are in my hair, her fingertips zapping electricity through my scalp. I fall onto my knees and drag her with me onto the grass. It's an unexpected struggle to get her bra off amidst the tangle of limbs we have become, but I want her naked beneath me more than I've wanted anything in my life.

I think about the times I laid down next to her on this indestructible patch of grass, dreaming up the courage to do something about the heat that throbbed under my skin.

Between the mad frenzy of tugging off our clothes and getting our hands on each other's flesh, I see all of my dreams come to life. I see it in Amy's eyes. The same desire I once suffered from, now sizzling between us, years too late but, simultaneously, right on time.

I marvel at the strong muscles gleaming beneath the skin of Amy's thighs as I strip off her trousers. Her legs are tanned, and why wouldn't they be with a backyard like this. Before I rid her of the last piece of clothing—her panties—I make sure I'm as half-dressed as she is and take everything off except my knickers.

Stretching my arms alongside her head, I look down at her, at the desire chasing away any doubt from her face and the ripple of her biceps as she brings her hands to my hair again. I'm beyond words, so I let my mouth crash down on hers and I kiss her.

Amy's elbows lock around my neck and the way she holds me close to her couldn't express my own emotions better. It's as if I found something I didn't even know was missing, but can never let go of again.

"Do it," she hisses into my ear when our lips break apart for a split second. "Fuck me, Eli."

And maybe it's in the way she pronounces my childhood nickname, or maybe it's the heat coming off her skin mixed with the nostalgic power of our surroundings, but the tears start stinging again. I'm quick to swallow them away and peck a moist path down her shoulder, over her exquisite collarbones, stopping at her breasts. I bend my elbows so my own nipples skate along her stomach. They're hard and stiffen further as they meet the soft skin of her belly. I suck one of her nipples into my mouth and rub my teeth against it.

"Ooh," she moans, and it's enough to set my pussy on fire. My entire body seems to vibrate as I nibble on Amy's nipples. And then the scent of the grass hits my nose and a light breeze rushes over us, making my skin break out in goosebumps, and the picture is complete.

I travel lower, kissing my way along Amy's belly button until my lips reach the hem of her panties. My tongue slips under briefly and already her muscles contract. I take the hour of foreplay she experienced when she fucked me on her massage table into consideration, and proceed. I place a trail of light kisses on the panel of her panties, before pulling it aside and exposing her pussy to the air. Then a whole new perfume hits my nose, pure arousal blending with the promise of a beautiful late summer night.

I look at her puffy, shiny lips. At how pink and perfect they are, and how wet they are for me, but before I threaten to get over-emotional again, I press my mouth to her pussy and inhale.

"Oh god, yes." Amy breathes heavily, twining her fingers through my hair.

I push myself up and, while removing her panties from her legs, find her gaze. I remember how she hardly blinked earlier that afternoon as her fingers meandered towards my pussy. We have a lot to talk about. Later.

After positioning myself comfortably between her legs, my arms cradling her hips for support, I lick Amy Waters's pussy for the first time. I believe it must affect me much more than her, despite the fact that, the instant my tongue connects, her pelvis shoots up and her nails may leave permanent scratch marks on my scalp.

I trail my tongue all the way along her lips and let it circle around her clit. Every time I repeat the action, my tongue burrows a bit deeper between her folds and I taste her musky, heady perfume.

"Eli," I hear her murmur, and I'm so lost in the trance licking her puts me in, she has to grab me by the hair to get my attention.

"What?" I scan her face for signs of pain or discomfort, but a big grin awaits.

"Straddle me, please. I need to taste you."

I begin to think I know exactly what went wrong in Amy's two marriages, providing they involved the opposite sex. The way she fucked me so assuredly earlier and now this question are hardly signs of someone new to the lesbian life-style. I'm also beginning to wonder how much of my life I wasted by leaving Amy behind twenty years ago.

Happily, I oblige. I slip out of my soaked underwear and crawl up to her.

"Are you sure?" I ask, more to tease than to know, because I recognise certainty when I see it and it's staring right back at me.

In response, she pulls me on top of her and there I sit,

my legs wide above Amy's mouth, hers spread in front of me. Never in my wildest dreams, I think, before lowering myself, my knees sinking into the grass of our youth.

When her tongue grazes against my lips the first time, I nearly crash through my elbows. My nipples press into Amy's belly as I position my mouth over her pussy. When she sucks my clit into her mouth, white heat crackles through my skull and I all but lose it again.

I have Amy's pussy to attend to, though, and this is not an opportunity I want to waste. I'm in no position to add fingers to the mix, so I put all my effort into licking her. Every time Amy sucks my lips or clit into her mouth, I do the same, until my brain reaches the point at which it can't compute anymore. Amy's tongue flicks my clit, while my own face is buried between her legs, breathing her in, lapping at her essence. And then it's too much again.

I come. My knees shuddering against her shoulders, and I could scold myself for my lack of self-control, because I certainly haven't given as good as I have gotten yet, but really, who could blame me for that?

I regroup quickly, because it's also a little bit a matter of pride, me being the out and proud lesbian in this alfresco sixty-nine position. I launch a fresh onslaught of licks on her clit, because she can't be that far off. I trill my tongue against her swollen bud and I feel her fingertips scrape my buttocks.

"Yes," she says and it spurs me on. Her body trembles underneath mine, her nipples hard pebbles against my stomach. "Oh god." And I sense the climax making its way through her body, pulsing through her muscles, but I only stop licking when she gives me a light pat on the backside.

I topple off her onto the grass and I can feel a fit of giggles build inside of me. This is what it came down to? A quick rumble by the pond?

"Come here," she says, and opens her arms as wide as her legs earlier.

I nestle in the crook of her elbow, and we both lie in silence for a while, waiting for our breath to steady and for our brain to find the words. Amy speaks first.

"I do hope for your sake none of my neighbours have zoom lenses on their cameras."

In any other circumstance, a blind panic would have rushed through me at the mention of nosy neighbours, but not when I'm in Amy's arms.

"No one recognises me without my glasses and fancy tops on, anyway."

"I did." Amy draws me closer, and a million questions race through my mind, but, perhaps because of the early-evening sun dipping lower behind the trees, I'm all of a sudden very aware of the reason for my visit and how I might not make it to my father's big birthday party on time and in a presentable way.

"I don't suppose you want to be my date tonight?" Reluctantly, I wrestle myself free from Amy's embrace.

She pulls me back in. "Don't we have some lesbian processing to do first?" Her hands shoot up my back and, instantly, set my skin on fire again.

"Not the kind you have in mind right now." I smile against her neck. "I have to go."

"Will you come back after?" I revel in the obvious tension in Amy's biceps, a big indicator she doesn't want me to go.

"I don't have to tell you what the Frosts are like, do I? It might be a late one."

"As long as you don't leave town without a word of warning." Amy's voice is a whisper, barely able to be heard above the rustle of the wind.

That's exactly what I did years ago. One day, I simply couldn't take it anymore. I couldn't be witness to Amy and

Brett's blossoming romance one minute longer. So I left. It was as much self-preservation as it was cowardice, because I failed to say goodbye.

"I promise." This conversation should not take place while we're both naked in Amy's backyard. "I really have to go now."

As I scramble for my clothes, sadness overtakes me. What if twenty years is not enough to forget the hurt I've caused her? What is this, anyway? Because, I may want to bring Amy breakfast in bed tomorrow morning, but as far as I know she's still a twice-divorced heterosexual woman—and nothing has changed at all, except for the few grey hairs sprouting from my scalp and the deepening laughter lines Joe, my make-up guy, always makes fun of.

Amy watches me leave. She's still naked, not making any effort to cover herself up. I bend down to kiss her on the forehead—and to commit the scent of this afternoon to memory.

It was the beginning of summer after our high school graduation. Amy and I both knew we'd be going our separate ways at the end of it, each to colleges miles away from one another. But we had one last summer of lounging by the pond, talking about boys—in Amy's case—and trying to muster up the courage to tell her how much I loved her—on my part. We had big plans to visit each other during breaks, and the Christmas reunions we'd stage would be epic.

Because I couldn't bring myself to tell her, I felt more like a fraud every day. One afternoon, something inside me broke. I was sitting by the edge of the water, eyeing Amy as she ducked above and below the surface. When she pulled herself out, a million water drops clinging to her skin and reflecting the summer sun, the vision I had of her was too much.

No one knew how I felt, and I couldn't tell my best friend. Insecurity, teenage hormones and the overwhelming sense of not having a clue as to who or what I was, knotted into a ball in the pit of my stomach. It sat there growing every time I looked at Amy. And I looked at Amy a lot those days.

"Brett's bringing his friend Paul tonight. You know, the handsome one from basketball." Amy plunged herself down next to me, spraying my skin with water drops. "Surely, he must be good-looking enough for you, Eli."

I resented the fact that she just didn't see. That she felt the need to set me up with boys I wasn't even remotely interested in. That she assumed I was just like her. At the same time, I knew it was wrong to feel that way. And I wanted her so much. I wanted to kiss her and tell her to forget about Brett and Paul. We spent all of our time together and we got along so well. Why was that not enough?

But I knew it didn't work that way.

"I have to go." I started getting up, for once almost more repulsed by Amy's half-naked body than turned-on.

"Now? Why?" Amy arched up her eyebrows. "You are coming tonight, aren't you?"

"I'll see." Suddenly, I couldn't get out of there fast enough. "I'll let you know," I said more to myself than to her, as I made my way out of Amy's yard.

When I arrived home I told my parents I had changed my mind and did want to enrol in the summer school programme my college offered. They'd been keen for me to attend, and shipped me off a week later. Six weeks before I was supposed to. I saw Amy one more time before I left.

· · ·

Throughout my dad's birthday party, my mind is on Amy. On how her fingers dipped so eagerly between my legs during the massage, and how, despite the undeniable intimacy we shared, everything else has been left unspoken.

I have to skip town early enough the next day to make it to the newsroom on Monday. I feel as if time is slipping away from me again, just like it did that last summer. The same kind of pressure builds in my gut, and by the time the party ends, I'm torn. It would be so easy to sneak off the next day, and pretend it never happened. To not have to face any consequences and just move on.

But I saw the fire in Amy's eyes—a fire I might have been too young to see when we were teenagers, if it was there at all. I've felt her fingers inside of me and her tongue between my legs. And how can I possibly run away from that, no matter what she has to say?

Instead of going to bed after the last guests have left, I borrow my mother's bike, because I'm too tipsy to drive a car, and cycle to Amy's house.

It's late and the air has cooled off, but an alcohol blush burns on my face and I have the memory of my afternoon with Amy to keep me warm.

When I arrive at Amy's house, everything is quiet and dark. For an instant, I wonder if it's appropriate to disturb her night rest, but I tell myself she'd want me to. I park my bike against a bunch of low shrubbery and, not wanting to ring a loud and intrusive doorbell, go round the back.

As I approach I hear a crackling noise I quickly identify as fire. To my surprise, Amy lounges in a deck chair, wrapped in a quilt, by an iron fire pit I hadn't noticed before—understandably, as earlier I was suffering from a severe case of tunnel vision.

"I was hoping you'd show up," she says as if she's been expecting me. "This time." There's no malice in her voice, only a playfulness and maybe a hint of hope. She looks up at me, a small smile tugging at the corners of her mouth. "I couldn't sleep."

A bit wobbly with too much wine in my blood, I crouch beside her. "I know an excellent remedy for that."

Amy's eyes sparkle in the light of the flames. She circles her fingers around my wrist again, and I'm glad for the extra support.

"This is all terribly romantic, isn't it?" I quip, because I have a lot of things I want to say but I don't really know where to begin.

"Let's go inside, anyway." Her fingertips already scorch my skin and I'd follow her anywhere. This time, I would.

The day I said goodbye to Amy without her knowing was an ordinary Wednesday. I was leaving for summer school the next Monday, but Amy was joining her family on a road trip to the coast the day after and wouldn't be back before I left.

We sat in the kitchen at my house, eating scones my auntie Ella had brought over. Amy loved scones, mostly because no one in her family knew how to make them properly. A big dollop of cream stuck to her nose, but I didn't tell her because it looked so adorable. I believed that if I remembered her face like that, more goofy than sexy, I'd get over her quicker.

For Amy, the summer still seemed to stretch itself out endlessly. A few weeks of no responsibilities and expectations had that effect. I sat there, looking at her and the cream on her nose, and the thought of leaving her behind made all the words die in my throat.

I let her rattle on about another party she was planning next week when she got back. I'd have to bring scones—preferably the ones my mother made—and everyone had to wear a white t-shirt, but I shouldn't forget to bring my bathing suit. And could I possibly get my hands on some beer?

I just nodded and watched her being Amy, cringing every time she mentioned Brett, and even more so when Paul's name came up.

At a bit past four—I remember because we had an old cuckoo clock in the kitchen that had just chimed four times —she got up because she had to take her little brother candy shopping for the road trip.

We didn't hug, because we weren't that type of people. Just a quick wave, and she was gone, out of the kitchen, our house, and my life.

I stayed glued to my chair until my mother came home from work an hour later, debating if I should go over that night to say something. But I knew I couldn't do that because I couldn't possibly face the accompanying questions.

I should have, but I couldn't.

"I should have told you," I say as I stand in Amy's kitchen. It's a dimly lit, stark white, handleless cupboards affair with lots of stainless steel and a host of Smeg appliances lining the countertops.

"I can't disagree." Amy leans against the fridge, out of which she has taken two beers. She hands me one—as if I need more booze. "But I understand why you didn't."

"Look, um, Amy…" I start to stutter. "I can't help but wonder if you, um, you know…"

"You couldn't ask me then, and you still can't ask me now." Amy's fingers hug the neck of her beer bottle. I stare at her hands because I can't look her in the eyes. She steps closer, puts her bottle on the counter, and lifts my chin up with one finger. "Ask me, Eli."

It reminds me of how she begged me to fuck her earlier today. I didn't hesitate then.

"Are you…" I begin. Her eyes are on me, just like they were when she slipped her fingers inside of me, and I suddenly realise I'm about to ask the most redundant question ever. So, I kiss her instead. I trail my lips from her mouth to her ear. "If you're not into women, I'm not either," I say.

"My sexuality is very fluid," she whispers back. "Always has been."

I snicker at the cliché. "You could have said." My lips descend to the hollow of her neck.

"I had no idea back then, Eli. Don't you think I would have told you otherwise?"

"To sum things up." My eyes have caught sight of the swell of her breasts. "I knew but I didn't say and you didn't know, but you would have said."

"Whatever you say, Eli." Amy's hands tug at my jacket. "All I know is that when you came into my spa, my heart started beating like mad and I wanted to tear your clothes off."

She's doing a good job of that now. Her fingers start unbuttoning my blouse, while my own hoist up her sweater.

"Good thing you're in the right profession for that then." After I pull her top over her head, our eyes meet. I see something shimmer in them, and I don't know if it's regret or promise, infatuation or pure lust, but it doesn't matter. We're Amy and Eli and we spent endless summers in this house. We ate dinner in this kitchen, which doesn't remind me at all of the kitchen of our youth, and I push Amy against her fancy Smeg refrigerator and flip open her jeans. And nothing could feel more right, more full-circle than this.

My hand moves quickly under the waistband of her panties and she's so wet it astounds me, but I don't let that deter me, because I realise I haven't done what she's asked me yet. I haven't fucked her yet.

"Stay," she mumbles in my ear, when I slip a trembling finger in between her hot, moist folds. "Not for the night, but for a week, or a month. Don't go, Eli. Please."

And as her words transform into throaty groans, I know I won't be going anywhere soon. As I fuck Amy, at last, there's nothing else I want to do but stay with her. The walls of her pussy clutch around my fingers and I dig deep, as deep as I can, as if the deeper I go, the more it will make up for lost time.

When I look at her, her eyes are already starting to glaze over. Maybe she's waited for this as long as I have.

"Yes," I say. "I'll stay." In the back of my mind, all the arrangements I have to make start rearing their head, but I ignore them easily, because, at my fingertips, a miracle is about to happen. I can sense Amy is about to come already, that her body has been on the brink all day from fondling me —and seeing me again. And I feel heat rise through my own flesh before it pools between my legs. I'm with Amy—I feel what she feels—when her knees buckle and an incredulous look takes over her face. And I can hardly believe it either, but it's happening right in front of me—to me, to us.

"Oh fuck," she says, and I swear I can feel my own pussy unclench as she lets loose on me. As she bangs the back of her head against the door of her refrigerator and the climax roars through her muscles.

I stare at the delicate skin of her neck while Amy catches her breath—my fingers still inside and her head still tilted back—and a knot I had long ago deemed not there anymore fizzles away to nothing in the pit of my stomach. When I exhale, it's not only used-up air that gets expelled from my body, but years of repressed feelings and, from the corner of my eyes, a few tears of relief and pure happiness.

Gently, I slide my fingers out of Amy and I press myself against her, finding her neck with my lips. After I've kissed a path to her ear, I whisper, "What will we do when I stay?"

I feel her body contract against me when she giggles. "I'll teach you how to give the perfect massage." Amy's voice is low and husky, and I might be bone-tired and drunk—my head swimming from too much booze and finally sinking my fingers into Amy—but this night is not over yet.

———

After calling my producer at the network to lie about a family emergency and claiming I need a week off, I head back to the bedroom where Amy still lounges.

She arches up her eyebrows when I walk through the door, her face lit up by the sun because there was no time to close the curtains last night.

"We have seven days to figure this out." I have no idea what I mean when I say it, but the prospect of spending a week with Amy makes me want to burst out of my skin.

Amy's quizzical expression transforms into a wide smile. She extends her arm and I grip her wrist so she can pull me back into bed with her.

"Who knew," she says as she draws me on top of her, "that it could be so easy to make you stay?"

I realise I'd best get used to wisecracks about me leaving town so stealthily twenty years ago. "Let's go outside." I kiss Amy on the tip of her nose. "I want to swim in the pond like old times."

"Old times, huh?" Amy paints a wicked grin on her face. "You mean lusting after me silently while I pretend I don't notice how you stare when I wear a bikini?"

"Absolutely not." I sink my teeth into the soft flesh of her earlobe. "No bathing suits allowed." I push myself up from the bed and the robe I borrowed from Amy splits open.

Amy eyes me. "I can hardly say no to that." She jumps from under the covers and snatches the fabric off me. Stark naked, we run down the stairs, through the kitchen and into the playground of our youth.

I'm sixteen again when I dip my toes into the water to test the temperature.

I first felt it when I sat in my familiar spot by the edge of the pond, timing Amy as she tried to swim as fast as she could from one side to the other. My job was to focus on my water-proof watch—something I'd always done with great determination before—but this time around, I couldn't keep my eyes off Amy as her body cut through the water towards me. It was an afternoon of just us, before Brett appeared on the scene and stole precious moments of our time together.

I didn't know what a lesbian was and I had no idea it was even possible for a woman to fall in love with another woman. But when Amy pulled herself out of the water, drops raining down her skin and lingering in her hair, I knew I was in love. I knew because not only did the sun catching the hazelnut in her eyes look like the most beautiful sight in the world, but later that afternoon, when I had to go home for supper, it suddenly hurt that I couldn't spend every waking moment with her.

"You weren't timing me," Amy said, her hands on her hips and, to punish me, she swung her head from left to right so the cool drops of water splattered from her hair onto my hot skin.

"Stop it." I looked up at her, at the grin on her face, which all of a sudden seemed unbearable as well as totally addictive. Because I had no idea how to handle myself, I pushed her back into the water, jumping in right after her, because I didn't want her to swim away from me.

She ducked under and yanked me down by the ankles and, just like that, an innocent game we'd played all of our lives, caused my body to pulse in places I'd never paid much attention to before.

This time, it's Amy who pushes *me* into the water. It's freezing cold, but not for long, as she dives in and wraps her body around me. I feel her pubes rub against my skin and her nails scrape along my back.

"I love this pond so much," Amy says before she kisses me and the world seems to disappear for a moment. "We have so many memories here," she whispers when her lips reach my ear.

She embraces me under water and it hits me, exactly like it did on that afternoon twenty years ago, that I'm in love with her. Maybe I still am or maybe it's just nostalgia mixing with confused memories. Maybe she was the one all along or perhaps she'll always have the same effect on me, either way, I rake my nails over her skin and bury them in the lush flesh of her behind, my body all fired up again. Because Amy in this pond might be the closest I'll come to everything I've ever wanted in my life.

With one hand, I cup her buttocks, while the other travels to her belly. Her legs are spread out in front of me, her body enveloping me, her breath on my neck as her lips nip at my skin. Despite being surrounded by water, I feel how wet she is for me again. There's not a hint of hesitation as my fingers find her opening and I slip and curl them inside. Her body tenses around me, her nails burrowing deeper into my flesh.

"Ooh," she exhales, her mouth so near.

My body takes over because my brain has shut off. This

is as close to primal as I've ever been. I fasten my pace, exploring her under water, her mouth now on mine, her moans disappearing down my throat. Her nipples are hard, wet peaks against mine, moving up and down with the rise and fall of her body as she rides my fingers. I press my thumb against her clit, circling it slowly every time I thrust deep. The sensation of having her in my arms, her body so close she almost melts into me, while my fingers are buried inside of her, is enough to make my muscles tremble and my knees go weak.

Amy holds onto me for dear life as I try to stay standing in the water, bucking under the force of her approaching climax. The sound of splashing water mixes with her groans in my ear, until she goes silent and her body clamps down on mine, nearly squeezing the breath out of me, and her pussy clenches around my fingers.

"Jesus Christ, Eli," she says, "I think I might fall in love with you."

The sun colours the water around us pale yellow as I slip my fingers out of her. Amy's legs are still wrapped around my waist, as if she can't let go, and I trace my fingertips along her sides and hold her close.

I commit the moment to memory, the soft slapping and the magical tint of the water, the pressure of Amy's body against mine, the words she just spoke, and decide that from now on, this will be my benchmark for happiness.

A Higher Education

I KNEW Professor Ferguson would be at this conference, but I hadn't prepared for this encounter. Because she faces the check-in clerk I only hear her voice, which never failed to reach the back of the auditorium.

"I don't want two single beds. I have no need for them," she says in a tone that bears no contesting. As sorry as I feel for the person behind the desk, I can't help but enjoy Professor Ferguson's attitude. She won't back down. Professor Joanne Ferguson was never known for backing down.

"I'm sorry, Mrs. Ferguson," the guy behind reception says in a practiced, calm voice with a very strained undertone. "We're fully booked because of the conference."

I shuffle forward a bit—get a whiff of her nutty, heavy perfume in the process—and try to catch the clerk's attention. "If it's any help, I'll happily swap." I hold out my printed confirmation, which clearly states that my room has a king-sized bed.

Professor Ferguson turns to face me. Her eyes narrow as she looks at me, but I can't say if she immediately recognizes me.

"Gail?" With one finger she shoves her dark, thick-rimmed glasses up the bridge of her nose. A gesture I, after all these years, still know so well. "Or should I say Professor Garvey?"

I guess she does know who I am.

Her face breaks out into a smile. "I was looking forward to seeing you again."

She was? Something unidentifiable is already happening in the pit of my stomach.

"Ahem." The clerk clears his throat. We both redirect our attention to him.

"Oh, it's fine," Professor Ferguson says, accompanying her statement with a dismissive hand gesture.

"No, I insist." I hand the clerk my confirmation. "Please put Professor Ferguson in my room." I'm a bit thrown off guard by how that sounds, so I quickly add, "And vice versa."

"That's very kind of you, Gail." Her spectacles have taken a dive down her nose again and she peers at me over the rim of them. "Completely unnecessary, but very kind." She sends me a smile that makes me feel twenty years old again. "I insist on buying you a drink tonight. Shall we say"—she breaks to check her watch—"in about one hour in the upstairs bar? It'd be great to catch up now that we're peers." She purses her lips together in a way that leaves me guessing if she's impressed by that last statement or not.

"Sure." I find myself nodding eagerly.

"Mrs. Ferguson. Mrs. Garvey." The clerk addresses us together. "Here are your keys." He holds out a small envelope to each of us.

"Best make sure you have the right one, Gail," Professor Ferguson jokes.

"Room 703 and 905," the clerk says. "The elevators are over there." He points redundantly to the bank of elevators on the other side of the lobby. "Enjoy your stay with us."

Professor Ferguson and I walk to the elevators together, each of us dragging our carry-on trolly behind us. I handed the bag with the two suits I brought to the bell boy earlier, and I suspect Professor Ferguson has done the same. Unless she plans on addressing her audience in the jeans and blazer she's wearing now—just like she did when I took her class. Personally, I wouldn't mind at all.

"I've followed your rise within our ranks with a keen eye, Gail. I guess we were destined to meet at one of these sooner rather than later."

For a stunned moment, I don't know what to say. Before I can reply, she continues, while stabbing the elevator call button twice.

"I read your paper on Accounting Theory and I was thoroughly impressed with it."

A beeping sound announces the arrival of the elevator and we both step in. I've had similar kinds of conversations numerous times before, but never with a professor whose classes I enjoyed for many more reasons than what she had to teach me.

"I was taught by the best." The instant the words come out of my mouth, I catch myself wondering if that was a reply with a flirty undertone.

Professor Ferguson lets out a hearty chuckle. It's just the two of us in the elevator cage, and I can clearly feel the tell-tale signs of an embarrassing blush coming on.

A bell chimes again, indicating that we've arrived on the seventh floor. "That's me." Professor Ferguson shoots me a quick smile. "See you soon, Gail."

Once the elevator doors close behind her, I take a deep breath. Again, I feel as though I've gone back in time twenty years. But I'm not the same person anymore. I hold a PhD in the same subject as Professor Ferguson. Just like she already was twenty years ago, I'm now a professor myself, teaching youngsters the same things she taught me. Over the years I've learned, to my utter dismay, that when you're in front of a class explaining something, it's really very easy to pick out the students who have a crush on you. And I always believed I hid it so well.

In my room, I heave my small suitcase onto one of the single beds, which is almost queen-sized, and smile at the memory of Professor Ferguson arguing. It reminds me of how she visibly took pleasure in dissecting every argument a student ever made in class. If I've modeled myself after her in some areas of my career, I do believe my teaching methods are more encouraging than hers—not that hers didn't encourage someone like me, someone who loves a challenge.

While I wait for the bellboy to deliver the rest of my luggage, I go through the conference's program. As I am one of the youngest and most inexperienced speakers, my talk is up first tomorrow morning at ten-thirty. Professor Ferguson is, like at most conferences she attends, the keynote speaker and will close this two-day event with a speech I already look forward to, the day after tomorrow at three in the afternoon.

I'm secretly pleased that she's arrived already. I'm sure lots of our colleagues will only check in tomorrow, well after my rookie speech has finished. Although the offer to buy me a drink makes me nervous in its own way, I do welcome the distraction it provides. It beats going over my notes for tomorrow over and over again.

After I've taken a shower and put more effort into dressing than I normally would when going for a drink in a hotel bar, I can't help but acknowledge that strange feeling in my stomach again.

When I arrive at the bar, I find Professor Ferguson perched at the counter, sipping from, as far as I can see, a

Manhattan. Heavy stuff. She's in the same clothes as when I left her with, but a fresh coat of lipstick has been applied and her hair looks more put together.

"Let's get a table, shall we?" Professor Ferguson says when she spots me. "It's so much cozier."

"Sure." I turn to the bartender who looks at me expectantly. "I'll have the same, please."

"Coming right up, Ma'am." She nods curtly.

Professor Ferguson has grabbed her drink and found us a table by the window, overlooking a rather spectacular part of the city.

"Are you a conference speaking virgin, Gail?" she asks me as soon as I sit down opposite her.

I'm still recovering from the shock of finding myself at a table with the woman I pined for for months on end in my last year of college—when I'd reached an age that shouldn't allow for such teenage, hormonal occurrences anymore. And now she's being coy with me?

"It's my first time on the other end of the speaking platform in a situation like this, yes," I confirm.

"Nervous?"

"A little, but I've been teaching for quite some time now. I suspect it won't be that different."

"I, for one, can't wait to see you up there." Professor Ferguson reaches for her drink. "It was such a thrill to see a former student's name in the program. It means I must have been doing something right." She fixes her gaze on me as she sips from her Manhattan.

Where's my drink? Instinctively, I look away, pretending to search for the bartender—but mainly to take a deep breath and hope that the blush I feel creeping up my neck doesn't reach my cheeks. To my relief, the bartender is on her way over, carrying my cocktail on a round silver tray. I lean back to let her deposit it between us, and patiently wait for her to depart.

"You're a very inspiring woman," I hear myself say, although I have no idea where those words come from.

"I get that a lot." Professor Ferguson raises her glass. "But I wouldn't want to sound blasé."

Carefully, I clink the rim of my glass to hers. "Modesty is such an over-rated characteristic," I remember Professor Ferguson saying once. I can't remember in reference to what —and what it had to do with her lectures—but I clearly remember her saying it. It sounded as true as anything coming from her mouth. And I never was one to fall for the shrinking violet type. It made me wonder what she would be like in bed—hardly the shrinking violet type either, I suspected. And dreamed of.

Sitting opposite her now, I do wonder how many Manhattans she had before I arrived. Though it's not so much a drunk—or even tipsy—air I get from her, there's definitely a careless, flirty vibe coming off her. Or perhaps I'm imagining things again. I was always very good at that when it came to Professor Ferguson.

"But back to you, Gail. A tenure at Dartmouth is very impressive."

"It's not Princeton, but it'll do."

"Still in the top ten. Anyway, you should never sell yourself short. You were one of my most brilliant students. Apart from other things, I do remember that vividly."

Oh shit. Are we headed in that direction already? I drink again, trying to drown out that twenty-one-year-old inside of me rearing it's hormonal head. "Thanks, Professor Ferguson."

"Nuh-uh." She shakes her head. "I call you Gail, so you must call me Joanne."

This is a far cry from the speech Professor Ferguson gave at the beginning of the academic year. "Some professors don't mind being called by their first name. I'm not one of them." She'd delivered the message with that trademark lopsided smile—as much disarming as it was threatening.

"A hard habit to break." I try to get her name to roll from my lips. "Joanne." It feels too strange.

"I'm well aware of my superior-seeming teaching methods, Gail. You must remember, there's a distinct generation difference between the two of us."

Date of birth of faculty was never disclosed to students through official channels, but it wasn't hard to guess which age bracket a certain professor fitted into. Professor Ferguson, I mean Joanne, definitely shows signs of ageing, but certainly not in a less than elegant fashion. Her hair is not dyed, for starters, although it has surely lost its previous ash-blond color. She must be in her late fifties or early sixties now. Her eyes are still the same yellow-flecked, strong coffee-colored brown and she has updated her spectacles to a retro-chic, heavy-rimmed pair.

What if I were to start taking one of her classes now? Would she have the same effect on me? I was never one to fall head over heels. It's always a slow process. A culmination of appealing characteristics and aha-moments. It took me at least one term to realize that I looked forward to Professor Ferguson's lectures much more than to any of the others.

"Princeton is not that far from Dartmouth. Maybe I should swing by some time. Sit in on one of your lectures. See how you go about things."

Although this is the first conference I've been invited to speak at, I've attended quite a few in the past and, usually, bar chatter is nothing like this. If any flirting goes on, and I'm sure it does, it's mostly out of my earshot and I've never been on the receiving end of it. Or am I interpreting this wrongly?

"I'm sure a visit from you would be very much appreciated." I find it hard to look at her, so I let my eye wander to the bartender, who vaguely reminds me of Amy, a girl I dated while I was getting my PhD.

"Hm. If I were to decide to visit, it would most certainly be on the down-low. There's a time and place for pomp and circumstance, and I wouldn't want to put you off your game."

I take a few sips from my drink. She must have known that I had the hots for her, and clearly it's amusing her to throw me off guard. Whatever Professor Ferguson is trying to accomplish with this line of banter she has chosen, it's working. I'm not one for playing games, though—and I certainly don't enjoy being played.

"Pro—" I start, but quickly correct myself. "Joanne." I find her gaze. Her eyes are wide behind her glasses, her face relaxed.

"Yes, Gail." She quirks up her eyebrows, the way she used to during an exam, to indicate doubt about where my answer was going.

"Are you—" Before I can finish my question, the door to the bar swings open, distracting me—something I'm not entirely unhappy about. The man who checked us in earlier scans the room and fixes his eyes on our table before resolutely heading in my and Professor Ferguson's direction.

"Mrs. Garvey, I'm so sorry." He clears his throat and focuses his attention on me. "Something has happened in the room above yours, erm, making your room unavailable for the time being. We *are* fully booked and are working very hard to find a solution, but we may have to ask you to move to the Plaza a few blocks from here. I do sincerely apologize for this ordeal. You will, of course, get a full refund."

"What?" I'm still trying to process the information. "What happened?"

"I'm afraid I'm not at liberty to say, Ma'am." The receptionist tilts his head a bit. "I would like your permission to enter your room and collect your belongings, Ma'am."

"This is all very odd," I protest. "And I can gather my own stuff, thank you very much."

"It would really be better if you didn't enter your room, Ma'am. I'm very happy to take any instructions." The check-in guy is unshakeable.

Then, suddenly, I feel a hand on my shoulder. "It's all right, Gail," Professor Ferguson says. "Put her luggage in my room," she addresses the receptionist next. "We'll share."

I turn to Professor Ferguson, my jaw slacking. When, flabbergasted, I face the check-in clerk again, he looks at me expectantly. "We'll take care of everything for you, Ma'am. And any expenses you incur during your stay will be taken care of by us."

"Well," I sigh. "Is anything damaged in my room? My laptop is in there. I must go and have a look."

A hand on my shoulder again, fingers pressing into my flesh. "I understand you're worried, Gail, but let them take care of it. We'll go check on your stuff as soon as they've moved it."

"Okay. Fine." I shrug, but Professor Ferguson's hand remains firmly planted on my shoulder.

"Thank you, Mrs. Garvey." The receptionist all but bows before speeding off.

"What the hell?" I turn to Professor Ferguson, whose hand really has no choice but to slip off me now.

"It's best not to let these things get to you, Gail." She leans back in her chair. "But I bet you're regretting that chivalrous move of swapping rooms with me now."

Rub it in, why don't you? "I suppose I'm the one who should be thanking you now, for saving me the shenanigans that come with staying in another hotel."

"If you want privacy, I can easily make myself scarce, you know?"

I blink twice, not getting what Professor Ferguson is trying to say.

"That woman perched on the furthest barstool to your left has been giving me the eye since I arrived. This is a conference, Gail. Things happen. And I'm a single lady."

It's my turn to hike up my eyebrows in an inquisitive expression.

"Don't play the innocent with me." Professor Ferguson drains the last of her cocktail and waves at the bartender. "We're all adults here. You're not my smitten student anymore."

I have half a mind to get up and storm out, but I have no room to flee to.

"What were you going to ask me before Mister Efficiency barged in?" Professor Ferguson cocks her head. The bartender approaches, buying me some time.

"I'll have another," Professor Ferguson says.

"Me too, please." I wonder if, instead of attending the Antitrust Economics and Competition Policy Conference, I've somehow landed myself in a parallel universe—or the Dinah. I wait for the barkeep to saunter off, before casting my glance on Professor Ferguson, who is nothing like the distinguished, discreet teacher I remember.

"Well?" she eyes me with that dark stare of hers. You certainly couldn't tell by looking at her. She sits there all elegant, the long fingers of her one hand spread wide on the edge of the table, tapping lightly with maroon varnished nails.

"I was going to ask you if you were flirting with me, but

the question no longer seems relevant." All pretense of being coy went out of the window five minutes ago.

"Why's that?"

"Because you obviously have your eye on someone else," I blurt out, suddenly realizing I'm jealous. Then, in a flash, it hits me that Professor Ferguson played me well.

She chuckles. It's a very womanly laugh, high-pitched and bubbly and a little bit polite. "The answer to your question is 'yes', by the way." Her eyes stay on me, her stare unwavering.

"But," I hear myself protesting again. "You don't know anything about me. You don't even know——"

"I know more than enough. Or should I say: I remember more than enough." She taps a finger against her right temple. "I may be getting on a bit but all the grays in here are still intact."

"Jesus Christ." I don't know what else to say. I look behind me, to check out if the potential bedfellow Professor Ferguson used to lure me in is even real. I only see an empty cocktail glass, alone on the countertop of the bar, on a half-shredded napkin.

"She could probably tell I had my sights set on someone else." Professor Ferguson has an amused smile on her face. "I go to a lot of these conferences, Gail. I try to keep things interesting. It's so easy to get bored. And really, life's too short to sit around and wonder about the virtues of your actions for too long."

"I didn't know you'd changed subjects, *Joanne*." Suddenly, I have no problem calling her by her first name. "Life Lessons with Professor Ferguson."

"No need to attach such importance to it. It's just a bit of fun." Her smile shifts into more of a sly grin. A satisfied one. No doubt because I'm playing along. Am I, though?

Just as the bartender brings over our fresh round of drinks, the receptionist storms back into the bar.

"Here's an extra key to room 703, Mrs. Garvey. You will find all your luggage there."

I take the key from him and stare at it undecidedly for a few seconds. "Thanks."

"Please don't hesitate to call the front desk if you need assistance with anything."

"Sure."

He nods and speeds off.

I put the key on the table and reach for my drink. It's a welcome sight. My nerves feel a little fraught and my shoulders are tense. Somehow, I wouldn't mind feeling Professor Ferguson's hand on them again.

"Here's to an interesting two days," Professor Ferguson says. "And, potentially, two even more interesting nights."

I clink the rim of my cocktail glass against hers, determined to not have the joy sucked out of my meeting with Professor Ferguson because of recent events. After all, one of my most frequent tween dreams is about to come true. Tonight, I'll be sharing a bed with Professor Joanne Ferguson.

"What do you think happened?" I ask. "In the room above mine?"

"This is a hotel. The options are unlimited." Professor Ferguson grins.

"Care to hazard a guess?" No matter where this line of conversation goes next, I'm starting to feel glad I won't have to stay in the room assigned to me as morbid images pop up in my brain.

Professor Ferguson shakes her head. "Just let it go, Gail." She draws her lips into a pout. "And I promise I will be nothing but a lady tonight. Unless you don't want me to." She giggles at her own words.

My brain is trying very hard to digest all this flirty banter. And here I was thinking we'd be discussing economics tonight. What do I want, though? A question so easily answered twenty years ago, even though, back then, my tortured desire for Professor Ferguson was as much based on her unavailability as anything else. It's so easy—even comforting at times—to pine for someone who can't possibly ruin your expectations of them, because it's all just a fantasy anyway.

"Let's see how the evening progresses," I say, not shying away from Professor Ferguson's glance.

"I take it you're a conference virgin in more than one sense of the word then." It's as though Professor Ferguson can't find the off-button for innuendo.

I huff out some air, stifle a chuckle. "And I take it you're not." When I was in college, I hardly ever questioned her sexual orientation. It didn't matter to the sort of crush I was cultivating. It only mattered in my daydreams, which had nothing to do with reality. I'd come to terms with my own preference long before I even clasped eyes on Professor Ferguson.

"I'm a scholar. I live to work. To research. To become as much of an expert in my field as I possibly can. I travel a lot, and I've never been particularly interested in the ludicrous concept of monogamy, anyway." She chews on her bottom lip for a fraction of a second. "But what I love most of all, is to make the best of any given situation."

If only I had known that twenty years ago. "So, let's say I wasn't here. What would you be doing now?"

"That's not a hypothesis I'm willing to entertain, Gail. You're here. Why would I even try to imagine that you're not?"

"Let me ask you another question then…" Something is tightening below my stomach. "Why me?"

Professor Ferguson draws her lips into a crooked smirk. "Okay. Sure," she says. "I'll go there." She takes a sip from her Manhattan before continuing. "You're my former student, so there's that. Not just any student, though." She narrows her eyes a bit when she says that. "And I'm not referring to the obvious crush you had on me. I'm talking about how easily you grasped complex formulas and economic models. As a student, you really excited me. Nothing is more sexy than a woman with a brain."

"Tell me about it." Professor Ferguson always seemed plenty sexy to me just by appearance. Although, in this case, it's completely impossible to separate the two. I get her point.

"Not that sometimes I don't have to settle for less, but conferences like these are excellent spots for finding smart women." She relaxes into her chair a bit more. "Despite the fact that our field is still so largely dominated by men." A shake of the head. "But let's not go there. I'd like to keep conversation light tonight."

"Have you always been, huh, interested in women?" A blush warms my neck as I ask the question.

"Always," Professor Ferguson confirms.

Am I supposed to see her as some sort of female Lothario now? A woman leaving a trail of broken hearts as she travels cross country, and around the world? I sometimes check Professor Ferguson's website for a peek at her schedule, and she's very much sought after as a speaker all over the globe.

"That can't have always been as easy as you make it out to be?"

"I don't know. How *do* I make it out to be?"

I break out into a light chuckle. "Gosh. Even though we're trying to keep the topic light, somehow, I'm still getting flashbacks to exams with you."

"Ah." Briefly, she chews her lip again. "Always such a pleasant experience when you entered the room."

The blush that I had hoped to keep confined to my neck is swiftly creeping upward. I'm also still a bit stuck on her comment on monogamy, seeing as I'm a firm believer in the concept myself.

"Not that it matters that much to me, Gail, but are you single?" There she is with a question from left field again. On top of that, she's making it sound as if seducing me is a foregone conclusion.

"I, huh, I am," I stammer.

"Good. Less messy. Don't you think?"

What I think is that Professor Ferguson is verging on the edge of being obnoxious. "This is all very strange, Professor."

"Joanne," she's quick to say.

"Joanne," I repeat, testing again how it feels to let her first name roll off my tongue. At the moment she's much more Joanne to me than Professor Ferguson. "You're very cocky and I'm not a big fan of over-the-top personas like that."

She nods pensively, like she used to do in class. "Oh, I see. Is this going to be a fight for top?"

My re-ignited attraction to Professor Ferguson, which is quickly starting to slip out of grasp, was still largely based on the crush I once had on her. Now, we both seem to be totally different people.

"You're making the Plaza seem very appealing right now, Joanne." Still, if I really wanted to walk away, I would. I decide to stay, which is telling in itself. "What's with the act?" I find it very difficult to believe that a woman I so admired would turn out to be this arrogant. Even slightly bitter. "Don't tell me that actually works on people?"

She opens her palms and pulls up her shoulders. "Believe it or not… it does."

"Well, it won't work on me." I see her crumble a little bit as I drain the last of my cocktail. But suddenly, I *have* had enough. "I think I will call it a night. I would appreciate a bit of privacy. Have another on me." With any luck, I'll be asleep by the time she comes up. I don't really want to go through the hassle of checking in to another hotel. I just want to go over my presentation for tomorrow, and try to get some sleep. Although the chances of the latter have been seriously dwindling in the past hour.

"Sure." She tilts her head. "Call reception and tell them to let me know when it's safe for me to enter *my* room." She's only being semi-gracious about me denying her access to her room, which was my room to begin with. But the reason why she so eagerly invited me to stay with her is now a bit too clear for my comfort.

"Fine," I say curtly before heading to the bar, telling the cute bartender to put all drinks on my tab, and exiting the establishment. On my way down to 'our room', I curse my lack of privacy, and run through the review of this hotel I want to write on TripAdvisor. Most of all, I'm disappointed. Having to witness someone I've looked up to all my adult life fall off their pedestal is an unpleasant reality check I could have lived without. Part of me wanted to stay, perhaps try to get to the bottom of it, but the other part—the rigid economist bit, I guess—was so appalled by what came out of Joanne's mouth, it started to seem like the exact opposite of flirting.

The room I gave up is the same size as the one I had to move out of, and I find my luggage neatly arranged next to the huge bed. First, I check if all my belongings have made it to my new digs, and once I'm reassured that everything has been transported, I instinctively head for the minibar. I need something to unwind. Two Manhattans have not done the trick. I pour myself a glass of wine from the half bottle of white I find in the tiny fridge, and settle behind the desk, arranging my notes in front of me while I power up my laptop.

I can't relax with the prospect of Joanne arriving any minute. I hardly trust her to wait until I make the call. It's probably just another one of the non-monogamous games she likes to play. I feel silly practicing my speech out loud, so I whisper it to myself. I know the words by heart by now. I know where to make my voice go up, and where to put a bit of a humorous inflection in my tone.

Satisfied that I've practiced enough, I kick off my shoes, finish the rest of the wine, and dig into my suitcase to unearth my pajamas. To my dismay, I find none.

In a flash, an image of the powder blue pair I had intended to pack lying on my bed pops up into my head. In the picture in my mind, they're next to my trolly, waiting to be put in. They never made it that far.

"Shoot," I holler at no one in particular. "Can this evening get any bloody worse?" I guess Joanne could choose this exact moment to return to her room. But she seems to be sticking to the plan. I rummage through my luggage and the only thing I find that I can comfortably sleep in is the tank top I wore underneath my blouse for traveling, because I always get cold on the plane. It's short and tight, though, and doesn't come with matching pants.

Sighing heavily, I undress and slip into the tank top. After brushing my teeth and washing my face, I arrange the robe provided by the hotel on a chair next to the side of the bed I've chosen—the one closest to the bathroom—and slip under the sheets. As I lay down, I realize I've forgotten to make the call to reception. What happens if I don't call? I'll probably just lie here waiting for Joanne, anyway, so I push myself up and call the front desk.

With Joanne's arrival imminent—or not—any signs that I'm ready for sleep soon escape me. I grab my Kindle from the night stand, close the lesbian erotic romance novel I was reading before, and try to find something un-arousing to read. Not an easy feat when your main means of relaxation is being absorbed in books with a heavy sexual undertone. I'm also very much in the habit of keeping my eReader tidy, thus deleting books I've read as soon as I've finished them. Right now it's a choice between dry works on macro-economy and whatever I found on my latest rampage through Amazon's Lesbian Romance Best Sellers List. *Why don't I enjoy classic literature more?* I ask myself, as I scroll through title after title with an image of two women on the cover.

Then I'm startled by a knock on the door.

"Are you decent?" Joanne asks. To my surprise, she waits for my reply to enter the room.

"Yes." I switch on the lamp on my bedside table so she can at least see where's she's going. I stay neatly tucked underneath the duvet, though.

"Hey, Gail." Joanne heads straight for the edge of the bed furthest away from me, and sits. "Look, I'm sorry about earlier. I was out of line. I fully realize that."

"It's fine. Really." It's a bit disconcerting to have Professor Ferguson apologize to me.

"It's important to me that you accept my apology. Some-times"—she clears her throat—"I get a bit defensive and too forward. Can't stop the words from coming out of my mouth. I sit there, listening to myself being all cocky while inwardly, and trust me on this, I hang my head in shame."

This makes me sit up. Joanne's words have made me forget about only wearing a tank top, but I soon remember as her eyes seem momentarily transfixed by my shoulder line. "I accept your apology, Joanne."

"This life I've chosen, it cost me a lot." A grimace slips over her lips. "Being a rockstar of economics is not easy, you know?"

"Because half of the people you encounter think you're the dullest person on the planet, while the ones you meet at conferences like this think you're a goddess?"

"It's mainly the interviews with Fox News. They really leave me with no sense of dignity intact." A wider smile starts breaking through on her face.

"You're on Fox News?" I feign surprise.

"The fact that you didn't know shines an even more flattering light on you." Joanne plays along, and I start feeling it again. A tingle in my stomach. A flutter underneath my skin. "Do you want to go over your notes for tomorrow? Or practice with me as your audience? I'm quite experienced at this lecturing at conferences thing. I could give you a pointer or two."

"I'm not exactly dressed to give a rehearsal speech." I dip my chin to look at my own chest. "Forgot my pajamas."

"Ah." She tips her head to the right a little, but doesn't say anything else. Perhaps she's biting back a lewd comment.

"Either way, I've gone over my speech enough times. I should be good."

"There's no doubt in my mind." Joanne gets up from the bed and walks to her suitcase. "You're welcome to use my pajamas, although that would leave me rather exposed."

"I'll make do with what I have." I smile sheepishly as Joanne presents a pair of lilac silk pajamas to me.

"I can be considerate and sleep in my underwear as well, so you don't feel too naked next to me." This time, her comment doesn't sound half as obnoxious as before. The atmosphere has changed. Her apology has taken the sting out of her words. She also delivers them with an almost goofy grin on her face.

"No need." I shoot her another smile. A reassuring one this time. "But thanks for the offer."

"Well then, excuse me while I slip into something more comfortable." From behind her spectacles, she winks at me. I'm definitely feeling the flutter now. I'm not one for aggressive come-ons, but give me some playful banter and I can be up for some fun.

While Joanne retreats to the bathroom, I revel in the anticipation of seeing her appear in the room in sleep wear. Specializing in economics might be considered not very exciting by a lot of people, but look at me now. Nothing boring about this situation. *Economics brought us together*, I think, and chuckle inwardly.

I put my Kindle to the side, quite confident I shouldn't be reading any of the steamy titles on there tonight. It would only blur my boundaries.

When Joanne reemerges from the bathroom a few minutes later, her face scrubbed clean of make-up, and the indentations of her lanky body showing easily through the silk fabric of her pajamas, I feel an unexpected tenderness engulf me. As a student, especially as a student with a massive crush, it's so easy to assign other-worldly characteristics to professors. They seem to have all the answers. They look so good up there explaining all these complex theories. And, in Professor Ferguson's case, she wasn't just in possession of great intelligence, she was also very easy on the eyes.

Now, as she stands in front of me, totally humanized, stripped of the power of the class room and the bravado of earlier in the bar, she's just another woman. One I still appear to be quite fond of, but no longer the professor I was so infatuated with twenty years ago.

"Ta-dah," she says unselfconsciously, spreading her

palms. "The economics slumber party is about to commence. Shall we discuss Political Economy or the global financial crisis? Whatever floats your boat, Gail."

"How about we just get some sleep?"

"That's probably the best way to go." Joanne seems reluctant to slip under the covers with me. "Would you like a sleeping aid? And by that I mean a pill, nothing else." She winks at me again.

"No, thanks. I'm not very big on medication."

"Aah, more the herbal kind, are you?" She takes a step closer to the bed, but doesn't hop in yet.

"I just want a clear head tomorrow. Kind of a big day for me."

"Of course." At last, she lifts the tip of her side of the duvet.

Perhaps we should have asked for separate blankets. The thought only crosses my mind briefly. Lying under the covers with Professor Ferguson, doing nothing, in this suspended state of will-we won't-we, is highly arousing. Definitely more erotic than any fantasy I dreamed up when I was still her student. The shifting of the sheets, the movements of her limbs inches away from mine, the possibility of everything so near, yet, in its immediacy, also quite faraway.

"Good night, Gail." I watch as Joanne deposits her glasses on the night stand beside her and lets her head drop to the pillow. "Feel free to read. I don't mind."

"That's all right." I flip off the light on my side and sink lower beneath the covers, careful to stay on my side of the bed. This creates a rigidness in my muscles hardly beneficial for sleep, but perhaps I should just give my mind up to the possibilities running frantically through my brain. My mind only, though. Nothing else.

Lying there, in the dark next to her, I can't help but wonder what she is thinking. I'm flabbergasted to find that, within minutes, I hear a slight purr come from my left. And this from the same person who was aggressively pursuing me mere hours ago. For an instant, it does make me feel like a dull economics professor—albeit one in a tank top.

My own behavior stays nicely within the boundaries of expectations. Sleep seems so far away, I reach for my Kindle. I can't just lie awake for hours going crazier as the night progresses. I need to take my mind off my speech, at least. So I start reading the novel I was engrossed in on the plane over here. But when, rather unexpectedly, the two main characters start engaging in some mild, but very stimulating BDSM, the images in my mind become too graphic for me to enjoy them in my current situation.

"What are you reading?" Joanne's voice comes out of nowhere. I've probably been too absorbed in the book to notice that the heavy breathing next to me has stopped.

"Oh, just something light."

"Judging from how you were sighing, it didn't sound very light." Joanne turns on to her back. It's odd to have her stare at me without glasses, a little moon dust gathered in the corner of her eyes.

I clap my Kindle shut in its magnetic case and am grateful for the sudden darkness around us. "There was a rather unexpected scene." My voice has gone a bit hoarse.

"Oh, that kind of book." I hear the chuckle in Joanne's tone. "Do you need some privacy?"

"No," I squeak. I can't help myself. I wonder what I would do if she were to put a hand on my thigh now, or brush a finger against my arm. Joanne remains the perfect gentlewoman she earlier claimed she would be, though, and I'm not sure if I feel happy or sad about that.

"Be sure to give me the title of that book tomorrow. I'm rather fond of 'unexpected scenes' myself."

"Sure." My voice is beginning to sound normal again. "I'm sorry if I woke you."

"It's not your fault. It's more the rather unexpected scene we find ourselves in, I guess."

"It *is* a bit odd." I'm anxious to keep the conversation going. In my gut, I can sense the desire building instead of subsiding. I'm going with my instinct. Trying to hang on to this feeling. Should I, in the end, make the first move? I turn on my side a bit more, facing her. "But it's not as if neither one of us doesn't want to be here."

Joanne smiles a slow, sly smile. "It's clear that you're aroused at the moment, Gail. I don't want to take advantage of that. I also want you to be well rested for tomorrow." She lifts herself up a bit and props her head onto her upturned palm, resting on her elbow. "We have another night. Let's see how you feel then." She runs the tip of her tongue over her upper lip quickly. "But just so we're clear: this is by no means a rejection."

"Only a very sadistic form of foreplay," I offer, feeling the sting of rejection coursing through me a little nonetheless.

"Perhaps also a very effective one." She shuffles a bit closer in my direction. "I'm sure you'll see what I mean tomorrow." With that, she slants her head toward me and presses a quick kiss on my forehead. It only confirms how much I want her now, how much I want her lips on me in other places as well. But, as though I'm still compelled to do so after all these years, I listen to her, and let the back of my head crash into the pillow.

"Good night, Gail." Joanne doesn't move to the edge of the bed. It's big enough to not encumber my movements, but she has made her intentions clear. How will I ever fall asleep after that?

But, it turns out that, after listening to how Joanne falls asleep again—with an ease that astounds me—and how her breathing slows, I manage to get a few hours of sleep myself. The day has worn me out sufficiently to calm down my whirling brain.

———

When I wake up the next morning, frantically checking the alarm clock, Joanne is already up. I hear water streaming in the bathroom, and the curtains have been opened to a slit. To my relief, it's only eight a.m. and I have plenty of time to prepare myself for my maiden conference speech.

I lie back and take a few minutes to relax myself into the day, silently looking forward to the moment Joanne will enter the room, all put-together and refined. She takes her time in the bathroom, and I have to suppress the urge to reach for my Kindle and pass the time by immersing myself into 'that scene' again. But now is really not a good time.

I extend my arm to feel her spot in the bed. The sheets are still a little bit lukewarm, and make me revel in the very intimate sensation of sharing a bed with someone, even if thrust together due to vague circumstances in a hotel, which I've all but forgotten about.

My heart skips a beat when the bathroom door opens and Joanne steps out, as predicted, with her hair styled elegantly, her make-up carefully applied, and a crisp white blouse tucked neatly into a pair of jeans. Distinguished women wearing jeans is another thing I can't get enough of.

"Morning," she says, a bright, red-lipped smile painted on her face. "Managed to get some sleep?"

"A little." I can't shake the thrill of waking up to this sight of Professor Ferguson. Deep inside of me, the throbbing ignites.

"I'm having breakfast with some of the regulars. Care to

join?" She fastens a small golden ring to her earlobe while she speaks.

"No. I'll just stay here and fret in solitude." The sad face I pull should be exaggerated enough to convey irony.

"Okay. I'll see you at ten. I'll be there to cheer you on." She tips her head in the other direction, clicking the other earring in place. "You'll be great. I know it. And don't argue, please. This is an argument you can't possibly win." She sends me a rather flirty smile, displaying her upper teeth. The red of her lips curves deliciously over them, and I'm aware of how the throbbing intensifies.

"Thanks." I watch her grab her bag, check herself in the mirror, adjust a stray strand of hair, and head for the door and out of my sight. Once I hear the door fall into the lock, I crash back into the pillows. I can feel my heart beat between my legs. Should I? To take the edge off? Housekeeping will be changing the sheets soon. No one ever needs to know. And damn, I could do with a little bit of tension release.

A thrill of excitement chases up my spine as I slip off my panties. I kick the duvet off me and spread my legs, welcoming the rush of fresh air on my pulsing clit. I hike up my tank top as well, needing that sensation of exposure to air on my nipples. Just lying on the bed I shared with Professor Ferguson like that, legs spread, nipples instantly hard, pussy lips throbbing, immediately puts me in the right mood. I don't need to turn to my go-to fantasy of being watched, all I need is to think of Joanne's hand finding my thigh underneath the sheets. Of her finger dipping in between my legs.

I let my own finger do the work. The first touch is light. A tentative circle drawn around my clit. I spread my pussy lips with the fingers of my other hand, and get down to business. The motion of my finger intensifies, and I know this is not going to be a long, drawn-out session of solo sex. There's urgency in my movements as I imagine it's Professor Ferguson's finger on me there, caressing me the way I like it, but most of all, watching me from behind those spectacles, an amused smile on her face.

The door falling into the lock with a bang startles me. Shit. I only have time to retract my hands from between my legs before Joanne stands in front of me. I feel frozen, suspended in time. I watch her watch me and it mortifies and entices me at the same time. I'm on full display for a split second, an instant during which I can't move, before scrambling for the duvet and covering myself.

And then, instead of speaking, or apologizing for barging in like that, Joanne tilts her head and looks at me in the exact same way I was imagining she would just before she walked in.

I'm too flabbergasted to speak, and perhaps also too aroused. I'm not sure yet which sensation is winning.

"Looks like I'll be missing breakfast," Joanne says in a low voice. She inches closer, dropping her bag to the floor, sitting down next to me on the bed. Underneath the covers, my clit is growing even more bloodshot, despite—or perhaps because of—me pressing my legs shut. She starts by pulling the duvet back. I'm not wearing any panties and my tank top is still lodged above my breasts. "Why don't I take care of that for you?" She pushes my legs down while shooting me a glance that sets my skin on fire—as though the words she just spoke weren't enough.

With a tiny shift of my chin, I nod my approval. Horniness is definitely winning.

"Spread your legs," she commands. "Lie back. Relax."

I assume the position I was in before she walked in. What is she doing here anyway? Did she sense I was touching myself while thinking of her? Was she able to predict it by using an analytical economic formula?

"Show me how you like it, Gail." Her words are turning

my bones to liquid. "Show me, and I'll take over." What sets me off the most, even more than how she speaks to me, is the smirk on her face. A knowing, confident, slightly arrogant grin. Inside, it's ripping me to pieces already. My blood is hot for her. My clit so ready to be touched. My muscles ready to contract.

I bring my hands between my legs and, slowly, she looks away from my face, to my exposed pussy and how I'm touching it for her. It only takes a few seconds before I feel her hand on mine. Gently, she pushes it away, and replaces it with hers.

I gasp for air at the connection of her finger on my clit, and even more so when she fixes her gaze on me again.

"Don't close your eyes," she says, but I had no intention of doing so. Her eyes on me are all I need, while her finger works my clit. But then her finger stops, and she leaves me hanging for a second, her smile growing wider, her eyes glinting behind the glass of her spectacles. Then her finger travels lower, through the wetness that has pooled there.

"You're so wet." I watch her red lips form the most redundant words in the history of my sex life. Her smile tightens a bit. This must be arousing her as well. Then, she slips a finger inside of me, and I die a little bit. How many times have I dreamed of a moment like this? The same finger that used to point out mistakes in papers, or indicate something on the blackboard, or wave through the air while she was trying to make a point. That finger is inside me now, undoing me.

"Can you come for me like this, Gail?" It's more a command than a question, but I nod anyway. I could come just by her staring at me the way she does.

"Good." With that, she adds another finger, and starts stroking me with deeper, more insistent thrusts. Her fingers connect with something inside of me. Long lost memories.

Nostalgia for a time when all I needed for a burst of extreme happiness was to see her on campus, just floating by. Just her being Professor Ferguson.

Joanne ups the pace, before adding another finger. I still can't believe Professor Ferguson is fucking me. Dreams like that are not supposed to come true. But she delves deeper, curling her fingers inside of me, while spreading me wide.

"Oh jesus," I groan. "Joanne, I—" And I want her fingers inside of me forever, and her eyes on me for the rest of time, but I'm coming, the walls of my pussy clamping hard around her fingers as she strokes me more, and more. I want to keep looking into her eyes while the climax takes me, but I can't help but blink a few times, blacking out the sight of Joanne's relentless stare on me for split seconds. It's in these moments of blackness that I feel it most. The rush. The release. The silly sense of victory, of having won something, of being given a gift I never even knew existed.

Joanne doesn't immediately retract her fingers. She leaves them inside of me for a few moments longer while sinking her teeth into her bottom lip.

"Well, that was unexpected," she says finally, while ever so slowly slipping her fingers out of me. She casts them a quick glance and seems to nod appreciatively at how they're coated in my juices, before wiping them off on the sheets.

"Jesus christ," I groan, not having come back fully to my senses yet.

"Seems like I forgot more than my phone." She smiles and points at her side of the bed, where, when I follow her finger, I see the device lying on the night stand.

"I'm sorry, I—"

"You're not going to apologize for that, are you?" She tips her head again. "Well, it's a little late for that now, anyway." She slants her upper body in my direction. "I'll let you get ready in peace, but…" Her lips are so close to my face now. "It looks like we'll have an interesting night together." Briefly, she touches her lips to mine, only to push herself up swiftly after, and leave me wanting much much more, despite the crushing climax she just delivered.

Joanne makes a quick stop in the bathroom and is out of the room again before I've had the opportunity to gather my wits. I lay there panting languidly for a while longer, until, while twisting my head to the side, I catch sight of the alarm clock. Damn. Almost time to deliver my speech and I have a lot of putting together to do. Although Joanne's intervention has uncoiled some of the tension lodging in my stomach, it has also introduced many more feelings to deal with. Tonight. The two of us in this bed. Professor Ferguson fully undressed. The anticipation is almost too much to take, and I've yet to deliver a talk—with those same eyes boring into me while I speak.

I take a cold shower to wake up my body fully, and to wash off the last remnants of lust lingering in my flesh. To no avail, of course. But, I'm a professional, and I can refocus my attention when I need to. I dress in the pale grey suit I brought, munch on an apple from the fruit basket, not able to face a buffet breakfast because of the nervous tightness in my stomach, and glance at myself in the mirror. There's a hint of 'just-fucked' about me, but I suspect I'll be the only one who can see that. Apart from Joanne.

Satisfied with my appearance, I grab my notes and head for the conference room where, according to Joanne when she comes up to me just after, I deliver a perfect talk on Applied Microeconomics, giving the attendees plenty of food for thought. My own appraisal of myself is not as glowing, but I can easily forget about the few times I stumbled over my words, and the instant, just after glancing at Joanne for an instant too long, my throat went so dry I had to pause to take a sip of water. Because this whole conference has taken on an entirely different meaning for me now. As enthusiastic as I was to come here, my focus has shifted. All I can think of as I sit through the panel discussion in the afternoon, and a few more talks before dinner, is my approaching night with Joanne.

Because there's no 'if' about it anymore. It's happening, and the thought of it leaves my head spinning when I look in the mirror after a bathroom break. Dinner is a pre-arranged affair with the conference goers occupying all the tables in the hotel restaurant. Someone goes over the schedule for tomorrow, but my ears only perk up when he announces the keynote speaker: Professor Joanne Ferguson. And yet, I can only think of how she looked at me, and how she spoke to me. Will there be fighting for top? I recall her question from last night in the bar, when I was starting to feel at odds with her. A distant memory now.

Then, dinner is over and I hear how Joanne doesn't accept several offers to go up to the bar for a drink.

"I'm exhausted," she says to a man I recognize as Professor Sands, another rockstar of economics. "And I need to go over my speech for tomorrow." When she turns around and spots me, she shoots me a wink that connects with my clit instantly. There will be no fighting for top tonight. I'm all hers already.

When she walks past the table where I'm sitting with a couple of other relative newcomers, she lets her gaze linger on me for a split second.

"Damn," the man I've been seated next to throughout dinner says with a southern drawl. "That Ferguson. Oh yeah."

I don't honor him with a response. Instead, I make my excuses and get up. "See you tomorrow," I mumble, my mind already—entirely—elsewhere.

"Hi Gail," Joanne says as soon as I enter the room. Her

70

shoulder is slanted against the wall nearest to the door. "Let's go for a walk."

"What?" I hadn't expected that. "Where?"

"We've been cooped up all day. It's not healthy." Joanne doesn't wait for me to agree. She just walks to the door and holds it open for me.

"But this is Atlanta. It must be ninety degrees out there still."

"Did you think it was going to be any colder in here?" With that, a smile slips along her lips again, and I'm ready to do whatever she asks of me.

I follow her out of our room. Secretly, I feel flattered to be walking through this hotel's corridors with Professor Ferguson. Just like I used to feel when, back in college, she'd stop to quickly greet me, or even better, ask me a question out of the blue. It would always send a rush of blood straight to my clit, that tortured little bud she so briefly touched this morning, that is making its presence known again through thick, urgent pulses between my legs.

"Where are we going?" I ask, more to mask my excitement than anything else.

"I don't really know yet. Just outside for now." Joanne looks straight ahead, strutting along with great purpose. "There are bound to be some trees on this hotel's grounds, right?" She slows her pace and locks her eyes on mine, bringing her lips a little closer to my ear. "Or something else I can shove you up against."

Instantly, the memory of her fingers inside of me is back. How she spread me wide and is, now, promising to do again. The thought of having her do it to me outside, with the possibility of someone seeing us, and a breeze of fresh air chasing along my skin, pumps a fresh load of blood straight to my pussy lips.

Not a lot of people prefer the outside, stifling air to the

air-conditioned one inside the hotel. When we exit through a door opposite the hotel's entrance, the sky is black and what I can see from the hotel garden eerily silent.

"Perfect," Joanne says, and even that short word sends a shiver up my spine. "Come on."

She leads the way to the right, still following the tiled garden path. After only a few minutes outside, the mugginess of the air affects my breath, and I feel a few drops of sweat travel down the small of my back.

"Damn, it's hot." Joanne starts shrugging off her blazer. We're both still dressed in full conference attire.

I follow suit and slip my arms out of my jacket. Already, the back of my blouse clings to my skin.

Joanne stops to scan our surroundings, her head moving from left to right. "Oh yes," she says, as the movement of her head stops. I follow her gaze and my eyes land on a cluster of five trees behind a few low bushes. The spot is dark, but not entirely secluded.

With renewed vigor in her stride, Joanne marches onward, and, my legs already going a little weak, I trot behind her.

"Perfect. Don't you think so?" she asks, while assessing the trees. Which one will she shove me up against?

I can only nod, and wonder when the tables turned. The second she walked into our room again this morning and cast her eyes on what I was doing. By far, the most defining moment of our re-acquaintance. That split second changed everything, gave her the upper hand. A hand she'd been vying for since we met at the bar, but I would never have given her had she kept up her antics. Now, I'm all too eager, and she knows it. She knows she has me. She's known it ever since she perched next to me on the bed this morning.

She points her thumb at the tree in the middle of four others, as though planted here only for the purpose of having Joanne fuck me against it. "That one it is," she says. "Why don't you take off your blouse and have a little rest against it, Gail." An undertone of menace has slipped into her voice. A tone I've never heard before, not even when she caught someone cheating at an exam years ago, giving the person the earful he deserved, but always keeping a certain lightness to her tone. This is different. It's not all menace though. Through the darkness, I can hear the desire inside of her finding a voice.

I do as she says, unbuttoning my blouse quickly and positioning myself against the tree as requested.

"Come on, Gail. Nothing I haven't seen before underneath that bra. Don't be shy now." The memory of her eyes on me this morning hits me again with full force. Much more than the thought of her fingers inside of me, it makes my blood race through my veins, heating up my flesh.

Swiftly, I unhook my bra because, frankly, I can't wait to expose my breasts to the heavy Atlanta air.

"That's more like it." Joanne doesn't come for me immediately, instead she stands there for a while, eyeing my naked flesh. My nipples grow rock hard under her gaze. For all the staring she's done at my naked body, she has barely touched me. It's a strange sensation to have had a woman's fingers inside of me, but not having had her caress my breasts, or even lay a finger on my belly.

There's a faint hush of traffic in the distance, and a light rustling in some bushes a bit further away, but apart from that, there's not a sound around us. Even if there were, it's just me and Joanne in this moment. Her eyes glitter in the darkness as they roam across my skin. She steps closer, and I suck in a shallow breath.

"Well." There's that dark hint in her voice again, even noticeable in such a short word. It's enough for me to know that she's just as aroused as I am. "I can't help but think this is what you wanted all along, Gail."

Kissing is always considered such an intimate act, but, to me, staring into someone's eyes, not averting my gaze but really looking back, is just as much an act of closeness—if not more so. I gaze deep into Joanne's eyes, into the darkness of them. They're not just dark because of the absence of light, there's something else there. More than shadows. More than desire.

She brings her hand up to my chin, stroking a finger along my jawbone. "Is this what you dreamed of?" she asks.

My only reply is a further silent stare into her eyes. I can hardly give her the satisfaction of a response to that question. It would undo me instantly.

"There's no use in playing hard to get anymore." Joanne's finger trails lower, hovering over my collarbone now. "I saw you. I saw how much you wanted me when you spread your legs the second I left the room. Is that how much you want me, Gail? Hm?"

It's the last 'hm' that gets to me the most, that connects with the fire in my belly and sets it free to travel throughout my flesh.

Her finger dives even lower and has reached the curve of my breast. My nipples are so eager for her touch. For a caress or, even better, a daring pinch.

"Tell me," she insists, not just with her words, but by catching my nipple between two fingers and squeezing oh-so softly.

"If you want more, tell me now."

"Yes," I hiss, lust tumbling down my stomach. "I want you."

She nods, a smug little smile on her face. "Good. We're getting somewhere." With that, her fingers lock hard around my nipple, pressing it into a hard, taut mass of exquisite pain. Meanwhile, her eyes are still on me, still blazing fire—and I blaze right back with mine.

"I'm going to undress you," she says, in between violent pinches. "You're going to stand here naked against this tree, for anyone who wishes to see. But mostly for me, Gail. I knew you wanted me from the second you offered to switch rooms. Hell, I knew it twenty years ago, when you came to my class all coy, but really, it couldn't have been more obvious."

She releases my nipple from her painful grasp, and her hand thunders down to the button of my trousers. With a fast, confident flip, she opens it, not waiting long to lower the zipper.

"Kick off your shoes," she commands, and, as though in a trance during which I have to automatically obey every command she utters, I heel them off. It leaves me standing a bit shorter than her, but not by much. Enough to make me feel smaller than her though, or at least in a complete submissive state.

She lets her gaze drop from mine for an instant while she guides my pants off my legs. Before she hikes down my underwear, she runs a finger across the soaked panel.

"Let's see how wet you are for me, huh?" These words coming from Professor Ferguson's mouth leave me wet like a river. "Damn." There's something new in her voice again. Awe? Surprise at exactly how drenched I am for her? "Jesus."

Next thing I know, my knickers are part of the pile of clothing next to my feet. And there I stand: completely naked, and for no one else but her. Although, of course, I can't be sure. For all I know, the man I was sitting next to at dinner might be gazing out of his window, casually staring into the garden, only to find me on full display. But I believe we're hidden enough. Still, the hint of doubt arouses me, and contributes greatly to that hot river running between my thighs.

"Spread your legs," Joanne says, her voice shot to pieces, and that ignites an even fiercer kind of throbbing in my clit. "Bring your hands above your head and hold on to the tree."

Again, I do as I'm told. Positioning myself the way she asks and, in the process, offering myself up to her. My breasts jut out and my cunt is completely accessible to her.

"Enjoy the show, Gail." Her eyes fixed on mine again, Joanne starts undoing the buttons of her own blouse. She doesn't exactly go about it in a sexy, slow manner. There's an urgency to her movements indicating that her own arousal is growing as well, that she's riding this wave of desire just as much as I am.

I haven't seen her naked yet, and my eyes are glued to her hands, to how they methodically unbutton her blouse and let it slide off her arms. Her bra is maroon-colored and, when she bares herself, her breasts are pale orbs in the darkness. Small domes I want to touch, cherish, kiss for hours. But I do have a strong tendency to believe I will have to wait quite some time before that happens.

She doesn't take off her pants. Instead, she brings her hands to her waist and stands there defiantly, as if asking, "Do you like what you see?" She doesn't say it out loud, and this question doesn't beg an answer. I started liking what I was seeing a long time ago, the wetness between my legs can attest to that.

It's also not the curvy shape of her breasts that arouses me the most, or their delicate paleness, or how hard her nipples poke upward; it's that she bared them to me at all. Of course, we have no manual here. She's playing by her rules, and hoping—gauging along the way—that they align with mine. So far, they do.

When she comes for me, I'm already half there. I'm

already half-suspended in that space leading to momentary oblivion, in that frame of mind where I know no boundaries, that addictive state of surrender, of giving it all up to someone else. I can feel my clit throb between my legs, reaching into the hot, thick air that surrounds it, as though vying for attention. I know she won't touch it. I know women like Joanne. It's only my luck that she turned out to be like this. But perhaps it was there all along since the moment we clasped eyes on each other again. Perhaps the opportunity presented itself in that instant when I addressed the reception clerk and offered up my room and, in offering that, she knew I was offering much more. Last night in the hotel bar is a distant memory now. Foreplay almost gone wrong. Or maybe it was part of her plan all along.

In situations like this, I'm not always the one submitting. I give as good as I get and because of that I try to guess what she'll do next. In my head, I'm still trying to outsmart her. Additionally, because I'm familiar with the thrill of being on the other side, my arousal increases.

"I have a question for you, Gail." To my utter surprise, her finger finds my clit. She rubs through my wetness creating tiny, tight circles around it, making me gasp for air instantly. "No need to raise your hand if you know the answer." A small chuckle in my ear. "How long can you resist? Show me now, and I'll give you everything I've got."

Is she asking me not to come? While her finger starts applying more pressure? It would be easier if I hadn't shown her how I liked it this morning—and if she wasn't pressing her breasts into mine when she asked this of me.

"Save yourself for the big one, Gail," she says. "I promise I won't disappoint you." With that, she locks her lips on mine, trapping my tortured moan in her mouth, and my knees buckle. If I was half-way there earlier, I'm only one quarter removed now. Joanne's kiss floors me more than

anything, more than I had expected. I want to simultaneously push my pelvis against her, and pull myself away. The
tree is hard against the delicate skin of my behind, and will
certainly leave scratches the way she has me squirming
against it. In the air, I smell late summer, a faint whiff of
flowers, Joanne's perfume, and trees. Although I'm not even
sure trees can be smelled. I'm not sure of anything anymore,
except that if she keeps kissing me like this, and rubbing my
clit like that, I'll come in a matter of seconds.

But then, she releases me, leaving me both frustrated and
relieved. Even though she promised me bigger things, I feel
deprived of something in that moment. I'm guessing that's
exactly how she wants it.

"Good girl," she says, in a husky voice. Because of our
kiss, her lipstick has been smeared across her lips and the skin
around it, giving her a dirty, devilish look. And in that
instant, I wish the tables were turned. Am I too far gone to
shove *her* up against a tree? I can barely still stand on my legs
—and she did an excellent job of making me submit. Would
she even allow it? The thought makes me go dizzy again.

One thing, however, is for sure: the woman standing in
front of me, about to 'give me all she has' is no longer
Professor Ferguson, my Applied Economics teacher of
twenty years ago. What I see now, is a woman possessed by
shadows, by the desire to take something from me while
giving me everything. In her eyes, I see how much she needs
this. How much she wants me. It's in the slant of her head, in
how her eyes have narrowed and, now, also, in the frenzy
with which she unbuttons her pants. She lets them drop to
the ground, no doubt soiling them, and kicks them off her
feet, along with her shoes. I never thought she'd go fully
naked for me, not here. She's still wearing her panties and
instead of slipping them off, she slides her hand underneath
the hem.

"I'm hot for you, Gail." She spreads her legs wider as she lets her hand sink deeper into her knickers. "Let's see how much more you can take."

Her arm crosses her chest in a diagonal line, and her hand and most of her wrist disappear into a pair of maroon knickers. Is this an invitation? Or another challenge?

"Take them off," I hiss, but I don't move. I stay moored in my spot against the tree, my hands still above my head. If anyone walked past now, they'd either get very aroused very quickly, or suffer a heart attack.

"Are you sure?" Joanne tips her head again. She looks like desire personified. Like someone about to lose the control she so carefully exercised all day. "Are you sure you can take that?"

Of course I'm not sure, but I'm not going to come just watching her touch herself, am I? What with my hands still obediently wrapped around the tree. "Yes. Please. I need to see."

"You need to see my pussy? You need to see how wet I am for you too?" She flicks her tongue along her lips, smudging the lipstick even more. It's the sight of a woman undone, of a woman surrendering to her own desire, and I know I won't be able to take it, not the way she asks.

With a few shakes of her behind, she wriggles out of her panties, and stands in front of me in all her naked glory. My eyes are instantly locked on her glistening pussy lips. Despite the darkness around us, I see enough. There's enough on display here to tip me over, and I can't help myself. As soon as Joanne brings her hand between her legs again, I do the same with mine. I watch her touch herself, her lips slightly parted, and flick a finger along my clit. It's too much. The whole scene and the lead-up to it. Joanne doesn't stop me—or order me to stop. Instead, we both touch ourselves, and I come in seconds while watching her.

Was this what she meant when she said she'd give me all she had?

My climax is violent and quick, tearing through me with compulsive need, and after I catch my breath, my back propped against the tree, I see my opportunity to turn the table.

"Stop," I say.

Joanne does so momentarily, locking her eyes on mine, but probably more from the shock of hearing me say it. She paints a grin on her lips and starts stroking herself again with slow, languorous strokes.

"Why don't you let me take care of that?" I ask, while stepping closer to her. Without the support of the tree, my legs are wobbly, and I'm more aware of my state of undress here out in the open, but the pull I feel toward her is too big to give that too much notice. I need to touch her now.

I put my hand over hers and take over, not waiting for permission. I'm floored a little more when my finger meets her wetness. Slowly, I walk her to the nearest tree, figuring we both need the extra support. When her back touches the trunk, Joanne fixes her eyes on me intently. Her hand, which she let slip from my grasp between her legs for a split second, is back.

"Fuck me, Gail," she says. I'm surprised at how she can still put more command than desire in her voice. "Put your fingers inside of me and fuck me."

I can't remember an instance in my life when I ever wanted to do something more. I'm looking at her face so I don't see what she does with her hand, but she keeps it there, circling around her clit by the feel of it, while I, without further ado, slip two fingers inside of her.

At the sound of Joanne's breath being cut off as I enter her deep from the start, my own throat closes as well. I press my lips to the frail skin of her neck, kissing her there, while I fuck her. The brushing of her fingers against my hand as she touches her own clit, while I thrust high inside of her, is an unexpected turn-on for me. I feel my clit swell again and, figuring I have a free hand anyway, I touch myself, again—it seems to have become a common thread for the weekend.

We're a tangled-up mass of intertwining arms, pumping hands, and busy fingers. Here, between these five trees outside our hotel, where anyone can see, but no one does.

"Oh, Gail." Joanne is starting to unravel now and with her free hand she latches on to my shoulder, digging her nails deep into my flesh. The mark will go nicely with the ones left by the rough surface of the tree.

The sight and sound of Joanne approaching climax enforces my own, but I hold off, lifting my finger from between my own legs to focus on her.

"Take me there," she says, and starts pushing me down.

Without giving it any further thought, I sink through my knees for her, for my first close-up encounter with her pussy. The angle of my strokes inside of her is different now, giving her some pause, but not for long as I touch my tongue to her clit. Joanne's hands are in my hair, pulling, grasping, twirling. I delve my fingers high and deep inside of her, while my tongue dances around her clit.

"Oh jesus," she moans. "Oh, damn." Her hands still in my hair, her fingertips trying to dent my scalp.

I halt my motion and give her clit one last devilish lick, which makes her knees buckle slightly, before slipping my fingers out of her and pushing myself up. At the sight of her —conquered, sated, pleased—I forget about my own pulsing clit for a moment.

"Jesus christ, Gail." Joanne's smudged lips form a half-smile.

"Just another conference night for you?" I send her a

smirk back. I can smile now because I already know the answer. What just happened between us here is not over yet.

She sinks her teeth into her bottom lip and slowly shakes her head. "I don't think so."

"As much as I'd like to stay here a few more hours, I think we'd be wise to go inside now."

Joanne quirks up her eyebrows. "Always the smart one." She starts scanning the ground for her clothes. "And the night has only just begun."

———

After we make it back to our room, smiling sheepishly at a few fellow guests we encounter along the way in our wrinkled clothes, we break out into spontaneous laughter. I look at Joanne's dirtied face, her disheveled blouse, her panties half-peeking out of her blazer pocket, and I just giggle—although I'm still acutely aware of a pulse between my legs.

"Best get this dry-cleaned," she says, while stepping out of her trousers again. The action is stripped of all eroticism in the half-light of our room. I'm not sure we can ever go back to the intensity we shared between those trees, but once again, Professor Ferguson displayed her genius when she took me outside to shove me against one.

"Do you want to shower first?" she asks, already half-naked. There's nothing left of the woman who stepped out of the bathroom in a pair of silk pajamas last night. Last night feels as though it took place months ago.

"You go first." I sink down on the bed, suddenly hit by a wave of fatigue. My speech. The day. What happened this morning. A slew of new emotions and experiences my brain is eager to process through sleep. And then there's the heat between my legs which still seems to consume me. The words Joanne uttered when she came still echo in my ears. And, again, I can't help myself. I wait until I hear the water of the shower beat down onto the tiles to slip my hand inside my unbuttoned pants. It's a wet mess down there and I realize, once again, that Joanne has barely touched me. Is this what she has specialized in during her conference tours? Driving women crazy by not touching them? No wonder I was so infatuated with her in college. The hold she can so easily have over someone, just by looking at them.

My finger circles around my clit, but my wrist is too constrained by the waistband of my panties. I quickly get up and push them off me before positioning myself on the edge of the bed, legs spread wide.

"Ahum." A noise by the bathroom door startles me. "Enough of that for one day, Gail."

She tricked me again, letting the water run to fool me into thinking I was alone. I don't care this time. I even revel in the blush that, inadvertently, creeps from my neck to my cheeks.

"Unfinished business," I say, and bring my hands ostentatiously between my legs.

"Come on." Joanne extends her hand. "Let me show you what I can do with a shower head."

I swallow hard, her words not missing their effect. Automatically, I rise to my feet, astounded by the lust that keeps building in my gut. I let her coax the rest of my dirty clothes off me and guide me to the shower, which is steaming already.

Underneath the spray of water, Joanne grabs me by the back of the head and pulls me close for a kiss. Although she kissed me once before, this one feels like the first kiss we skipped. It goes on and on, as the water cascades onto our faces and shoulders, lubricating the expanse of our skin.

And if I feared we could never get back to the intense atmosphere we shared outside earlier, I was wrong, because I feel it in my blood again, and I see it in Joanne's gaze when we break for air. Her hair is matted against her head, strands of it streaking her forehead, but beyond that screen of water, I see it clearly. I think I'll invite her to Dartmouth sooner rather than later. There's lots of greenery there. Loads of trees which she can shove me up against. And if she stays long enough, I may even acquaint her with the good sides of monogamy. But I'm getting ahead of myself, as she pushes my back against the wall of the shower, shoots me a longing glance, and kneels down before me.

A Hard Day's Work

"FEMALE BOSSES ARE THE WORST," Ann says before carefully allowing a tiny lettuce leaf into her mouth. She chews it as if eating is a forbidden activity.

"I disagree." Kenneth draws his lips into that leery look I despise. He fixes his gaze on me. His eyes are the colour of weak tea. "I'm sure Jo and I are on the same page."

After I first told him I'm exclusively into women, he didn't know what to do with that information for a few weeks. He would stare at me in silence for minutes and shake his head in disbelief, as if he couldn't figure out the physical practicalities of two women in bed together. I much preferred his ignorance over the delusional camaraderie he now believes we share.

I take a big bite out of my sandwich because I refuse to acknowledge Kenneth's insinuation. Ann arches up her eyebrows and shoots me a quizzical look. Silence is not going to get me off the hook this time.

I chew slowly, making sure she understands how much tastier my cheese sandwich is than her salad without dressing.

"Amanda has some issues." For starters, she's straight, I say only to myself. "But I've seen worse." I know that by stating this I'm essentially siding with Kenneth, but I can't agree with Ann on this one.

"Shht," Kenneth says before I can continue. "She's coming." He sits up straight in his chair, all but adjusting his tie.

"Hey team." Clearly, one of Amanda's issues is that she addresses us as *team*, as if we're taking part in a self-improvement seminar. "Do you mind if I join?"

"Of course not," Ann is quick to say. The fake smile on her face hurts my eyes.

Amanda unpacks her green salad. I spot a few drops of dressing. At least Ann is winning that particular battle.

"You ladies should eat more." Kenneth shuffles in his seat. Unlike him, I can keep my cool in Amanda's presence. "If that were my lunch," he points at Ann and Amanda's flimsy salads, "I'd pass out after three."

Amanda zones in on his pastrami sandwich. I detect a glimmer of disgust in her eyes, but I can't be sure. I might just be projecting. "After you're finished with that, you should have enough energy to finish the Haynes report I've been waiting for."

I catch a glimpse of Ann's triumphant grin before she stretches her mouth into a semi-indifferent pout again.

Kenneth's cheeks flush the tell-tale crimson red they always do when Amanda chastises him.

"Did you have a nice weekend, Amanda?" I quickly change the subject because I can't help but feel sorry for him. I also want to grab the opportunity to find out more about Amanda's personal life.

"Doug was away so I came into the office on Saturday to catch up on e-mails." She pauses to check if she has our full attention. Amanda likes it that way. "And yesterday I ran a half-marathon."

Silence ensues. It's a hard one to follow. I know Ann has been training for the company's annual 5K race taking place in two months. Kenneth—despite his love for unhealthy food —is so skinny his body seems only made up of flesh and bone with no room for fat or muscle tissue.

"How about you, Jo? Did you paint the town red?" Amanda's green eyes rest on me.

I don't know how I got the reputation of being a party animal. Maybe it's because I'm the youngest on the team, or because I'm single—or because I'm a lesbian. "My doubles partner and I got severely beaten in our tennis club's championship."

"Oh, I didn't know you played." Amanda's face lights up. It's common knowledge her two great loves in life—apart from work—are running and tennis. "Which club do you belong to?"

"Hennessy's. It's in Surrey." I only joined a month ago. I'm more a martial arts kind of person, but it was a strategic decision which is paying off already. I can practically feel Ann roll her eyes behind my back. I expect her to give me the cold shoulder for at least a day as punishment for fraternising with the enemy.

"We should—" The loud ring of her cellphone interrupts Amanda. "I'm sorry, I have to take this."

Uninterested in what's left of my sandwich, I lean back in my chair. Amanda rises from her seat and, as if it was only her in the break room, turns on her heels and leaves.

"Tennis, huh?" Ann shoves a dry stick of celery into her mouth. "That's a new one."

"What can I say," I joke. "I'm a woman of many talents."

"Is that what it's called these days?" A vacant look—the

one he gets whenever Amanda leaves the room—has taken over Kenneth's face.

"Just because she has a non-existent personal life, doesn't mean she has to sit here and declare how dedicated to her job she is. If I had a husband who's never around and no children, I'd have time to *catch up on e-mails* in the weekend as well." Ann's too busy being pissed at Amanda to direct more of her frustration at me.

Kenneth rolls the tin foil his lunch was packed in into a ball and tries to fling it in the waste basket in the corner. He misses. Without saying a word, he gets up and leaves.

"How's that 5K coming along, Ann?" I can't keep a mild sneer out of my voice.

"Just fine." She shoots up out of her chair and crosses to the sink to rinse off the plastic container her salad came in.

I wait until she leaves to close the lunch box Amanda carelessly left on the table. I put it in the fridge while humming the *Happy Days* theme tune.

———

Every day, at five on the dot, Ann and Kenneth rise from their desk and finish their work day. They have spouses to consider and children who need to be fed before bed. I usually linger on in the office the three of us share, enjoying the solitude and silence their absence brings. It also allows me the opportunity, every time I hear Amanda's footsteps clatter on the hallway floor outside, to imagine she'll walk in and say, "At last, they've gone," before hurling herself at me.

But Amanda is straight and she's my boss. I can pretend to play tennis all I want, she'll never be interested in me *that way*. It doesn't stop me from dreaming.

"You're on your own, Jo," Kenneth says and closes the door of our office behind him.

"Leave it open," I yell behind him—just like every night —but he lets it bang shut with the most annoying thud possible.

I push myself out of my chair but my toes catch behind the foot of my desk. My hip crashes into it, sending a half-empty coffee cup to the floor, its tepid contents spilling over my sweater.

"Fuck," I scream at no one but myself. I quickly grab a tissue from the box on Ann's desk and try to stop the stain from soaking all the way into the delicate fabric of my sweater. It doesn't help so I dash out of the office to the break room, which is closer than the wash room. I hoist my sweater over my head before yanking a tea towel off its hook and dousing it in water.

Engrossed in removing the stain from my sweater, I don't hear the footsteps approach from behind.

"Is it casual Friday already?" Amanda's voice beams.

Thank god I'm wearing a tank top, I think as I turn around. To my surprise, Amanda's eyes appear glued to my arms. Countless upper cuts and hooks a week haven't missed their effect.

"I didn't finish my lunch," she mumbles, completely out of character.

While she hides behind the refrigerator door, I stifle a chuckle. Instead of cursing Kenneth and his stupid game of slamming the door shut every night, I secretly thank him for landing me in this situation.

When Amanda re-emerges she has put herself together again. "You must have quite a serve with biceps like that."

This time, I'm the one nearly blushing. "I get by."

"What happened?" She nods in the direction of my sweater.

"Office clumsiness." Flustered, I hold my palms up, drop-ping the tea towel to the floor. It really isn't my day.

She scoots closer and crouches down to pick it up. As she hands it back to me, the tips of our fingers lightly touch. She redirects her attention to my sweater.

"You may want to use some vinegar on that when you get home." I hadn't pegged her for someone with detailed knowledge on removing stains. "Doug is terribly clumsy. It seems all I do is run after him and clean up his mess."

The mention of her husband's name zaps me back into reality. I doubt Amanda is the sort of woman who does a lot of running around for her husband—the mysterious Doug whose name gets dropped occasionally, but who never shows up for office parties or other work-related social events. I want to quiz her about him, but the circumstances don't strike me as ideal. It's also none of my business.

"Thanks for the tip." I smile and glance at my sweater, which I fear might now be ruined.

"Here's another one," she says as she heads for the door. "You should wear short sleeves more often."

I have to keep my jaw from dropping. If I didn't know any better, I'd swear she was flirting.

———

"Happy three months, Jo," Kenneth says. "Looks like you're a keeper."

"Don't speak too soon," Ann butts in. "She hasn't had *the talk* yet."

It's Friday morning and I've been officially employed by the company for three months, thus ending my trial period.

"You'd best hope she's in a good mood today. I remember my first performance review and, well, let's just say it's not the fondest of my many happy memories of this place." Ann feverishly tries to untangle a bunch of paperclips. "And not because I was performing below par, mind you. Just because—"

"Yes, Ann, we know already," Kenneth cuts her off. "Because you're a woman. Blah blah blah."

"She wasn't horrible to you though, was she?" Ann tosses the paperclips to the side. "Because she's not threatened by you. It's so classic."

I stop listening because, in the three months that I've shared an office with them, I've heard it all a million times. Ann and Kenneth love to bicker, but strangely enough, they work well together. I suspect they keep the quarrelling going because they fear it may affect their performance if they stop.

A knock on the frame of our open door interrupts their current spat.

"My office in five minutes, Jo?" I instantly notice Amanda is wearing a different shade of lipstick. It's redder than usual, making her lips look fuller—and more attractive to chew.

"You got it, boss." I shoot her what I think is a confident smile.

She disappears into the hallway and I'm left counting down the seconds.

"Good luck," Ann says when I get up four minutes later.

"She doesn't need it." Kenneth winks at me and it almost moves me.

It's Friday so I'm dressed casually in a pair of dark, tight jeans and a sleeveless blouse. I make sure the blouse is neatly tucked into my trousers before knocking on Amanda's door.

"Come in." The different versions of this scenario that have played in my head are countless, but they always ended up with both of us half-naked on the floor. "Close the door behind you and take a seat."

I've never had any reason to believe Amanda hates the

other women on her team. Most of the rivalry between her
and Ann takes place solely in Ann's head, just as Kenneth's
firm belief that Amanda has a soft spot for him is merely a
figment of his imagination.

I sit down in the chair opposite Amanda's desk. She
glances at a sheet of paper in her hands. I stop myself from
tapping my fingers on the arm rest of the chair, but I can't
consciously slow down the mad pitter-patter of my heart.

Amanda is wearing a tight black blouse today—one of
my favourites on her. It's open at the throat and it's hard to
keep my eyes off the exquisite hollow of her neck.

"I only have one question for you." Amanda leans back
in her plush leather chair. It's as if I can feel her glance move
over the skin of my arms. She shoots me a quick smile before
continuing. Moments alone with Amanda are so rare—I can
count the times I've been alone with her in her office behind
a closed door on the fingers of one hand—and the situation
makes my stomach knot. I shuffle in my seat, expecting a
query on why I handled a case a certain way or how I feel I
fit into the team. "Why are you single?"

Her question has the effect of a bolt of lightning
connecting between my legs. Amanda looks at me as if she
just asked me how I feel about the endless rain we've been
having this summer.

"W-why?" I stammer, sufficiently taken aback. The cool I
always prided myself on keeping in her presence quickly slips
away. I may even feel a blush creeping up my cheeks. "I
mean, erm, why do you want to know?"

"It's not a trick question, Jo. I was single when I was your
age, but I had ulterior motives. I worked late to impress the
higher-ups, always making sure I exceeded my monthly
targets by at least fifty percent." She brings her fingers to her
neck, as if wanting to fiddle with a necklace that's not there.
"I'm just curious about your motivation and ambition." Her

smile shifts from neutral to flirtatious, her teeth sinking into her bottom lip.

I may be young but I recognise a come-on when I see one. If she hadn't painted on that seductive grin I might have believed her question was born from pure professional curiosity, but her eyes have lingered on my arms a few seconds too long and her smile grows even wider.

"You've made it abundantly clear you don't believe in a work system that focuses on reaching targets alone." I'm not sure how to play this so I decide to stick to a semi-profes-sional angle for now. "And I don't believe that working hard should exclude one from having a fulfilling personal life." I channel my taekwondo teacher Stan's mantra. "Everything in life is about balance."

"So," Amanda leans forward, placing her elbows on the surface of her desk. A whiff of her perfume enters my nose. I have no idea which brand it is because I'm not the kind of girl who has a working knowledge of things like that, but I do enjoy the smell of it very much. She clasps her hands together and intertwines her fingers. "You're not single out of ambition. That's good." She draws her mouth into an indecipherable pout. "Life's too short for that, trust me."

This is my first proper job so I don't have any experience with performance reviews but I'm fairly certain this is not how they usually go. I notice a slight hesitation in her eyes before she continues.

"But seriously, Jo. How can you be single with arms like that?" She cocks her head to the left a bit and curls her lips into a silly grin.

And then it hits me. She's giving me an opening to flirt with her. This is as much a performance review as it is an audience with the pope. In front of me sits a woman on the prowl—and I haven't even had my morning coffee yet. I feel all the power shift to me in that moment. The energy in the room changes and I have my confidence back. Amanda is too smart to come on to me too ostentatiously. Or maybe she just has a bicep fetish.

"I spend too much time doing push-ups, I guess." Stan makes me do a hundred regular ones before every training and a hundred with elevated feet after. "Not enough time in clubs." I make sure to flex my biceps when I say it. I can't help but wonder if I'm such a dead giveaway when it comes to crushes or if Amanda's just going out on a limb. I do know for a fact that my push-up statement will impress her.

"I'm certainly glad you took my advice on office attire."

Another opening. Am I supposed to ask her out? What about her husband? And the small detail that she's my boss? Maybe I should challenge her to a game of tennis, but then she'll soon notice I'm as much a novice on the court as I am at office flirting.

"What are you doing after work?" I may never get a chance like this again and I can't let it pass. As Amanda just reminded me, life's too short for that.

"Going for a run." Her chin rests on her hands. "Want to come?"

I nod. My throat has gone too dry for speaking—as if all the moisture in my body is suddenly occupied elsewhere.

"Good." She slants back into her chair. "Now about your first three months with us." Her eyes narrow to slits as she focuses her attention on the sheet of paper she was holding when I first entered her office. "Excellent work. HR will have you sign some papers. I sincerely hope you'll stay with the company a very long time." Her face is drawn into a mask of professionalism but her eyes sparkle with mischief. "That's it." She taps a key on her keyboard to wake up her computer. "Close the door on your way out, please. I need some privacy this morning."

I'm not sure my legs will hold me when I get up. My core

seems molten and a wild pulse throbs in every cell of my body. The fantasies I indulged in before this meeting suddenly seem nothing compared to what really happened.

"Thanks," I mumble and make my way out. After I gently close the door, I take a deep breath before returning to my colleagues and the questions they will surely bombard me with. This morning, when I dressed for work, pondering if I should really go for that sleeveless blouse, I had no way of knowing I'd end up on a date with my boss.

———

The rest of the day goes by slowly and it doesn't help that Ann eyes me suspiciously every time I get up to go to the bathroom or take a break. Amanda failed to discuss any details with me for tonight and I have no idea how this is going to play out. I can't focus on the figures I'm supposed to analyse. They dance in front of my eyes, always mysteriously shaping themselves into the form of Amanda's smile. I can't stop thinking about how she chewed her bottom lip, how she cocked her head and drew me in, making me believe I was in charge, but actually manipulating me—while taking advantage of the crush I so obviously have on her—into making a move.

"What on earth did she say to you, Jo?" Kenneth can't help himself. "You've been spaced out all day."

If Amanda was aware of my crush on her, it wouldn't be too far a stretch of the imagination for the two people I spend all my working hours with to know.

"Pff," Ann bristles. "I mean this in the nicest way possible, but obviously Amanda is not threatened by lesbians as much as she is by her own kind."

Her own kind? If only Ann knew. I check the clock on

my computer screen. It's ten to five. Ann and Kenneth are just killing time before they head home for the weekend.

"Dear Ann, I wish you and your kind a lovely weekend." I shoot her a small smile because she doesn't deserve more. Then I fix my gaze on Kenneth.

"It was just an uneventful performance review. I was barely in there ten minutes." Ten minutes of which I'll remember every second for the rest of my life.

Kenneth shrugs and Ann starts packing up her stuff. She screws the cap onto her bottle of water before placing it into her bag, arranges her pens just so in their basket and switches off her computer. I conclude that they don't have a clue.

A few minutes later they're both out of the door, but instead of relaxing into my seat while enjoying the first real silence of the day, my nerves are rattled and I can almost feel my blood pump its way through my veins.

Apart from the physical discomfort and the stress Amanda's words are causing me, my imagination isn't exactly playing nice either. I keep wondering about the length of her running shorts and the delicate tracks the sweat dripping from her hair will leave on her face. I'm also fairly worried about not being able to keep up with her. Despite being in good shape, I'm not a runner. In the dojo, I train barefoot and the only gym shoes I own are the cheap pair of tennis shoes I bought last month.

"Hey." Amanda startles me when she appears in the door frame. "Are we still on for tonight?" She's not exceptionally tall, but when she stands in front of me like that, her shoulder leaning against the door frame, her face relaxed but her upper body always held up straight, there's something so regal about her.

"Sure." I let her take the lead, not by choice but because I feel as if I have no other option.

"I'm knocking off early today. Shall we meet at the south entrance of Hampstead Heath at…" She pauses to check her wristwatch. "…seven?"

I should have had the audacity to ask her out for a drink instead. What else are Friday nights for if not for downing the pint or two I don't allow myself on weekdays? Do people who run half-marathons even drink alcohol?

"I'll be there." I've never seen Amanda in anything else but a dark pencil skirt and a tight blouse in either baby-blue, light pink, black, or white. Her work uniform doesn't vary and I hardly mind it—she pulls it off so well—but it will be strange to see her outside of work and in a sports outfit.

"Can't wait." She winks at me before turning on her heels and leaving me in a puddle of my own desire.

"It's a running date," I tell myself. "You'll both be sweaty and wet and highly unattractive." I have trouble believing myself.

I scramble for my stuff, save the document I was working on and rush out of the office. I have time to stop at a shop to buy a decent pair of running shoes.

————

When I arrive at the park entrance five minutes early— already exhausted by the slightly uphill trek from the tube station and the stress of not knowing where to put my keys, money, and Oyster card—Amanda's already there, stretching her calves in a highly intimidating manner.

She's wearing a pair of tight, knee-length running pants and a matching black top. My new shoes are making my right little toe itch—the first sign of a burgeoning blister. As I approach I count all the ways in which this was the worst idea ever.

"Hey." Her eyes instantly wander to my bare arms. She

really can't seem to get enough of them. "Did you find it easily?" Her demeanour seems different. There's less of an edge to her voice and her spine doesn't appear to be stretched so tautly.

"Yeah. No problem." I fumble with the small pouch holding my stuff. "I love it here. It's beautiful at this time of the day."

"My car's right over there." She points at a golden SUV parked a few feet away by the curb. I had pictured her driving a less practical car—something a bit more show-offy. "If you want to get rid of that." She opens a small pocket on the side of her running pants in which a car key is velcroed to the fabric. So that's how it's done.

"Thanks." I quickly head to the car, all the while feeling Amanda's gaze burn my backside. While dropping my pouch on the passenger seat of her car I do a quick scan for signs of Doug, but I only see a bottle of water, a few towels and back-pack tucked away on the back seat.

"How often do you run?" Amanda's already moving in place when I get back.

It's a question I should have anticipated, but somehow—because my brain was too busy focusing on less practical issues—I haven't. "Not very often." I smile sheepishly.

"You're clearly in good shape and you have quite a few years on me." She taps my shoulder lightly with her finger-tips. "You'll be fine. How does five miles sound?"

"Like a piece of cake," I lie and follow her into the park to a small path curving around the trees.

The first ten minutes are surprisingly easy. I realise I must be high on adrenalin. I let Amanda lead the way as the sun dips lower in the sky. The rain has stopped and it's an accept-able summer evening. Amanda is quiet when she runs, her face focused, her bent arms swinging by her side in fluent motions. The pace she sets is one I can keep up with—not effortlessly, but I do a lot of boxing training and, although very different from running, I am quite quick on my feet.

After fifteen minutes the first beads of sweat start making their way down her arms. That's when it gets difficult. I haven't forgotten what I'm here for, but I do wonder if I'll have energy left later to take this where I want it to go.

The Heath is quite deserted because it's a Friday evening and most people have better things to do than work on their fitness levels. Ordinarily, I'd be in the pub, contemplating a big night out but deciding on going home at a decent time because I always train with Stan on Saturday morning.

Maybe Amanda and I have more in common than I first thought. She also has a husband, though. In that respect, we couldn't be more different.

After what feels like three hours of running, but must, in reality, not be more than a good thirty minutes, I've fallen behind a little. It gives me a good view of Amanda's flexing calves and sculpted shoulder line. Her right arm is a bit wider than her left, indicating hours of tennis practice.

Then, all of a sudden, she stops. I breathe heavily when I reach the secluded spot she chose to halt our run at. My white tank top is completely soaked through and the muscles in my legs tremble.

"Are you all right?" she inquires. Her brow is coated in sweat, but there's no sign of a blush on her face. "I didn't mean to go so fast, but sometimes I stop thinking when I run and I just go for it."

I take a few deep breaths. "That wasn't five miles, was it?"

"No." She plants her palms against a tree and starts stretching her legs. "I made an executive decision to cut our run short."

I arch up my eyebrows. "Oh really? Why's that?"

"Come on, stretch," is her only answer.

I take position at the other side of the tree. It's thin enough to not obstruct too much of my view. Amanda's top is sufficiently drenched for me to see how hard her nipples are. I mimic her stretching movements, which gives me a good excuse to keep my eyes on her.

"Turn around," she says. With one step she's by my side. "With your back against the tree."

Heat radiates off her body. My skin crackles when her palms connect with my shoulders. Her fingertips dig into my flesh and I instantly know this is not some special sort of stretch. This is foreplay.

"Quick question," she breathes into my ear. "Can I kiss you now?"

In a flash, my hands move to her neck and I pull her close. A storm brews in her eyes in the instant before she closes them, the moment before our lips touch and everything changes.

Desire rips through me as her stiff nipples crash against my chest. We're about the same height and the pressure of her breasts against mine while she lets her tongue slip inside my mouth for the first time, is enough to make my knees buckle.

The air around us is suddenly heavy with moist heat. The sun disappears behind a building in the distance, casting a sudden shadow over us. I want all of her at once. I want to tear off her wet clothes and fuck her right on this spot. But what about Doug? And maybe all she wants to do is kiss. Exactly how straight is she, anyway?

A million questions race through my mind and, despite the buzzing sensation creeping along my skin and the fire exploding in my belly as she kisses me over and over again, I can't make them stop.

Gently, I push her away. "I know you know that I want nothing more than what is happening right now."

"But…" She swallows before speaking. "You want to know what on earth I'm playing at."

I let my hands drop to her side and curl my fingers around hers to bridge the sudden distance.

"I'm all for a quick romp in the bushes, Amanda, but on Monday you'll be my boss again and what will happen then?" After dreaming of a moment like this for months, I could slap myself for saying this.

Her lips quirk into an almost shy smile that melts every bit of me that hasn't surrendered yet. She squeezes my fingers in hers and I know I still have a chance.

"I do apologise for my very un-boss-like behaviour." She presses her body against mine. "Will you go home with me so we can talk about it?"

Home? Talk? What about Doug? "You want to take me home?"

"I do." She nods as if it's the most logical question in the world. "Will you come?"

"Yes." If she's going to be all casual about it, so will I. I'm also dying to see her house… and to see if there's any sign of her husband. Speaking of which. Surely, this could not be some lame set-up for a threesome with him? What if he's waiting for his wife to bring home a young piece of meat. I realise I haven't thought this through. "What about your husband?"

She pulls back, letting my hand dangle in the air. "There's no need to worry about Doug." She sighs before straightening her spine, as if drawing strength from the action of lifting her shoulders and standing tall. "He's not in town and we're only a few signatures away from being divorced."

We start walking down the path. I have no idea where we are, if the car is far away, and what sort of walk this will turn out to be. Is Amanda on the rebound? It would explain her sudden interest. Maybe my crush on her, which I thought I was hiding so capably under my cool veneer, flattered her and she wondered why the hell not.

Dusk is falling as we silently head to the exit of the park. Does this change anything? It's not as if I didn't know about Doug before I came here tonight. If anything, at least I know now that he's as good as out of the picture.

This isn't just about Doug and Amanda and whatever's going on with them. This is about me being on my way to my boss's house after she kissed me against a tree. She kissed me. She invited me here. She wants this just as much as I do.

———

Amanda's house is much warmer than I had expected. I'd always envisioned her in a factory-conversion loft with sleek white designs and not a thing out of place. To my surprise, she has two cats who mewl excitedly as she enters. She scratches them behind the ears and the sight of it transforms my crush into something a lot deeper.

"Sorry about the mess," she says as we venture from the hallway into the lounge. "I wasn't expecting company." She smiles apologetically. I spot an empty mug on the table and a few pairs of discarded shoes on the rug. It's hardly my idea of a mess. "Do you want to take a shower? I can fix us something to eat. Spaghetti maybe?" She babbles.

I want to take a shower all right. It's my turn to make a move now, anyway. Amanda looks as if she's about to shatter with nerves. Something furry drags against my legs as I position myself right in front of her.

"Yes, please." I peck her on the cheek. "I'll take a shower…" I plant a soft kiss against the delicate skin of her neck. "…but only if you join me."

"But—" I can feel her body relax in my grasp. "Don't you want to talk?"

"You've told me all I needed to know," I breathe into her ear. "I didn't want a quick shag against a tree on the Heath and then have you drive home to your husband."

"And have me call you into my office on Monday claiming it was a big mistake and threatening to fire you if you ever told anyone."

There goes my false sense of security again. Every time I think I have the situation in hand—which I clearly never have but my acute lust would like me to believe otherwise— she slaps me in the face with a truth so obvious, it makes me feel like a hormonal teenager.

My muscles tense and a deflated sigh escapes me.

"Hey." She draws me back in, her fingers on the back of my neck zapping electricity through my body. "I was just kidding. I won't claim I know exactly what I'm doing here, Jo. Far from it. But you have no idea how long I've wanted this."

Amanda wanted this?

"How about that shower?" I ask.

Her hands trail down the sides of my body. "I'll have to get you out of these dirty clothes first." She hoists up my tank top and I instinctively raise my arms over my head. With the back of her hand, she caresses my stomach. "Jesus…" she hisses while she discovers my abs.

I hook my fingers under the tight fabric of her top and roll it upwards.

"There are two things you should know," she whispers after I've removed her top off her body. Her green eyes shine as they bore into mine. "One." She brings her hands behind her back and unclasps her bra. "I've never been with a woman before, but I've always wanted to." Her bra falls to the floor with a soft thud as she releases it. "And two." She heels off her running shoes. "I haven't had sex in a very…" She pauses to remove the headband keeping her hair in place. "…very long time."

I don't know what to think of her impromptu confessions. Frankly, the time for thinking has passed. Amanda stands in front of me half-naked, as good as throwing herself at me. I'm more than willing to receive, and be her first of everything she wants me to be—her first woman, her first lover in ages.

I crash my body in to hers, my hands in her loose hair and my lips on her mouth, and I'm not sure we'll have time to shower. I inhale her scent. The musky sweat clinging to her skin and the remnants of the day's perfume—I remember how it hit my nostrils this morning, instantly making my clit ache for her. I shove her against the nearest wall and catch a nipple between my fingers.

She moans, her breath hot against my neck, and I'm torn between ravaging her right there and then, or allowing us both to slow down. I remember my first time—with a woman—and the slowness of it, the deliberate hesitation of fingers on skin, the heat mounting in my blood with every tender caress of my girlfriend, and I want this for Amanda as well. I want her to feel this is not a quick rumble for me. I want her to feel my intentions behind it. Not because this is —suddenly—love, but it's not just sex either. Moreover, I don't want her jammed against a wall when I first slip my fingers inside of her. I want it to be more than that.

I release the pressure on her nipple and trail my lips down her neck to her breast. She tastes salty and her scent sets off something in my blood. A chemical reaction freeing me of inhibitions. The sudden certainty of knowing exactly what to do.

"Where's the bathroom?" I ask as I stare up into her eyes.

This is going to be a slow one—one we'll both never want to forget.

She takes my hand and leads me through the hallway, up the stairs into the master bedroom. I let her take off my bra, but I have other things in mind than slowly peeling off our sweaty clothes. I get out of my shorts and underwear quickly and wait until we're both completely naked.

"Come on." To my relief the en-suite boasts a large walk-in shower. Definitely something I can work with. I turn on the tap and wait for the water to turn warm before pulling her in with me. Instantly, her skin is on mine—hot and wet and sticky.

I kiss her under the relentless stream of water, drops leaking into our mouths while our tongues meet over and over again. Her fingernails scrape along my back and my skin breaks out in goosebumps.

I locate the soap behind her in a small alcove in the tiled wall. Reaching for it, I push her closer to the wall until I'm able to squirt a good amount into the palm of my hand.

"Time to wash." I rub the flower-scented soap all over her back, creating large bubbles of foam. Slowly, my hands travel to the front and my slippery fingers massage her breasts. I find her eyes and see nothing but desire. The woman who's melting under my hands has nothing in common with the woman who presides staff meetings and tells my colleagues and me what to do. Stripped of her office uniform—and running clothes—Amanda is a woman with god knows how many months of pent up lust coursing through her veins.

Her lips widen when my fingertips encircle her nipples, soft and slick. She sends me a wicked grin before turning towards the soap container and squirting some into her own hand. Soon, she's mimicking my motions and we're both caught in a massive cloud of foam, our bodies fragrant, moist and ready for more.

The first time her hands land on my breasts, it's my turn to gasp for air. Somehow, in my late-night fantasies, I've always focused on touching Amanda, never on her having her hands all over me. Reluctantly, I remember to go slow. To make an unforgettable memory for both of us, as opposed to a frenzy of lust gone in seconds.

Her hands become bold and travel lower, cupping my buttocks. Our breasts squish together, soap lathering in between. She digs her fingertips into my glutes and slants her lips towards my ear.

"Those cheeks in my palms is what my dreams are made of." She giggles and nips at my neck.

Her words send shivers up my spine. This first act of foreplay has gone on long enough. I need to move on to the next stage before I explode with desire.

Amanda's hair clings to her face and shoulders in dark strands. Drops of water slide down her skin to places I'll want to explore very soon. I reach for the tap behind her and turn it off.

"Clean enough to proceed?" she asks. Mischief glints in her eyes, but her face is serious. She sinks her teeth into her bottom lip and sucks it into her mouth. Her nipples point forward and underneath the wet layer of water, her skin crinkles up in goosebumps.

"You're gorgeous," I want to say, but the words don't come—they somehow die on the way out of my throat—so instead of saying it out loud, I lunge at her and draw her near. The smell of her sweat has been replaced by the scent of her soap. I start licking drops of water off her neck until my tongue reaches her mouth.

The kiss that follows leaves me trembling against her. It's full of everything I've always wanted from her—

passion, lust, and need. This time it's her turn to take the lead.

"Let's get you dry." She cups my chin in her hands and plants a soft kiss on my lips. "You're shivering." She leads the way out of the shower, pulls a big towel off a rack on the wall and covers me in it. Gently, she rubs my arms and back dry, but I'm still half-drenched when she quickly soaks up some water from her own body with it before coaxing me towards the bed.

It's big and plush and—in a flash—I see myself waking up in it in the morning, Amanda's body glued to my skin.

She backs up on to the bed until she's fully on it. I take in the scene. Amanda's wet hair dripping all over, her naked breasts heaving with the force of her quickened breath, her hand reaching out for me. I feel moist heat spreading through my body and throbbing between my legs.

I take her hand and let her drag me onto the bed. I kneel in front of her and her hands reach for my breasts. While inching forward to straddle her, she pinches my nipple between her fingers and a white flash of pure lust crackles in my blood.

Moisture trickles down my thighs as I spread my legs wide over hers. Amanda replaces her fingers with her lips and sucks my nipple deep into her mouth. I can't but throw my head back, my body already shattering with ecstasy. With my nipple still firmly lodged between her lips, I push her body down into the pillows. She rakes her nails along my thighs and my body shudders as if a jolt of pure electricity shoots from every single one of her fingertips.

I bend my legs further and my burning pussy kisses the skin of her upper thighs. The connection seems to trigger something in Amanda and she releases my nipple from her mouth, draws my face in and slips her tongue in my mouth. The occasional friction of her flesh against my clit is enough to reduce me to nothing but a puddle of desire, but, at that point, I still have enough control to push myself up.

Amanda does not agree though, and, with her hands on my hips, she bucks up against me, pasting her body to my feverish lips. It's as if, now that she has touched pussy for the first time, she needs much more of it—and I know exactly how that feels. So I give her more. I slide myself up and down along her moist, muscly thighs, careful not to apply too much pressure to my clit. As wonderful as it feels, I want her lips on my clit when I come, not her legs.

Gradually, I free myself from her grasp and start slithering down, kissing every inch of skin on the journey. I pause to bathe her nipples in my mouth, tasting how hard they are for me. Her body ripples underneath me as I make my way further down. My tongue catches a few last drops of water from her stomach and when my lips reach the edge of her trimmed bush, her body tenses.

I lock eyes with her to check if she's still with me—if she still wants this as much as she claimed earlier. Then her hands are in my hair, pressing me down in the direction of her pussy. Her legs are still closed beneath me and I don't let my lips wander lower than just above the hood of her clit. It's enough to send her body spasming and squirming beneath me.

I lift myself off of her to take position between her legs. She draws up her knees and spreads wide. When I lower my head, I instantly smell the heady scent of her arousal. Her breath comes ragged and her body jerks this way and that. There's no more time for postponing now. This is it.

Slowly, I drag my tongue all the way up her pussy lips, stopping at her clit. I repeat the process, slipping my tongue between her wet folds a little deeper every time. She tastes tangy and fruity and I know I'm already addicted to the smell of pure woman emanating from her.

"Good god," she moans and I take it as a signal to go one step further. I've waited for this moment as well, and I take a deep breath before gently touching my tongue to her clit. Her body goes rigid for a fraction of a second, then relaxes beneath the touch of my tongue. I give her clit a few tentative licks before swirling my tongue around it and sucking it all the way between my lips. With her clit inside my mouth, I flick my tongue from left to right, until her muscles tremble so hard, I have to let go. But I'm not done with her yet.

I look down at her glistening pussy lips, at how they seem to open themselves up for me. I readjust my position so I lean on one elbow, giving free reign to my right hand. I find her eyes at the moment the tip of my finger circles around her entrance. Her pussy seems to suck me in and I don't tease her any longer. One finger slips inside the wet, moist heat of her pussy and, in response, I feel my own pussy releasing a gulp of warm juice.

While I add another finger, I lower my lips and my tongue connects with her clit.

"Oh yes," she moans, and I slip my fingers deep inside while my tongue dances over her clit. I quickly settle into a rhythm of licks and strokes until her body goes completely still for an instant.

"Oh god yes, yes," she cries as the walls of her pussy contract around my fingers. A warm heat washes over me as Amanda comes all over my fingers. Her nails dig into my skull and I thrust deeper, until she can't take it anymore and pushes my head away, then pulls it up.

Her body has gone limp when our faces meet.

"That…" I wait until she catches her breath. "…was every inch as spectacular as I imagined it to be."

"Oh, so you've been imagining things." I kiss her on the temple. "How presumptuous of you, boss."

She smiles lazily while dragging a fingertip over my cheek. "What have you been imagining, Jo?"

"Who, Miss? Me, Miss?" I paint a surprised expression on my face.

"It's okay. You don't have to tell me." In a flash, she topples me over until my back hits the mattress. "I'll find out for myself."

Her knee is lodged between my legs and it feels so hot down there, I fear I might burn it with the sheer force of my lust for her. I have no more repartee because I'm lost beneath her gaze, beneath that look of pure longing in her eyes. She drops her body to the side, draping herself half over me.

"You have the most exquisite body." Her fingers travel over my breasts to my abs. "I may have to ask you to start wearing long sleeves again, especially on Fridays." Her grin is wicked and sly as her finger dips down between my legs. She tickles my inner thighs while her eyes linger on mine.

"Please," I say, because I can't wait any longer. I need more of her, need her inside.

She licks her lips and her fingers zone in, stroking along my thigh, through the wetness clinging everywhere.

Her eyes narrow to slits as she pushes two fingers inside of me.

It feels as if a month-long thirst is being quenched. As if every wish I ever had has been granted. Her fingers move inside of me unhurried and I arch my back to push myself towards her.

"You're so gloriously wet." Her eyes are still on me, wonder dancing in the green of her irises. Her wet hair clings to her skin and her breasts bounce with her movement.

And it's all I need to let go. Her voice. Her eyes. Her fingers inside of me, rocking me to my core. She intensifies the pace of her strokes, meeting my need, reading me, and I go with her. I go where she takes me.

"Come for me, Jo," she says, and I do. It crashes through me, unstoppably, for her. Lightning in my bones and thunder in my blood. My climax makes me shiver in my skin, makes my pussy clamp down on her fingers, makes my eyes moist with tears.

Even after my muscles relax she keeps her fingers inside, as if she doesn't want to let go and stay in the moment. Satisfaction glows beneath my skin as I pull her close and kiss her until she finally lets her fingers slip out of me.

"This was without a doubt the best run of my life," she whispers in my ear before wrapping her body around mine. "Let's keep on training, though."

Suddenly exhausted, I sink into the mattress, Amanda's skin all over mine, her hair in my mouth and her scent in my nose. "Whatever you say, boss."

———

I wake up in a panic with cramps in my calves. My eyes scan the room for an alarm clock, but before I have the chance to check the time, Amanda's arms draw me in for a hug.

"Morning," she breathes into my ear, her teeth already nipping at my earlobe. "I hope you have nowhere to be today."

I turn to face her. Her eyes are barely open and her hair is a tangled mess framing her face on the pillow, but she looks ready to eat. "Hey." My voice is a mere whisper. "What time is it?"

"Does it matter?" Her fingers trail along my spine, arousing my sleepy body.

"Don't you have a marathon to run?" My lips quirk into a smile.

"I have my mind set on a different kind of marathon this

weekend." One of her fingers has reached a sensitive spot on my buttocks and I'm already melting.

"But what will you say on Monday when someone at work asks how your weekend was." I push my pelvis against her, wanting to feel as much of her warm skin as possible.

"Depends. The weekend has only just begun." Her fingertip travels down and slips between my legs. Any shyness —or reservations about sex with another woman—on Amanda's part seems to have been dissolved by the night because her finger goes straight for my pussy lips. "I think it's going to be a wet one."

"I don't mean to rain on your parade, boss." The tip of her finger circles my entrance. "But I have training at ten." My coach Stan does not accept any excuses.

"Can I write you a note?" She slips in an inch. Her finger can't go further in the position we're in.

I have to regroup before I can reply. "No," I pant. "But think of how toned my arms will look when I get back."

"I can think of plenty of arm toning exercises that don't require you leaving my bed." She shoots me a wicked grin, retracts her finger and pulls me on top of her. "Spread your legs."

I straddle her, my arms stretched on either side of her face.

"Do a push-up every time my finger slips inside of you." Her eyes sparkle and she doesn't give me time to reflect. "It's the perfect exercise." As promised, her finger enters.

When I bend my elbows to perform the required push-up, the angle with which her finger probes me changes and a burst of pleasure sparks in my blood.

"One," she says, her voice unfocused and her other hand clasping my right tricep.

She thrusts again and it's hard to keep my balance when

I press down. My face hovers over hers and her nails dig into my muscle as I flex.

"Two." The angle of her finger inside of me shifts again and as I push myself up, she adds another.

We both lose count as she fucks me faster and harder. Our breath meets as I come down and her nails leave marks on my skin. My body transforms into a mass of pure joy. My arms tremble and my shoulders hurt while my pussy burns around her fingers. All I see are her green eyes and the astonished expression on her face as she keeps upping the pace until I can't keep up and crash down on top her. Her fingers burrow inside and she takes me until I'm nothing but a shuddering, sweaty mess covering her body.

"I suppose I could call in sick," I stammer once I've found my voice again.

"Excellent plan." Her hands are in my hair, caressing my scalp. "As long as you never pull that trick at work."

"I wouldn't dare." I kiss her on the shoulder. "Have you met my boss?"

Younger Than Yesterday

THE GARDEN LOOKS beautiful under the setting sun, gorgeous but empty. A lone cricket launches into its raspy evening song, just like every night. The sameness of the days is comforting but sometimes, after dozing off for a brief moment, when I open my eyes, I expect him to sit across from me, his lips curled into a playful smile.

"You're getting old, darling," he would say. "And I had planned to keep you up all night."

I put my book down, trying to make it last longer because it's the only one I brought. Gazing into the black-green of the pine trees hedging off the garden, I let my mind wander freely. I allow myself to think about Michael and the times we spent here. This is his house, after all.

The loud jeer of my mobile startles me. So much for reminiscing. You can't really escape life anywhere anymore these days, no matter how remote your Tuscan refuge.

"Rose, my dear," John's voice beams into my ear. "How are you?"

"Looking forward to hosting you and your lovely wife next week, as ever." Solitude is good, necessary even, but

Helen and John's annual visit is always a cathartic trip down memory lane. John and Michael were best friends and John, although repeated hundreds of times, has the best stories to tell.

"Would you mind terribly if our Catherine came along? Her holiday plans with Jenny have fallen through and she's in desperate need of some healing sunshine." John's always been a good sport about Catherine's misfortunes in romance. Most fathers aren't half as apt at picking up the pieces of their daughter's broken heart.

"Of course not. Tell Cat she's most welcome."

Despite Michael being Cat's brother's godfather, she was his favourite member of the Archer clan. Every year, when John and Helen visited and we sat around the teak garden table, glass in hand and brain pleasantly fogged by alcohol, he would look at the old oak tree in the furthest corner of the yard and recount the story of how Cat climbed all the way up and broke her wrist on her way down.

"She was a fearless child," he would say. "Just like me." He'd peer deep into Helen's glazed-over eyes and taunt her. "If I didn't know any better, I'd say she was mine." He'd wink and Helen would never know what to say. "Billy stood watching at the bottom of the tree as his sister conquered it with her tiny little hands and feet, agile as a cat. Good name choice by the way." He'd smack John on the thigh. "And then she went flying. It must have only taken two seconds but I remember it in slow-motion. Her red t-shirt flashing between branches on the way down. The soft thud and crack with which she landed on the grass. The slight tremble of her bottom lip as she fought back the tears." He'd shake his head and smile. "Such a rascal."

"I should have known there and then she wasn't like other girls," Helen had said the last summer we were all together at the villa, two months before Michael's heart attack. She was never good at hiding the disappointment in her voice.

"Honestly, Helen," Michael butted in, louder than was necessary but unable to conceal his anger. "A little acceptance goes a long way."

Spurred on by the alcohol in her blood, Helen lashed out. "You may think she's yours. But she's not, so mind your own business."

John, always fiercely protective of his youngest child, rose to his feet and shot them both his well-practiced headmaster look. "Enough." That usually put a stop to the perpetual row between Michael and Helen about Cat's sexuality. Frankly, I never understood what all the fuss was about, then again, Helen has more than a decade on me—more than ten years to grow more ignorant, even when it concerns her own daughter.

Long after I put down the phone I contemplate the special relationship Michael had with Cat. They were always whispering in a corner, up to no good, plotting ways to get on Helen's nerves.

Cat never goes shopping with Helen. They don't trade sponge cake recipes or make-up tips. Instead, she smokes cigars with her dad and Billy and played football with Michael until it got so dark they couldn't see the ball anymore. Always rowdy and giggling, testing Helen's patience when they sat down in her beige couch with grass-stained shorts.

"If only you could see her now," I say to the empty space inhabiting Michael's chair. "You'd be proud. Often heart-broken, but definitely proud."

———

"Have you really never considered another man?" John asks,

his face earnest and his intentions good. The question doesn't come completely out of the blue. He's been trying to set me up with a new member of his tennis club for months, but I haven't been able to muster up any interest. I tear my gaze away from Cat's naked shoulder, unsure of how long it has lingered there. She's been quite withdrawn since they arrived. Nursing a relationship hangover can do that to a person, but her dad's question seems to peak her interest. I shoot her a small smile when she looks at me, curiosity brimming in her eyes. She responds with a wink and suddenly the hair on the back of my neck stands up.

"I've dated." It feels so incredibly silly to say that. "But you know better than anyone else Michael's shoes are hard to fill."

"Maybe you're looking at it the wrong way." John's voice wavers. He loved Michael just as much as I did. "It's not about replacing Michael. It's about companionship. You're too young to go through life alone." Every year, I get the same speech from John, but this one has come mighty early. They've only been here a day.

"If it makes you feel any better, dear John, I'll come watch one of your and Lionel's tennis matches when I'm back in London." I give him a weary smile.

"Wonderful," Helen cooes as if it's a done deal. "I'll make cucumber sandwiches and we can all have tea afterwards."

John draws his hands up in defence. "This is hardly about me. I only want you to be happy."

"I'm perfectly all right." I shoot a quick glance in Cat's direction, eager to see her reaction to all of this. She rolls her eyes at me. She must sit through these kinds of conversations on the state of her love life regularly. As unlikely as it may be, I feel as if I've found a kindred spirit.

"Dad, please." Cat straightens her posture. "Leave her

alone." She turns towards me. "You must forgive him. He's still adjusting to retirement and you know his job was basically sticking his nose into everyone's affairs. It's been a rough transition."

John taps his daughter playfully on the arm. She could say anything and he'd still smile.

"Sometimes all it takes is a little meddling," Helen chimes in.

"Most people are not that fond of it, mum." Cat chastises her mother with a harsh glance. Undoubtedly, she must have had to endure an avalanche of comments on her love life that, judging by what I've heard, hasn't exactly been a bed of roses lately—if ever.

Inadvertently, I put a hand on Cat's knee. I do it without thinking, as a gesture of gratitude because she's siding with me, but the touch of her skin on my fingertips jerks through me and releases a slew of unexpected butterflies in my stomach. For a split second I sit there stunned, not knowing what to do with myself. When I look up I catch Cat glaring at my hand so I quickly retract it. I narrow my eyes and fake a confident smile.

"How about we go into town tomorrow?" I change the subject. "There's a marvellous new restaurant owned by an adorable young couple. I'm sure you'll love it." Helen and John both nod enthusiastically while Cat stares into the distance.

The memory of walking past the open window of Cat's room the day before surprises me again. It wasn't entirely unplanned but I had no idea she would be half-naked. It was still easy to keep my cool then. I just made a joke about her choice of underwear and dashed off. That was before I knew I'd be awake half the night thinking about her bare breasts.

———

When the clock in my bedroom strikes three, I get up. I pull a dress over my naked body and open the French windows as quietly as I can. I walk to the pool and let my feet dangle in the water, careful not to make too much noise. Helen and John's room is on the other side of the hallway but Cat's room is next to mine and I don't want to wake her. She must have some sleep to catch up on.

Yesterday, when doing the dishes together, I clearly noticed the pain in her eyes. All I could do was hold her close and give her a hug. Her tears wet my blouse and, unexpectedly, heated the skin underneath. I wanted her head to stay on my shoulder much longer than she left it there. But I understood the moment was getting awkward. Now all I can do is think about how her breath landed on my neck and how I wanted to trap it with my mouth.

I draw ripples in the water with my toes and wonder what is happening to me. The thought of stealing another intimate embrace with Cat excites me much more—even disproportionally so—than the prospect of watching John and his pal Lionel play an old man's game of tennis. Maybe it's her youth and, despite the fact she's hurting, the energy that comes with it. She'll get over Jenny. She'll love again. At least she can be certain of that. I, on the other hand, have no clue what's been stopping me.

Michael was not an easy man to lose. Of course, I hold every new person of interest to the standard he set. It's not because I'm getting older that I have to settle for less. Still, it doesn't explain this thing with Cat. The pure physicality of it —how that snuck up on me and made my heart rumble in my chest when I put my arms around her—has thrown me for such a loop. As far as I can remember, and I've been racking my brain, I've never been attracted to another woman before.

It must be that I recognise myself in her pain. I feel for

her and want to protect her. Also, perhaps after seven years of mourning, I'm finally ready for something new. And Cat symbolises my rebirth into the world of romance.

Thoughts like this have been racing through my mind since I went to bed. Thoughts I can't place. Emotions so far buried I can't recall ever having them. Emotions from before Michael died, so suddenly, and left me to deal with life on my own.

I stare up at the moon and guess the time—not that the moon can help me with that. It must be closer to four now. Cat only woke up around noon yesterday. I caught myself checking my watch impatiently. As if my day couldn't start properly until I'd made her some scrambled eggs.

––––––

"Morning." Cat rubs the sleep from her eyes. I've been eyeing her window for an hour. John and Helen took their rental car into the village to do some grocery shopping and I've been battling with myself ever since. The selfish, crazy, inexplicably hormonal part of me wanted to wake her up so we could spend a little time alone. I didn't give in, though. I let her have her lie-in. She's on holiday and I couldn't think of a valid excuse to rouse her.

When I walked past her bedroom door half an hour ago, I had to stop myself from gently opening it and peeking my head in, but for all I knew she was hiding in there, dreaming of Jenny and better times. Also, that's no way for a hostess to behave.

"Sleep well?" I inquire, masking the grin that wants to burst all over my face. She sports a sexy bed-head, short black hair pushed up by sleep, and her athletic body is only covered by a skimpy pair of shorts and a crumpled tank top. No bra as far as I can see—and I'm looking.

"On and off." Barefoot, she pads over to a chair and pulls it back, her eyes searching for coffee. "Still getting used to the bed. It's strange coming back here after so many years. Everything is different now." She pours herself some coffee and stirs in two teaspoons of sugar. "Have mum and dad left me in your care?" She fixes her blue eyes on me, as blue as the sky reflecting in the water of the pool, and smiles. Her hair is starting to come down and a strand falls over her eyes. She has one of those unevenly cut hairstyles, short in the back and longer in the front.

"I promised them no harm would come to you." I suppress the urge to make her a sandwich, the desire to look after her and make her forget about her sudden break-up.

"Sorry they kept going on about Lionel last night." She crosses one leg over the other and cradles her coffee cup in the palm of her hand. "They can get carried away some-times, and honestly, if you want my opinion, you're way too hot for him." She winks at me and I'm sure it's meant inno-cently but I have trouble taking it that way. I don't blush easily, but I feel the heat creeping up my cheeks.

"I know they mean well. They just want to keep me from turning into an old maid." I accompany my statement with a little chuckle.

"I'm sure you don't need John and Helen Archer's help with that." She gives me a once-over and, if I'm not mistaken, fixes her eyes on my cleavage for a moment. "You must be fending off advances." The sparkle in her glance fills me with joy. "A woman like you." She says it as if it's an irrefutable truth and I try not to beam too much.

"Oh, stop it, Catherine." I flutter my eyes. "You're making me blush."

"Mum may disagree, but I have impeccable taste in women." Suddenly, her eyes get cloudy and I can see her

122

mood darken on her face. "Although I could be a better judge of character, I guess."

There's that pain again. I want to make it go away, kiss it away if I have to. Or even if I don't have to. I get a grip on myself and push these nonsensical thoughts to the back of my head. My day's already been made, anyway. Five minutes of semi-flirting with Cat is all it takes.

"Do you want some eggs?" I want to do something for her. It's stronger than myself. "Some toast, maybe?" I also want to get her mind off Jenny.

"I'll wait for lunch." She drains her coffee and stands up. Already, I feel the emptiness. "Let me clear this off."

"I'll take care of that." I rise out of my chair and stand next to her, her body heat glowing against me. Simultaneously, our hands reach for the same plate and when our fingers collide sparks shiver up my spine. If I didn't know any better I'd think I was falling in love.

"Come on, Rose." She turns her face towards me and her mouth is so close, her lips so curvy. "You're saving my holiday. Let me at least do something." Our hands are still touching so I don't want to let go of the plate. I peer into her eyes and my heart starts throbbing again, the same senseless thudding as the night before when I put my hand on her knee.

"Let's do it together."

"Deal." Cat lets go of the plate and focuses her attention on the rest of the table. Tires hiss as a car pulls up on the driveway. The moment is gone. It was good enough to hold onto for a while.

———

In the afternoon we're all lounging by the pool. I peer over my sunglasses as Cat swims laps, her strong shoulders gliding in and out of the water. The drops cascading down from them every time she comes up for air stir a funny sensation in my belly. I can't wait for the moment she exits the pool, her skin all wet and her muscles pumped from exercise. John and Helen are dozing in the shadow of the oak tree and I imagine they aren't here. I picture Cat pushing herself out of the water while pinning her eyes on me. She walks over to me with long confident strides and the drops of water falling out of her hair stain the book I'm reading. She bends over and places a moist hand on my neck.

"Come here," she says before pressing her lips against mine. "This has been a long time coming."

She takes the book from my hands and tosses it to the side. She pulls me down on the sun-bed until I'm flat on my back and straddles me, her wet bikini cooling my thighs. She kisses me again as if it's the most natural course of action, as if there's no other conceivable way for us to spend the rest of the afternoon. With wet hands she cups my breasts, stiffening my nipples. My blood races through my veins and I'm ready to surrender.

"Drink?"

"What?" I open my eyes, which I appear to have closed in the midst of my fantasy, and find Cat towering over me, a towel wrapped chastely around her body.

"Oh sorry, did I wake you?"

I scold myself for having missed her exit out of the water. And also a little for the inappropriate thoughts flooding my brain.

"I was just resting my eyes." The lesbian detective book she lent me sits in my lap. It's not half as saucy as I wanted it to be. "I'll have a G&T, please."

"Never too early for that." She shoots me a sly smile and heads into the kitchen. I catch my breath and am aware of the throbbing between my legs. I sit up and compose myself.

Helen and John are still snoozing. I berate myself for wishing my dear friends weren't here. I just really want to kiss their daughter.

John and Helen visit me every year, so I'm used to their company. Cat hasn't been here since she was a teenager and having her around has unsettled me. I haven't been myself with all this daydreaming I do about her undressing me, taking charge of me, really.

"Here you go, madam." She thrusts a large G&T into my hand. The towel has descended to her hips and I have to pull my gaze away from her wet bikini top. As the drink cools my throat, I'm beginning to think I've lost my mind. I haven't experienced this kind of instant attraction in years. I rack my brain for explanations but always come up empty. I've known Cat since she was sixteen, since she was a rampant tomboy with a mouth that—to Michael's delight—drove her mother crazy. When I'm in London, I see her at least once a month, and never has even the slightest inkling of this kind of inappropriateness surfaced before.

She settles on a deck chair a few feet away from me and leafs through one of Helen's Hello Magazines. Her wet bangs cling to her forehead and I'm eager to continue the fantasy I was indulging in before she interrupted, but I can't do it when she's sitting so close to me. Too much reality is mixed in with the dream.

Her skin is already turning golden-brown, setting off her blue eyes even more. She doesn't have the typical pale British complexion that goes red after two hours in the sun. Instead, there's a darkness about her. Not just in her looks—her hair and her tan—but also in her brooding air. Although bruised —her affair with Jenny was not the first that ended badly— she still has that easy-going flair of youth. A flexibility that seems to diminish with age. A nonchalance that drives me crazy.

I imagine what I would say to her if I had free reign. If John and Helen weren't her parents and it was just the two of us here, in the sun-drenched garden of this house I inherited from Michael. Would I go up to her, put my hands on her neck and whisper something in her ear? Something outrageous like, "I need you to fuck me now."

"Are you all right?" Cat catches me staring at her and I don't avert my gaze. Surely I deserve a bit of fun.

"Perfectly." My voice sounds a bit hoarse and I quickly sip from my drink.

"You look a bit flushed. It's not the book, is it?" Her smile is so disarming. I do wonder what got into Jenny that she ditched Cat for someone else. Clearly, it doesn't make any sense. I want to tell her she didn't deserve to get cheated on, that it's ludicrous, but I know it's not my place.

"Heavens no." I shake my head. "My drink must be too strong."

She looks at me as if she knows I'm hiding something. If only she would punish me for it. Pin my wrists to the chair with the palm of her hands and stare me down. At some point, I will need some chastising.

"Please, excuse me." I have to walk away. I need to remove myself from this explosive situation before I burst a vein.

"Sure." Carelessly, she turns her attention back to her magazine and my heart breaks a little.

I walk into my bedroom and close the curtains. I sit down on the edge of the bed and pant as if I've just run half a marathon. I scan myself in the mirror and hardly recognise the person sitting there. I recognise the familiar face, of course, and my curls rioting in all directions. But the passion in those eyes, that blatant want, is completely foreign to me. I nod at my reflection and I know it's time for something I haven't done in a long time.

I shuffle backwards onto the bed until my body is totally supported. I pull my legs up and let my hands wander between my upper thighs. I'm surprised by the heat glowing through my bikini bottoms when I let a finger slide over the seam. I realise I've neglected certain body parts for years, willed certain desires to take a back seat. I can't explain why Cat seems to be the catalyst for this sexual awakening I'm experiencing, but the fact of the matter is that just watching her has made me so wet I can't ignore it. I need to do something about this frustration that hasn't reared its head in seven years but has now decided to ambush me with unstoppable force.

I can't stand any fabric covering my swollen pussy lips anymore and tug off my bikini bottoms. I close my eyes and think of Cat. Her smile and the occasional sparkle in her eyes. I dream I am the cause of her pleasure, that I make her smile, make her feel better. I imagine her eyes peering down at me as her hands discover my body, as her fingers play with my nipples.

My clit is rock hard and pulsing for attention. When I dip a finger between my pussy lips I discover my wetness and, although expected, the heat of it still surprises me. I screw my eyes shut and envision Cat's finger doing to me what I'm doing to myself. I bet she'd do it better. I bet she has some secret lesbian tricks that would make me come five times in a row.

"I'll fuck you," I make her whisper in my ear. "It's all I wanted to do since I arrived."

I flick a wet finger over my clit, cautiously, but with plenty of determination and pretend Cat makes me moan with pleasure. I'm at her mercy. She can do whatever she wants with me as long as she never stops, as long as she keeps doing it and I can go back for more.

"Oh Cat," I grunt, and saying her name sparks bursts of electricity to pop in my veins.

"I want you so much, Rose," I have her say, while I imagine her fingers going deep.

From the depths of my gut, a fire builds and spreads through me, enflaming my muscles and skin. I nudge my clit quicker and quicker, to the rhythm of the sparks dancing in my belly. My muscles contract and I toss my head back into the pillows. My mind focuses on the image of Cat holding out her hand for me earlier. Instead of offering me a drink, she holds it open expectantly, her eyes forcing me to follow her into the bedroom. Drops of water rain down her shoulders and crash down onto the fabric of her bikini.

My clit and fingers are so wet from my juices. If only it was Cat's tongue setting me on fire like this. Cat's tongue there. The mere thought of it pushes me over the edge. I come while I mutter a muffled cry for Cat. My orgasm spasms through me and, though satisfying, I already know it's not enough. It will never be enough as long as it's not Cat giving it to me. Because it's too blatant to ignore, I'm ready to acknowledge my desire for her. I don't need to know why, don't need to analyse the origin of this madness. I just need to do something about it. If I boil everything down to its essence, which I'm more than willing to do, we're both single adults and we don't need anyone's approval. Now all that's left to do is seduce her.

———

On Saturday, John and Helen's thirty-seventh wedding anniversary, I set my plan into motion. I convince Cat's parents to enjoy their special day by themselves and take Cat on the road with me. She appears relaxed when we cruise down the country roads, happy even, or at least content in the moment. I make myself believe it's my company perking her up. I need all the confidence I can get for this.

I start things off in a relaxed manner by taking her to a winery where I engage in some innocent flirting and Cat, to my delight, has no apparent qualms about flirting back. We get a little tipsy but sober up before continuing our odyssey. I drive her to a secluded spot near a small forest where Michael asked me to marry him. It's quite significant for me to, of all places, take her there. But I feel as if I need to make an emotional investment. I'm not half-hearted about this. For the first time in many years I've found the freedom to give in to my desires, to needs buried along with Michael, and I refuse to question my motives any longer. This is no time to hold back.

We share a bottle of wine I brought in a cool box. I try to keep it casual but automatically, as if I have no control over what comes out of my mouth, I tell her about how Michael proposed to me here. It adds a graveness to the situation, a solemnness I wasn't really going for. In all honesty, I have no idea what I'm doing. I suppose I sort of believed the moment would present itself.

When I take the bottle back from her, in desperate need of a few more gulps, I let my hands rest on hers. She doesn't immediately retract, which I take as a good sign. My heart thumps in my ears. I wait for her to look into my eyes and I know it's now or never. I mentally prepared myself for this moment all week, for this split second in which I change my life.

I let go of the bottle and cup her right cheek.

"Tell me if you want me to stop." I trace my fingers over her ear and feeling her skin on my fingertips makes me gasp for air. I scan Cat's eyes for a sign of something—hopefully surrender—and wait for her reaction.

"Have you ever kissed—" she starts.

"Does it matter?" I cut her off. There's plenty of time later for questions like that. I just want this moment between us to develop into something more—a kiss, at least. I've been dreaming of her lips for days, been touching myself with a frequency I never even deemed possible because of them. "I want you. I think that's obvious." There. It's out in the open, in the glorious mid-afternoon Tuscan country-side no less. There is no better scenery for this kind of romance—or pent-up lust, if you will. I've laid my cards on the table. I've said the words. My heart is in her hands now.

"It's not that I don't want to."

That's not what I wanted to hear. I was hoping for a wordless answer, an inevitable breathless one. I haven't put my ego, my self, on the line like this in fifteen years. So this is what it feels like to crash and burn.

"I'm so sorry. I shouldn't have." I feel so silly for thinking this would be easy, for getting so caught up in my own desire. The girl just had her heart broken, for heaven's sake. My late husband was like a favourite uncle to her. What on earth was I thinking? "Embarrassed doesn't even begin to describe it." I cover my face with my hands, afraid to face this outrageous situation head-on. If Helen saw this, she'd pack her bags straight away and walk back to London.

Cat inches closer and puts her arm around my shoulder. "It's perfectly all right." I know she's trying to make me feel better, she probably feels sorry for me. I feel quite sorry for myself as well. It's clear she doesn't really know what to say. "I just—I don't know—" she stammers and I wish I had a magic wand to erase this awkwardness with.

I look at her, silly tears dripping down my cheeks. "I've been foolish, but it's been so long since I felt something like this." I shake my head. "You must think I've lost my mind." I shoot her a small smile.

"How about a date?"

"What?" The adrenalin levels in my blood spike again.

"We've been pussyfooting around it all day, with all the innuendo and such. Let's make it less awkward by making it official." Cat treats me to one of her trademark smiles, one of the irresistible ones and, once again, I'm baffled by how much sheer want courses through my body. "I'm asking you out on a date. Tonight."

"And that will make it less awkward?" I quip. I must be beaming goofiness. My head feels dangerously light while my stomach somersaults. That's when it hits me that I've fallen victim to a crush. Maybe it's one of those things that was bound to occur and Cat happens to be in the right place at the right time.

"Sorry to be so lesbian about it, but I need to process first."

"At least you are one." I grab her hand, which is still curved around my shoulders. I want to keep it there, wallow in its act of kindness. "There goes my fantasy of some woman love out in the open," I joke, wanting to make light of the situation, contrary to how I feel inside.

"We can always come back." She gives me a definite opening and I need to restrain myself. I want to push her down on the blanket and kiss her senseless, kiss her like I haven't kissed anyone in my life. "Depending on how the date goes."

"My dating skills may be a bit rusty," I admit.

"Judging by the current state of my love life, mine aren't exactly top-notch either."

————

It turns out we're both quite dating-challenged at this time in our lives. Dinner is a tension-laden disaster, an unpleasant affair sapping all energy from me. I sense Cat's reticence, her doubts about all of this, and I can't blame her. But, despite the refusal in her words and the hesitation in her voice, there's still a flicker of hope to hold on to. I decide to put my fantasy of Cat taking control of the situation—of her seducing me—aside and take her to Fabio's, my pub of choice. Maybe all this situation needs is for the edge to be taken off of it.

"Have you ever had feelings for a woman before?" Cat asks again. I'm not sure if a lot depends on my answer, if a definite 'yes' would sway her, but I can hardly lie about something so significant and obviously important to her.

Fabio buys me some time by bringing us a jug of Limoncello. We drain a shot each and the liquor is so strong it makes my eyes water.

"The answer is no." I have to look away, afraid to find more dismissal in her glance. "I haven't felt anything like this for anyone in a very long time." I figure the truth is my best ally. The Limoncello burns in my stomach. I should have actually eaten something at dinner instead of giving in to my disappointment, which only resulted in a lot of left-over pizza. I refill our glasses and find Cat's eyes. She immediately reaches for her glass and brings it to her lips. "Perhaps I should feel foolish, but you know what?" Some liquor spills over the glass onto my fingers. "I honestly don't." I do a little, but more because of her lack of desire to enthusiastically reciprocate than anything else. I down my shot and lick my fingers.

"Good for you."

What does that mean? I bear my soul to her and a generic semi-encouragement is all I get?

"The only thing I regret is spooking you out of sleeping with me."

My brazen words shock her into almost choking on her

drink, but what else can I be but straightforward at this point?

"I should have used more subtlety." It's easy to say after the fact, when regret is about to clobber me senseless. "Would you have gone for that?" I need to mock myself. It helps with the bitter sting of rejection. What was I thinking, anyway? That because she's a lesbian she'd go for it?

"I'm going to powder my nose." Cat stands up, imitating Helen's way of announcing she needs the toilet. "Follow me in one minute."

It's my turn to be flabbergasted. Adrenalin rushes through my veins. I nod eagerly and Cat heads off to the washroom. I try to count to sixty, but the prospect of Cat waiting for me in there, of her wanting me—of my dream coming true—makes it challenging. I follow in her footsteps and open the door. Before either of us can say anything, I push her into a cubicle and lock the door.

"Yes?" I ask, but I don't wait for her reply. I can't. Days of lusting after her have boiled down to this. I feel the familiar pulsing between my legs—familiar since a few days. If ever I wanted to kiss someone, it can't have been with more desire than this. I press my body against her and tilt her chin up. Then I kiss her and I know it's right. Sparks soar through me as our lips touch. Her tongue is soft and her cheeks smooth. Everything seems fluid and meant to be. If that's what kissing a woman feels like, I wonder what I've been waiting for all my life.

I pull back. I need to see her face. See if the blue of her eyes has changed. See if she wants me as much as I want her.

"Where can we go?" Cat asks and reality slaps me hard in the face. I choose to ignore it for as long as I can and kiss her again. I can't get enough of her sweet lips, the tenderness of her tongue and what it promises it can do to me. But I know I need to keep a clear head.

"We're in no condition to drive and the house is miles away. We need a taxi." I check my watch. "And we can't stay in here for too long. This is rural Italy, after all."

Cat leans in for another kiss and the sight of her lust sets my blood on fire. I hold her off, though. I need to get us out of here and back to the house, where she can ravage me the way I dreamed she would.

"Trust me. It'll be all right." We exit the bathroom and I wonder if Fabio or any of his patrons will notice. I wonder if I care at all. I arrange a cab and sit next to the driver in the front seat, afraid of what might happen if I'm in the back with Cat. I come to this town every summer and I'm not sure I'm ready for a lesbian scandal.

———

Once we're back at the house I half-drag Cat to my room. Long lost emotions confuse my brain, but I'm sure about one thing. I want nothing more than Catherine Archer in my bed tonight. Of course, it's not my parents sleeping at the other end of the hallway, but I block out any thoughts of John and Helen. As far as I'm concerned, they're not here. It's just me and Cat now, and this delicious anticipation riding in my veins. I have some inkling of what to expect. I've seen movies and read books, and am well-endowed with a vivid imagination, but this is the real deal. This is it.

"No, not in there," Cat says and pulls me towards the door of her bedroom. I don't care where we do it. It might as well be on the hallway carpet, though I'm not sure Cat would agree. I realise she's taking a big step, while I'm overcome by desire, by this new energy that has taken hold of me, obliterating any questions of wrong or right.

"They're over sixty, but hardly deaf," Cat whispers. "We'll have to be really quiet."

"No problem." I reach out my hand and Cat takes it. Slowly, I inch two fingers along the inside of her arm, the touch zapping electric shocks through my flesh. That's the last bit of control I'm able to exercise. I need her inside of me as quickly as possible. I've had days of foreplay, days of imagining what lies beneath the fabric of her bikini, of wondering what her skin will feel like on mine. I yank her top over her head and the sight of her stiff nipples nearly bursting through her bra makes my breath hitch in my throat. Then, at last, Cat takes charge.

She pulls me close and kisses me with new determination. I can't press my lips close enough to hers. I need more, more of her, something to quench this thirst inside of me.

We undress each other frantically, until only panties and bras keep us from being totally naked. Cat drags me on the bed with her and I'm suddenly overcome with emotion, with raw lust mixed with the friendly affection I've felt for her for years.

"I can't believe this is happening," I whisper.

Cat responds by curling her hands around my back and undoing my bra. I quickly get rid of hers, finally allowed to gawk at her breasts without having to be sneaky about it. Our nipples touch and the softness of her skin, the way her breasts mould into mine, floors me.

An impatient desire shimmers in Cat's eyes as she pulls down my panties. I let her take the lead. After all, she knows what she's doing. Her hand travels down, to the part of me that's gone untouched too long. I can feel my wetness on her fingers and push my pelvis towards them to let her know I'm ready for whatever she has in mind.

Cat shrugs off her underwear and I don't know where to look first. At her breasts, still young and supple, lit from the side by a sliver of moonlight, or between her legs, where tiny curls guard her pussy lips. I can't stop myself from reaching out. I have to touch her. She's so wet and it's all for me. It feels like the biggest compliment I've had in ages.

She pushes herself up to her knees and I follow her until we face each other. While we kiss, Cat's hands find my breasts and my nipples go as stiff as I've ever felt them. This is already a night of superlatives for me. I realise it's not just about satisfying each other—although I can't wait for that bit. It's about the connection between us. How we stare into each other's eyes while we discover one another's body. How her glance seems to gut me.

Cat's finger goes down, back between my legs. She circles my swollen clit and I can't help but cry out.

"Shhh," she says, but the grin on her face tells me it doesn't matter anymore who hears what.

She looks me straight in the eyes as she pushes a finger inside of me. I catch my breath but don't avert my gaze. I want to experience this joy, this pleasure engulfing me, together with her.

My hand wanders down to her pussy and I find her wetness. Cat twirls the fingers of her other hand into my hair and pulls me close. I fold my free hand around her neck and we find a rhythm. I mirror Cat's movement and every time she adds a finger inside of me, I do the same. Our eyes connect whenever they can and every glimpse of the fire in her glance spurs me on. I can't believe I'm fucking her, that she's fucking me. I can't believe it feels so spectacular.

I groan into Cat's ear and she starts bucking down harder on my fingers. Her pussy seems to grab on to me, catching me inside of her. Her moans intensify and her breaths shorten and stutter as the walls of her pussy contract around me. She's so wet and soft and magical inside.

She holds onto me, tugging at my hair while the motion of her fingers stops. Her body shudders against mine.

"Yes, oh yes," she hisses into my ear. I can't believe I

made her come. The sensation overwhelms me, but Cat's fingers are still in me and she pushes me down.

"Your turn," she says and her mouth goes straight for my clit. I scream so loud I startle myself and cover my mouth with my hand. Cat's tongue on me like that, so close and intimate and brushing just the right spots, makes me lose all control. Her fingers go deep, while her tongue flicks over my clit and my body starts tensing up. It feels vaguely reminiscent of the orgasms I've been giving myself lately, alone in my room, but the power behind it, the intensity of the fire ripping through me, is a million times bigger. Grandiose seems like the right word. And obliterating, as in everything that came before.

I breathe heavily through it and Cat steps it up on all fronts. Her fingers move in and out of me quicker and her tongue laps at a furious pace until I can't hold back any longer. The climax crashes into me from everywhere, from above me, beneath me, from inside of me. Its power leaves me speechless, close to tears. For some reason I want to hide, make myself disappear in this moment. I shield my face with my hands and lay there as Cat tenderly hugs me.

"Fuck me," I say because I don't have any other words.

"I believe I just did." Cat pushes herself up and smiles down at me. I must look like a fool to her, with my eyes all watery and an incredulous expression on my face. I dreamed of this for days, but reality has outdone fantasy. It's not merely the orgasm, which was, after years of maybe one hesitant solo-sex session every few months, quite earth-shattering, but the emotions it has unleashed in me. I want to linger in her bed all night, all of tomorrow and the rest of the week she's here.

"Can I stay in your room tonight?" I don't know if I should ask or not. I don't even know if she wants me to stay. I wonder if it was as satisfying for her as it was for me. She does this all the time. I wonder if it was better than when she did it last with Jenny. I feel like an insecure teenager, which is quite unbecoming for a forty-eight-year-old woman.

"It's your house. You can do whatever you want."

"Really?" I take her reply as encouragement. "Because there are a few more things I'd like to try."

———

I spend the next few days processing my cross-over into lesbianism. I feel more guilty now, after the fact—or in the middle of many facts—than when I was secretly day-dreaming about Cat. In the end, it all comes down to John and Helen's presence. I can't find a way to justify my new position in their daughter's life, however undefined it is. It doesn't help that Cat gets very paranoid about them and repeatedly urges me they can never find out. In a way, the secrecy ignites the sexual tension between us, but, on the other hand, it's also a massive source of guilt.

"Looks like you're a late-bian, then," she says one night after I sneak into her bedroom. She has stayed very adamant about not sleeping with me in my room.

"A what?" I'm only half-listening, my brain already fraz-zled by the prospect of what waits for me beneath the sheets.

"A later-in-life lesbian." She smiles at me, but, as glorious as that cheeky grin looks on her face, my eyes are drawn to her exposed chest. It's only recently I found out that the sight of naked breasts actually makes my mouth water.

"Oh, I'm a lesbian now, am I?" If that's what the satisfac-tion of having a woman's body to cuddle up to at night makes me, then I really don't mind.

"You sure are behaving like one." I can hardly deny that. I slip into bed with her and curve my arm around her waist.

"Only because your pussy tastes so sweet." Lately, I've

been baffled more than once by the words coming out of my mouth. My theory is that my brain needs to compress years of sexual frustration into the few days I have left with Cat. Anything goes. It's also true that, while before I was always a mere—but happy—recipient of it, I now consider the pleasure of performing cunnilingus as one of the great discoveries of my late-forties. The power I can exercise over Cat just by licking her is intoxicating.

"I rest my case." She plants a kiss on my hair. "I want to get lost in your curls," she hums and her words set off that weak feeling in my stomach again. That hint at something more that instantly gets squashed by our circumstances. This isn't just about physicality, about getting my sexual needs met. Perhaps it's easy to confuse the tenderness between us for love, or something akin, but, ultimately, that's what it feels like. But I'm nowhere near ready to broach that subject with Cat. Mostly because she's still suffering from a broken heart, even though the name Jenny hasn't been spoken in days. But I realise that, for her, this can't be much more than a rebound affair.

"I want to get lost somewhere else." I tilt my head up and find her eyes. Three tiny laughter lines crinkle around her temples. She knows what I mean by now. I've all but licked her raw.

I kiss her breasts, spreading hot saliva over her nipples. Her body already feels familiar, as if it belongs here with me and nowhere else. Before making my way down, to my final destination, I search for her gaze once more. I want to witness her desire for me before I satisfy it. I want her to say it.

"Fuck me," she says, because she knows, and her words ignite tiny explosions in my blood. She slides her body down and opens her legs for me, a gesture so trivial but at the same time so intimate.

I smell my soap on her, the same one I've used for years, blending with the aroma of her juices. I trail a path of moist kisses along her inner thighs. Her hands are in my hair—she seems really fond of my hair—and tug at my curls.

Before zoning in on her pussy I lick along her pubes, the coarse texture of them tickling my tongue. Then I can't hold it in any longer and I wonder if she knows how much I want this, how much of a slave I've become to her. I take in the length of her pussy, her glistening lips, so blood-shot and swollen for me, and tuck in.

The first contact always overwhelms me, because, despite the familiarity of all of her by now, this is still new to me. Her softness on my tongue and how she gasps for air that first instant. It makes my own clit pulse for attention and I feel myself heating up, a moist glow radiating between my legs.

I lick her up and down with long tentative strokes and her hands grip my hair firmer, as if she's never letting go again. When I part her lips with my tongue and gently flick the tip over her clit, her muscles contract and she pushes herself upwards, closer to my eager mouth. She's mine now, which is all I want.

I revel in her moans as I suck her clit between my lips and nibble it gently. And then pure passion takes over. I need her to tremble for me, shake and writhe underneath me like no one else ever has. I unleash a tongue-dancing frenzy on her, feeling her pleasure on my soaking wet lips. It shivers through me as her muscles clench and release, a bit more intensely with every stroke of my tongue.

"Fuck me," she says again and this time she doesn't say it to please me. She says it to please herself. I bring two fingers to the rim of her pussy and lightly circle them around the opening before slowly letting them enter. I love being inside of her. It's the closest I can get.

With every thrust I drive my fingers deeper into her, coaxing louder groans from her throat. A few strands of my hair are curled around her fingers. It doesn't hurt the way it should. Instead, it engorges my clit because I know it means she's close. As much as I like to fuck her, and lick her, there's nothing like having her come all over my fingers, her juices spilling over my lips.

"Oh god," she whispers, then repeats it again and again. She loves drama in the bedroom, likes to make a spectacle of herself when she gets there, unlike me—but I'm still getting used to this new lease on my sex life. She thrashes her head from left to right and yanks at my hair while shoving my face as much into her as possible. Her body shakes itself free of any tension as her pussy clutches my fingers. Her orgasm rips through me, like a hurricane of satisfaction, pleasing me in ways I never knew existed. It's not a smug satisfaction and it has nothing to do with ego. It's more a gentle reaffirmation smouldering in my soul, knowing everything is within my grasp again. That I've found what I didn't even know I was looking for.

"What the fuck have you done to me?" Cat asks between gasps. I could ask her the same question. I crawl up to see her face. Tiny drops of sweat cling to her forehead and her cheeks are flushed bright red. I look into her eyes and I have to stop myself from saying it because I'm sure it would ruin the magic of the aftermath. But I would give everything to hold her in my arms and tell her I love her because, daft or not, true or not, that's what it feels like—and it's not a tiny feeling either.

———

The day before the Archers are set to leave, I change my flight back. I meant to stay in the villa for four more weeks, but the void I face after Cat's departure is too vast. It's more a symbolic gesture than anything else. My own departure from my old life. I don't tell Cat because I don't want to put any pressure on her. Despite John and Helen's presence this was essentially a holiday romance. This would never have happened in London.

For me, everything may have changed, but, as far as I know, for Cat it was only a way of getting over a broken heart. I'm afraid to ask, afraid to hear words that are too definite. The wise, rational part of me knows full well we don't stand a chance back in England, but the prospect of staying behind alone is even more gruelling. At least in London I can see her. Pop over to John and Helen's unannounced on Sunday when they have their weekly family dinner. They always have an extra plate for me.

When I wake up in Cat's bed on the morning of her flight home, her usual content wake-up smile is competing with a big frown. She looks all wrinkled and frumpy, as if she didn't sleep a wink.

"Never had a summer love before?" I ask, inwardly kicking myself for using the l-word.

Cat shakes her head and swallows hard. It's clear she doesn't know how to deal with this situation. Or maybe it's because I used the word love. But it's too late to backtrack now.

"Neither have I." I snuggle up to her, resting my head on her shoulder one last time, scouring my brain for a way to say goodbye properly.

"Maybe it doesn't have to be." Cat holds her breath and my heart jumps. "Confined to summer, I mean." Her body goes rigid with tension underneath mine.

"Is it time for the talk?" A strange kind of elation spreads through me. She doesn't have to say the words for me to know.

"I'm leaving in a few hours, so maybe we do need to discuss some things." Her voice trembles, insecurity leaking from her words.

"No need." I tilt my head up and find her eyes. "I booked a flight back home next week." My face bursts out into a beaming smile. The shock etched around her mouth is priceless. "I can't bear the thought of spending the rest of the summer here without you." My stomach suddenly feels funny. If this isn't a love confession, then I don't know what is.

"Are you serious?" I'm pretty sure that's pure joy running across her face.

"As if I'm the world's biggest prankster."

Cat responds by launching herself at me, crashing me under her bodyweight in the process, and showering me in an avalanche of kisses.

"Let's celebrate." Her fingers travel down, along my chest, between my legs. She gazes deep into my eyes as she finds my throbbing pussy lips. Happiness bubbles through me as she claims me, one last time.

A knock on the door startles us.

"Kit-Kat, darling?" John half-yells. "Are you up? We must go soon."

We try not to burst out into giggles at John's sudden interruption.

"I'll be ready in half an hour," Cat shouts back.

"All right." My heart thunders in my chest as I wait for John's footsteps to wither as he walks away. Thank god he's not one of those parents who don't give their children any privacy, no matter their age.

"Has that killed your hunger for me, Kit-Kat?" I smile, but at the same time vow to never call her that again.

"Never," she says and I gasp for air as her fingers enter me.

Learning Curve

"Ja?" Giselle asks.

"Yes Djeesel." I sneak a peek at my watch. It's two minutes to six and I pray she'll let me off the hook.

"What did you say?" She pins her sky blue eyes on me. The sky looks a bit icy today though.

"Sorry. Ghie-sel-le." I stress every syllable of her name as I pronounce it slowly.

In my head, the imaginary bell to signal the end of another gruelling lesson rings. Only, I'm not in school. I'm in private tutoring hell. Every Friday afternoon I leave work early to spend the last three hours of the week learning German. You'd think it would be easy for someone English-speaking, what with the two languages belonging to the same linguistic group, but let me assure you it's bloody hard. The main problem, I duly confess, is that when it comes to learning, I might be over the hill. Picking up practical skills isn't so much the issue, but studying exceptions to very rigid grammar rules—and remembering them—is proving quite difficult. The other issue is that I'm not convinced I need it and I find it hard to invest myself in useless activities.

My company sent me to Berlin five months ago and I've been having these weekly sessions with Giselle for the past fifteen weeks. That's a lot of hours spent gazing into the impossible blue of her eyes. If only I could pick up German by doing that.

"Watch the news on ZDF," Giselle says in impeccable English. I'm sure she does it to taunt me. I bet she's a genius who speaks at least seven languages with no sign of a native accent.

"And address people in German this week. Don't worry about making mistakes."

"Sure." I bury my books in my backpack with no intention of digging them up before next week's session. Giselle has told me many times that German is not a language you can learn without memorising vocabulary, articles, and the dreaded verb cases, but does she honestly believe I have nothing better to do?

"Any wild plans this weekend?" She takes off her dark-framed glasses with those long-fingered hands and I can feel my heart skip a beat before it starts thundering in my chest. It doesn't matter that those hands have pointed out countless mistakes and have, occasionally, slapped the desk in frustration with my apparent German learning disability. If Giselle wasn't my teacher, she'd be perfect. Apart from her hands, they're perfect already, regardless of our relationship.

"Just the usual speaking your fair language to everyone I encounter and maybe a few drinks in between." I grab my leather jacket from the back of the chair and sling it over my shoulder. I need to get out of here before I lose my cool completely. I can feel it slipping away as I skim her freckled face for a sign of a smile. She shoots me a small one at last. One that says—*I know you want to fuck me, but you'll have to learn German first.*

Granted, I could try harder with the flirting. Maybe ask

her out for a drink after class. It is Friday night after all, but what if she says no? It's already so excruciating to sit across from her every week, her dirty blonde hair caressing her face in all the places I want to touch it. I'm also ninety percent certain she's straight. She looks like she may have a dark-haired, square-jawed boyfriend, a bit of a bad boy maybe, on a motor bike.

"Viel Spass," she says. At least I know it means 'have fun'. I scour my brain for the German translation of 'like-wise' but it doesn't come so I just wink and walk out, but not without conflicting emotions. It happens every Friday at six. The elation linked to the start of the weekend courses through me, elevated by the relief of surviving another three-hour lesson, but then there's that crushing weight on my soul. A new cycle of seven days minus three hours begins before I see Giselle again.

I realise it's fairly immature for a thirty-year-old to have a teacher crush. Believe me, I've tried to stop it, but having to sit across from her every week doesn't help. And, crush or not, it doesn't inspire me to give German my best shot. It must be my rebellious streak. I've never been one to please.

Giselle teaches from a spacious basement studio in Pren-zlauer Berg, a ten-minute walk along broad boulevards from my flat. I breathe in the autumnal Berlin air and I couldn't be happier. I couldn't believe my luck when my company sent me here. I'd never made it a secret that relocating to Berlin was my ultimate goal. I just hadn't expected it to happen so soon. I work for an international architecture and design firm and they could have sent me to Poland or the Middle East instead, but here I am. The only caveat was that I had to learn German. "No biggie," I had said, full of swag and confidence, "I'll master that in no time."

I stroll along the Kastanienallee and consider a Friday night cocktail when my phone buzzes in my pocket to announce a text from my friend Max. He is one of those Germans who only want to speak English with foreigners. It reads, *Now your weekly all-expenses-paid lusting session is over, meet me at Der Hobby in half an hour.*

I'm not one to keep a crush a secret—and I'm sure Giselle was the first to know.

———

"I'm not kidding." I try to convince Max with a bold stare. "We need to speak German. What if Giselle flunks me and the firm sends me back to the UK?"

"How can she flunk you when you don't even have exams?"

"She must give them progress reports or something. This private teaching business isn't exactly cheap."

"Then try a little harder, darling."

My biggest misconception about Germans when I first arrived was that they would all speak with a gayish lispy accent. Max is one of the biggest poofs in Berlin and his English pronunciation is better than mine.

"Anyway, let's move on to more important subjects. Berghain tonight?" He bites his lip in anticipation of his monthly night of complete hedonistic escapism. I've only accompanied him once and it took me three months to recover. Berghain is such an assault on the senses. Of course, Max calls it a thrilling feast.

I grimace and scrunch my mouth into an indecisive pout. "I'm not sure I'm up for it tonight."

"Come on. Andreas is bringing Ellen and we both know she has the hots for you."

Ellen is a nice girl, a typical Berlin hipster wearing polkadot dresses under heavy leather jackets, with black-dyed bangs and huge brown eyes. I do find her attractive and even kissed her once, but truth be told, the second I closed my eyes all I saw was Giselle's face scolding me. *You can kiss them but you can't speak German with them?* It kind of put a damper on things. So much so, that I haven't popped my Berlin cherry yet.

"This teacher infatuation is getting out of hand. Give Ellen a chance."

Max has always championed Ellen as a prospective love interest for me. Judging from his rave reviews she's the second coming to lesbians around the world, but I can't help but wonder why she's single then. And going for me.

"You're right, Schatzie." Giselle would be so proud of me for utilising her language to address Max, instead of the endless affected 'darlings' we shower each other with in casual conversation. "I'll keep an open mind tonight, but don't you get her hopes up."

"As if." Max smirks and checks his watch. "One more drink followed by a disco nap. Let's meet at midnight. The queue should still be doable then and it gives us plenty of time to get into the groove."

————

I check myself in the mirror. I have a bit of a dark circle situation going on underneath my eyes and my eyelids sag slightly. If someone is drunk enough to want me tonight, they'll have to take me flaws and all. I remember Ellen and decide it's in the bag already, anyway. An unexpected shudder of anticipation creeps up my spine. It really has been a long time.

I head out wearing just a white tank top underneath my leather jacket—a big thing in Berlin—despite the early autumn chill. Golden-brown leaves tumble to the ground around me and I feel that surge of contentment rushing through me again. This is my city now and, if circumstances allow, I'm never leaving. I haven't been to many places in my life, but something tells me that, now that I live in Berlin, I don't have to anymore. There's always this buzz of possibility in the air. This electric enthusiasm infecting people and spurring them on to have one more drink and one more dance. Raves are not just for the young in this town and tonight we'll show them how it's done.

I recognise Max' green hoodie sticking out from under his jacket as I approach the tram stop. He'll take them both off the minute he walks inside the club, ready to show off his five-days-a-week-in-the-gym body. I spot Andreas' peroxide mane of hair and then, there she is, Ellen Kauer, my sort of date for the night.

"Guten Abend," I try and they look at me as if I'm speaking Chinese. So much for cultural integration.

"Hey, Ada." Ellen throws her arms around me and I must admit it feels pretty good. "Long time, no see," she whispers in my ear, her breath warming my skin.

Maybe we should skip the whole going out charade and head back to my place. It would make my liver happy, for starters, and I could spend my Saturday as a human being instead of a red-eyed zombie. I need some alcohol for this to work though and for whatever else Berghain has to offer. And I didn't move to Berlin to go home early on Friday evenings.

The tram arrives and we hop on. Max is a hyped-up bundle of excitement. It could be the promise of all his favourite things—boys, booze and blow jobs—crammed together in one club or he could already be on something.

"How are your German classes going?" Ellen asks and I wish she hadn't.

Her question transports me right back to the unrequited lust balling up inside of me every Friday afternoon, as if I'm some half-grown teenager who can't deal with her hormones yet. Maybe it's more than lust, I ponder. I spend more time with Giselle every week than I do with most of my friends. We sit across from each other, our hands almost touching and our breath audible.

"Wunderbar," I say and fix my eyes and attention on Ellen. She'll have to deliver tonight. I need some sort of release and she looks more than willing.

"What's the name of your teacher again?" I do wish she'd stop going on about that.

"Giselle Cromm," I say and the mention of her name, the ease with which it rolls from my lips, as if I'm meant to say it for the rest of my life, ignites the fire in my belly again. Ellen could well just have ruined her chances.

"A lanky, bohemian blonde, right?"

"Yes." My heart thuds violently. With icy blue eyes, I want to add, and three freckles on the side of her nose.

"I believe I may have met her a few weeks ago at a free-lance teachers' conference."

Of course, Ellen is a teacher as well, which, I'm beginning to think, might be the only reason I kissed her that time.

"Really?" Regardless of the fact that I don't want to have this conversation with Ellen, I am extremely intrigued.

"A group of us hit some bars afterwards and I remember she quite fancied herself some shots of tequila." Ellen smiles broadly at the memory.

I don't know whether to like her less or more now that she's divulged this bit of information. She had drinks with Giselle. It does make her more attractive-by-proxy. It also stirs an irrational bout of jealousy inside of me.

"She's a party girl, that one," Ellen continues and I'm confused.

Giselle has always struck me as anything but a raging night owl searching for cheap thrills after dark. She always seems so proper with her black-rimmed glasses and her endless array of purple-tinted scarves, so mature and above us mere mortal drunkards.

"Wouldn't be surprised to see her at Berghain tonight," Ellen concludes.

My pulse starts racing. I need to take a few sharp breaths to steady my heartbeat. Max winks at me and I don't know where to look. What I do know is I'll be roaming the club halls until I find her.

———

Queuing only takes half an hour—half an hour of anxiously keeping my eyes peeled for Giselle, who may not even show up. We walk into the grand concrete entrance hall and I'm floored again by its enormity. The ceilings are high and the lighting is red and dim. You'd expect people to be snobbish and aloof here, but they're not. They're just here to have a wild time.

We leave our coats in the cloak room and head for the Panorama Bar. It's not that busy yet, but Ellen already squeezes her body against my back when I order drinks. She obviously has a very physical plan of attack tonight.

"I'm so in the mood," Andreas says and drags his fingers through his unnaturally blond hair. He's wearing a tight red t-shirt saying 'Yours or mine?' He takes long drags from his bottle of beer until it's empty, plops it on the bar with a loud bang, and immediately orders another.

"Fuck pacing," Max agrees and drains his bottle too.

"Might as well." I peer into Ellen's eyes while I slurp greedily from the beer. I have no idea what to do with myself and drinking appears to be the easiest solution. Soon we've bought a round each and have over a litre of beer swirling inside our stomachs.

"Let's dance," Ellen, visibly tipsy, squeaks. She staggers

when we descend the stairs and I grab her arm in support. Her fingers instantly search for mine and we walk down hand in hand.

We reach the main dance floor, which is comfortably half-full. Around me naked torsos twirl and sweat, interspersed with a diverse blend of female bodies. Some wear high heels and dainty dresses, some tank tops like me, others hot pants and mini skirts. Most of them are probably straight but this is Berghain and anything can happen. That's why it's so popular. There's a danger to the atmosphere, an unknown element injecting the air with unpredictable possibilities. I've never been to a club where something so intangible is the main attraction.

Andreas arrives with more beers and Ellen devours hers. If she continues at this pace she'll be snoring beside me instead of showering me in my first night of Berlin passion. She has a funny way of dancing where she always bops just under the beat, as if she's perfectly capable of moving to it but has no interest in complying like that. I curl my fingers around hers and push forward until we sway to the music together, pelvis to pelvis. A pleasant beer buzz muddles my brain and I'm about to lean in for the first kiss when I see her.

Giselle stands with her back against the wall, one heel lifted and pressing into the concrete. Her fingers are curved around a bottle of beer. She brings it to her mouth in quick intervals. She's dressed in jeans and boots and one of her hippie scarves and she takes my breath away. I'm so tipsy I get emotional just by looking at her.

"Seen a ghost?" Ellen asks, a big smile plastered across her face. Doubt stiffens my limbs. I stand there for a second, torn between self-preservation and total foolishness. It's not a choice really because in my head I'm already there.

"I'll get us some more beers."

I duck out from under Ellen's embrace and head to the bar for a clearer view of Giselle. An oversized boat-neck top hangs on her frail frame as she looks out over the masses. My whole body throbs and I need to shake my head to snap out of it. My brain is too frazzled to come up with a plan of action so I just stand there a little while longer, gaping at my teacher and trying to catch my breath. I'd sacrifice a pinkie for a glimpse of her blue eyes, I think, just as she turns her head and finds me in the crowd. A slow smile sneaks around her lips and she acknowledges my presence with a tiny nod of the head. Then we lose eye-contact as she's joined by three women carrying more bottles and my chances—if ever I had any—feel blown.

"Need a hand?" Max materialises in front of me, his naked chest covered in sweat.

"I saw Giselle," I stammer. "Sorry for the wait." I direct my attention to the bar staff and place our order, ignoring Max' excited yelps.

"Ooh," he goes. "Where is this goddess who's made a puritan out of you?"

"Maybe I've always been one."

He narrows his eyes to slits. "Remember York, darling? There wasn't a woman in town you didn't put the moves on."

I met Max when he attended York University through a student exchange programme.

"That was ten years ago. I'd just come out and felt I needed to make the most of things." I point my chin in the direction of the wall against which Giselle is huddled with her friends.

"Blue eyes, blond hair," Max murmurs as he scans the room. "Okay, I get it. She's smoking hot. But—"

I know what he's going to say and I don't want to hear it. I pay for the beers and shove two bottles in his hand and, before he has a chance to continue, silence him with a well-practiced menacing eye-roll. When we get back to the dance floor I try to avoid Ellen but it's too late now. Her hands are all over me and she seems to have lost all sense of decorum.

"Would you mind taking me to the lounge?"

Her eyes are glazed over and her mouth droops down. I want to stay in the dance hall and try to catch glimpses of Giselle. I need to know how she dances, how her limbs respond to beats like this, but I have to go with Ellen. It's only common decency.

While we make our way out I search the room frantically for another sign of Giselle, but she seems to have moved on. I coax Ellen towards the lounge area and find her a space on one of the sofas.

"Don't move." I'm slightly annoyed by the situation, but I do realise that if I hadn't seen Giselle I'd probably be amused by Ellen's goofy drunkenness. "I'll get you some water."

Ellen grabs my hand and mouths 'thank you' and it makes me feel like a jerk. When I return with two bottles of water my heart stops. I only see their backs but I'd recognise that ash blond head of hair anywhere. It's wild and unruly and probably dyed and it makes my heart thump in my throat. I approach and hear them talk in quick German with lots of giggles in between.

"Here's your water," I say casually and then mentally kick myself for saying it in English.

"I thought that was you, Ada," Giselle says, her eyes shining brightly in the dimly lit lounge. Her body is slanted back on the sofa and one of her long legs is crossed over the other. This picture could be perfect, if only Ellen didn't have a starring role in it.

"You can speak German if you like." I try to look cool while sipping from my water bottle. They both glance up at me, their faces drawn into an amused expression. Giselle sports a lopsided grin edging between mockery and, I swear, flirting. Or maybe I'm just reading it wrong, even though wishful thinking is not one of my hobbies. I'm more of a doom and gloom kind of person. "I'm sure I'll understand."

"Don't be silly." Ellen shoots me a confused look and I wonder when the penny will drop. Or perhaps I'm the only one feeling the tension rise on our little corner island in the lounge.

"Do you come here often?" I ask Giselle, searching for the blue of her eyes and then steadying myself against the arm rest of the sofa to stop from metaphorically drowning in them.

"Maybe once a month. More often would take away from the magic."

It's the first time I hear a hint of an accent when she speaks and it sets my skin on fire.

"I'd better get back to my friends before I lose them. You know what this place is like." Giselle pushes herself up and stands mere inches away from me. Because she's wearing heels she towers over me a bit, sort of looking down on me, but her grin is anything but disdainful. "Hope to see you around," she says and brushes past me.

I follow her with my eyes as she struts away, her long lilac scarf curling behind her. I crash down next to Ellen and sigh audibly before I have a chance to consider her feelings.

"Do you like her?" she asks and my cheeks flush instantly. "There was this vibe between you."

I can't look at her so stare straight ahead, to the spot where Giselle stood a minute ago. "She's my teacher. You know how it is."

"My students don't tend to lose their nerve when I bump into them in a club."

"You Germans are such cool cucumbers."

Ellen bumps her elbow into my bicep. "And you Brits are

the most passionate people on the planet." She pats me on the knee. "At least now I know why I wasn't getting anywhere with you."

"What? No, no," I start. "That's not—"

"There's no need to insult my intelligence as well." She hoists herself out of the couch then shoots me a smirk. "Come on, we didn't come here for a heart to heart. Let's hit the dark room."

It's not a dark room as such, more like a maze with discreetly lit corners where heavy petting can easily morph into foreplay and more. Ellen doesn't appear fazed at all by my reluctant confession, if anything she seems to possess a new energy now we're approaching the naughty well of darkness. I shuffle behind her in silence and my eyes are drawn to the couples scattered along the grey walls. A heat starts tingling in my body and I wish I was cruising the maze with Giselle instead of Ellen.

"Check them out," Ellen whispers and fixes her gaze on the next corner where a guy is going down on another guy. The deeper we go, the more daring the people become. The moans are louder and the atmosphere more intense.

"Lesbians at two o'clock," Ellen says and I can't stop watching them.

The only thing I see are tongues slipping in and out of mouths and hands roaming across breasts. It awakes something inside of me, something untouched for months. How easy would it be to grab Ellen's hand and push her against the wall? Too easy, I conclude, and not right. Also, no matter how iconic, I don't want my first time in Berlin to take place in the dark room in Berghain. I'm not the most romantic of souls, but I do have certain standards. I let the sensual vibe wash over me, until it all becomes a bit too melancholic— and something between my legs is pulsing for attention.

"I need to get out of here." I tap Ellen on the shoulder

157

and she barely notices, her gaze transfixed on the two women against the wall. "Maybe you should join them," I joke.

"Maybe I should." She turns around to face me. "As I won't be getting any from you tonight."

"I'm sorry—"

"I'm kidding, Ada. Come on, time to dance our asses off."

We hurry out of the labyrinth, meandering through a thickening crowd of frisky people and find our way to the dance hall. Max and Andreas are going wild on the floor, twisting their head left and right, as if in unison, to the droning bass beats. Ellen and I join them and we shake and grind all night. Dawn is breaking when we exit the club and by the time I fall into my empty bed, my apartment is flooded with bright weekend light. I cover my eyes to block it out and sleep, exhausted and alone.

———

Next Friday after class, while I stuff my books deep into my bag with a small sigh of both reluctance and relief, Giselle suddenly puts a hand on my shoulder.

"Care for a drink?" she asks and I am dumbfounded.

"Sure," I say quickly, before she can change her mind and withdraw the invitation. "Where's your watering hole of choice around here?"

"I have a bottle of wine open upstairs. If you don't mind…"

I have to stop my chin from dropping down. Maybe there is a god, I think. Or maybe some deity is playing a real mean trick on me. I follow Giselle upstairs. She lives and teaches in a gigantic pre-war building with no lift, just endless staircases and the sound of footsteps clattering on polished wood. Her apartment is on the third floor and is mainly beige with touches of bright blue and orange to liven the place up. I had expected more purple. I scan the living room for obvious signs of lesbianism, but once I draw a blank on all the stereotypes I let it go. I'll find out soon enough.

"You've been studying, haven't you?" she asks as she hands me a glass of Riesling.

It's true. After shaking off my Berghain coma on Sunday afternoon, instead of settling on a terrace to watch people go by while listening to Max' comments on their attire, I excavated my text books and drilled German words into my head. Knowing I was doing it for Giselle made the experience not entirely unpleasant.

"Is that why I get a glass of wine after class?"

"I expect you to respond positively to such an incentive."

"Excellent teaching methods."

She sits down next to me. Our arms balance on our knees and our glasses—and hands—nearly touch. We both stare ahead.

"If only I'd thought of that sooner."

"That alcohol is the way to a Brit's heart?" I regret it the instant I say it. It's a silly lapse of the tongue. And I've only had two sips.

She leans backwards and treats me to a lazy smile. "As a teacher, I'd be more than happy with just your brain."

"No," I stammer, "I didn't mean it like that. It's just an expression." I fold my right leg under my thigh and sit back to get a better look at her.

"Sure." She brings her glass to her mouth without taking her eyes off me. "Was that your girlfriend I saw you with?"

"Ellen?" I shake my head. "We're just friends."

"I saw you stumble out of the labyrinth together. You looked quite flushed." She pauses. "As if you had a really good time in there."

"We were just window shopping." I draw my lips into a defiant smirk. "Do you ever go in?"

She doesn't reply immediately, just looks at me and bats her eyelashes a few times. "I'm not that much of a watcher."

She's wearing faded jeans and a simple grey sweater, looking more lesbian than I do today. Her scarf has some blue tones in it, bringing out her eyes. Her stare melts my insides and I feel an inappropriate shortness of breath coming on. Part of me wants to escape from this uncomfortable situation, but I'm chained to my seat. She must know. There must be a reason why I'm here.

"Do you think you can write a story about it?" She breaks the silence I left between us. "In German, of course."

"About Berghain?"

"The dark room." She shuffles her body forward, making rustling noises in the couch. "What you saw and how it made you feel. You should be able to do that with what you've learnt so far."

"What if I tell you now?" The wine is making me overzealous. "You can correct me as I go along."

"I'd feel so naked without my red marker." She moves closer until our knees touch. "But go on then."

In broken German I tell her about the maze, about how the deeper we penetrated, the more audacious the actions we witnessed became. She doesn't interrupt nor correct me, despite my many blatant assaults on her language.

"And all the while," I conclude my story, "I wished it was you in there with me."

It's Giselle's turn to swallow hard now. Or maybe I'm just projecting as my own throat goes dry. I look away, suddenly gripped by a desire to study the bottom of my wine glass. In agonising silence I wait for her response. It comes in the form of her hand on the back of my neck and her lips grazing my ear.

"Top marks for honesty."

My entire body starts throbbing, blood speeding through my veins. I take a deep calming breath that fails miserably and face her. Her eyes are so close, the clear blue of them slicing through me. Her lips are even closer as they touch mine for a split second I'll never forget. She pulls back to take the glass from my hand and puts it on the table next to the sofa. Both our hands are free now but I don't know what to do with mine. I don't know if I'm allowed to touch my teacher the way I want to—yet. She cups my face in her hands and stares into my eyes.

"How long have you known?" I ask.

She kisses me again, her lips brushing against mine before they trace a path of featherlight pecks to my ear. "How long have you?"

"Known what?" With great difficulty I withdraw from her embrace to scan her face.

"That this teacher has been improperly lusting after her Friday afternoon pupil for months."

"Are you kidding me?" I'm torn between laughing hysterically and crying over all the missed opportunities. I'm also baffled by my own glaring cluelessness.

"I've been the worst teacher ever. Disgracing myself and my profession by letting you off the hook every time you didn't put in any work. Not scolding you for refusing to study. That's not how it normally works."

"It's been a while since I was in school."

"I noticed."

"I'll get straight A's from now on, I swear."

"Not too straight, I hope."

The skin around Giselle's eyes crinkles as she smiles and the blue shines through the narrow slits of her eyelids. My heart is about to burst out of my chest with pure joy. I grab her head and kiss her, this time with parted lips. Our tongues dart in and out of each other's mouths and as the autumn sun starts setting outside Giselle's window I can't help but think this is the best Friday night feeling I've ever had.

"What's with the scarves?" I ask as I slip today's purple-and-blue specimen from around Giselle's neck. "Hippie fashion statement? I didn't know you were that old."

Giselle takes it from me and lets it slide through the gaps of her spread-out fingers. "I like to have one at the ready at all times." She gives it a demonstrative tug. "To restrain mouthy students."

"Do you have a lot of those?" I yank the scarf from her fingers and toss it away. I'll need my hands fully functioning tonight.

"Only one who really deserves it."

The next kiss is longer and deeper. Giselle's tongue trails along the edge of my teeth and even though it's not quite dark yet, a million stars twinkle on the back of my closed eyelids. Desire soars through me and I roam my hands through her hair. Her long fingers trace the outline of my my jaw. Despite the lust coursing through me like unmistakable naked need, I know this night has to be unhurried. I want to savour every split second of Giselle touching me. I want to etch it in my brain like sensual slow memories I couldn't forget if I wanted to.

"Take me to your bedroom," I whisper in her ear. The patch of skin beneath her earlobe smells musky and heady.

She weaves her fingers into mine and drags me off the couch. My legs are wobbly as I follow her into a room filled with the light of dusk. The bed is unmade and the violet sheets lay bunched together on one side. She sits down and pulls me on top of her. I bury my nose into her wavy golden hair and inhale the scent of camomile. She traces her tongue along my neck and stops at my ear.

"I want you so much," she exhales and my insides turn to liquid.

I push her down onto the bed and stare into her clear eyes before sinking my teeth gently into her bottom lip. I nibble and suck, and my tongue explores every inch of her mouth. Everything about her tastes sweet and all I want is more, much more. Her legs move underneath me and two soft thuds announce the removal of her shoes. She manoeuvres herself higher onto the bed and slides from under me. I quickly turn my body and take off my own shoes, then hurry to Giselle's side again. A soft smile graces her face. It's mysterious, full of promise and radiates the kind of easy confidence that drives me insane.

"Come here." She cradles her fingers around the nape of my neck and pulls me close for another kiss that infuses my entire body with a tingling sensation. Without breaking lip contact, she eases herself on top of me. I welcome the full weight and length of her body. I need to be covered in Giselle, every inch of her. Her knee parts my legs and I feel eighteen years old again, touched for the very first time.

Fully clothed we rub against each other, our limbs tangling up and our lips locking for moist hot kiss after kiss. Finally, her hands trail down and she opens the top button of my blouse. One finger dips into my cleavage and tickles the skin around my collar bone. Giselle pushes herself up some more and undoes the rest of my buttons. I stare at her fingers as they curl around the studs, gracefully coaxing them out of the buttonholes, as if one-handedly undressing women is all she does in life. The sides of my blouse slip off me and all that's left separating Giselle's luscious lips from kissing my nipples is the unremarkable black bra I chose to wear that morning. She snakes her hand up my belly, her fingers crawling their way up until they rest just under my breasts.

She traces short lines under the cups of my bra and I'm beginning to suffer from shortness of breath.

"Please, take it off." I lift my head slightly to emphasise my words but Giselle seems entranced by the half-naked curve of my chest and she ignores my request. Instead, her fingers meander over the fabric of my bra, avoiding my nipples, and reach the top where they pull down the cup slightly, but not low enough to bare my nipple. She leans down and brushes her lips over the skin she just exposed then adds teeth to lightly nibble. Every patch of skin she touches with fingers, teeth or lips feels electric and a damp heat rises from between my legs where her upper thigh digs into me.

Slowly she inches down the left cup of my bra. The skin around my nipple is stretched to its limits and the rush of air caressing it makes it stand even taller. Giselle lowers her lips unto the top of my breast and kisses her way to the dark, taut bud in the middle of it. The first contact with her mouth is explosive and I groan as if I'm about to come. She wraps her tongue around the stiffness of my nipple and sucks it into the wet heat of her mouth. Satisfied with her work she eyes my breast for a second and then moves on to the other one, repeating the torturous process.

At last, a hand creeps behind my back and unclasps my bra, slips it over my arms and tosses it to the floor. Relieved that at least my torso is naked now, I let a small gasp escape my lips. These pants I'm wearing need to come off as quickly as possible though. I push myself up and flip Giselle over to assert the top part of my personality, but she stops me.

"Let me," she says gently, as if stating the natural laws of this new universe we've entered.

With a tender touch she eases me back down onto the mattress and lets her eyes dance across my chest. Her scanning glance equals a hundred unbearably light touches on my skin and I'm beginning to believe in the possibility of a purely cerebral orgasm.

Giselle's hair frames her face and catches the light of a street lamp outside. She beams me an almost angelic smile, but not quite beatific enough to make me forget who's in charge.

She leans over, a hand hovering over my breast, and whispers, "Not long now."

The hand descends and I could cry. Emotion wells up inside of me and never in my life has the touch of a hand on my breast made me tearful. As far as first times go, this is the one that matters. My throat constricts and I let go. The back of my head buries itself into the pillows and I surrender to Giselle's long-fingered hands. They trail sizzling paths of excitement over my skin and roll my nipples between thumb and index finger. They apply pressure where it feels good and become featherlight when needed. She works me like a virtuoso does her prized instrument, coaxing only the right sounds from my mouth. When two fingers finally unzip my trousers, I fear they may drown in the puddle of wetness they'll find inside.

In one go, she lowers both my pants and underwear. I'm completely naked while she is fully dressed. Not used to being so vulnerable I press my legs together and reach for her top. I hitch it upwards and she leans back until she's on her knees and pulls it over her head. Her bra is lavender and, despite not having a special love for pastel colours, I can't keep my eyes off it. I push myself up, pressing my breasts against her, and unhook her bra. I retreat slightly and let the bra slide off her, revealing her breasts inch by inch. Before I allow myself to even touch them I need to get her jeans off. I go straight for the button and my blood boils when I flip it open. As I unzip I realise she's not wearing underwear and I can't help but wonder if she's been teaching me commando all this time.

I arch an eyebrow as I look up at her and she shoots me a devilish grin. She shifts her bodyweight backwards and slides out of the jeans. I pounce and pour my limbs over her, burying my lips in her neck before finding her mouth. I'm like a wild animal let loose and my hands drift across her skin savagely. I feel like I only have a minute to touch her and need to make the most of it.

"Calm down," she whispers in my ear. "I'm not going anywhere."

She steadies my arms and I don't protest. She rolls me over and tops me again, her eyes peering down at me, brazen and so blue. Her mouth comes down and she kisses me softly. Weeks of pent-up sexual energy racing through my blood make my body scream for release. She hovers over me on all fours, her hair tickling my face and neck. She breaks the lip lock and fixes her eyes on me. The back of her hand travels through the crevice between my breasts, over my belly button to the gaping wetness between my legs. My skin is on fire and my bones ache with need. Apart from her hair and her hand we barely touch and her entire presence rests in her eyes, locked on mine. She chews her lip as a finger digs into the heat of my pussy.

Her finger inches deeper and a low moan escapes my throat. Her body seems so far away while her finger and her eyes delve into me, closer than ever. Her finger hardly moves and she shoots me a tender smile. She inserts another finger and I must be soaking wet—I know I am—because she immediately adds another. Her breasts shake to the rhythm of her thrusts as she gradually increases the pace. I feel so full of Giselle and I want to touch her and pull her close but I know better. She's the teacher and I'm the student. Her fingers beg louder groans of me with every stroke. I stare up into her eyes while she fucks me and the intimacy of her glance floors me. It connects to the sensation starting at my pussy and spreads through me. The intensity of my sighs increases and I start panting heavily.

"Oh yes." I push my pelvis up to meet her and then she slows down. Her eyes bore deep into mine, her lips are parted from the effort and a thin film of sweat pearls on her forehead. She steadies her pace until I catch my breath, licks her lips and starts again, driving her fingers inside of me with feverish passion until I'm on the brink of orgasm. I feel it coming at me from every extremity of my body, pulsing towards my pussy and beating back through my blood. I'm almost there and fingers pound and pound and I accept them greedily. When she pulls back again I stare at her, trying to convey the anguish cramping through my muscles. Her eyes haven't left mine and they scour my naked skin and the despair leaking from every pore of my body.

There she goes again and, before I have the chance to hope she won't retreat this time, the beginning of an orgasm grips me. It rolls over me and I cast a furtive glance in Giselle's direction, noticing the determination etched in the fine lines around her mouth. She's going to let me have it. I relax into it and let her fingers take me to newer heights. They plunge into me time after time as my breath catches and releases. I try to keep my gaze on her but my eyes involuntarily close when my muscles contract. The intimacy of her fingers inside me, stretching me while Giselle floats over me and scorches me with her stare blends with the desire I have had for her for weeks.

Because my climax was postponed twice I seem to come doubly hard, drenching her fingers with juice, the walls of my pussy pulsing and releasing more fluids with every wave. I dig my nails into the pillow behind my head and every thrust elicits a more carnal cry from my throat. Giselle keeps fucking me until I have nothing left, until my body has trembled itself rid of any tension. This really is the first time, I think as I sink into the mattress, reduced to a puddle of silly giddiness. The first time I came this hard.

Giselle drapes her body over mine, her arm across my chest and her bent leg across my knees. I feel her pubes tickle my thigh and her breath in my ear.

"You're gorgeous," she says and the 's' in gorgeous is long and lispy and sounds so German and it drives me crazy.

I pant underneath her until I feel I can talk and move again. I could lie like this forever, protected by Giselle's limbs after a mind-blowing orgasm, but I have my pride and I want to witness her pleasure. This time I won't roll over without a fight.

"You're such a top." I turn my head to face her.

"Don't be silly." She traces a finger along my mouth. "You were begging for it."

I start to protest but she moves in again, covering my mouth with hers, stifling my words.

"Please, Miss," I say after biting her tongue playfully, causing it to disappear from my mouth. "Can I have a taste now?"

Her eyes glisten and she holds back a smile.

"What?" I start easing myself out from under her embrace.

"I do hope you give better head than you speak German."

She bursts out laughing and I can't control myself either. I bury my nose in her wild mane of hair and find her ear.

"I've had better teachers than you."

I have my eyes back on her face just in time to see the look of playful indignation expressed in the 'o' of her mouth. I wink at her and move down to taste her nipples.

I cover them in hot saliva and trail my tongue along

every inch of her breasts. The magnetic pull of her pussy is too strong though and I abandon her chest. I lock my eyes on hers while I travel south. Her face is bunched together in a look of pure desire, her lips puckered and open and her eyes covered by slitted eyelids. I smell her tangy juices before I taste them. I want to dive in and savour them but, if anything, I know she likes it slow so I restrain myself. I treat her inner thighs to a shower of wet kisses while my nose drinks in her heady perfume. I anticipate the special moment of licking a new lover's pussy for the first time. The mere thought of it makes my head spin. I sat across from this woman for weeks, dreaming of this while she tried to drill the difference between 'Die' and 'Der' into my distracted brain. To bury my lips between her legs now feels like an unex-pected triumph, a victory of the heart, but I'm getting slightly ahead of myself.

My tongue slicks alongside her pubic hair and I let it tickle my nose. I position my hands under her buttocks and run my thumbs over that delicate curve where the behind joins the legs. My own juices start flowing again. The memory of how Giselle slowly drove me to orgasm earlier, so controlled and confident in the outcome, nudges my clit to attention. I glance up at her and strands of hair cling to her face. I don't have the patience to make her wait any longer. My lips swell at the prospect of licking her and I take posi-tion. I blow gently over the length of her pussy and drink in the pink glistening sight of it. I circle my tongue around her clit and the aroma of her juices unleashes a long-buried passion inside of me. No matter what stands to happen after this, it's already much more than sex for me now.

The first contact of my tongue on her clit sends a shiver up my own spine and Giselle's quiet moan adds to the excite-ment. I sense fluids trickling down my thighs. My thumbs are so close to Giselle's pussy they're soon covered in her wetness.

I'm startled by two hands tugging at my hair, pulling my face up.

"Turn around," Giselle hisses, her breath hitching in her throat. "Sit on my face."

Her eyes remind me of the blue heat of a flame before it starts flickering. A little reluctantly I desert my spot between her legs. The promise of what's to come, however, squashes that initial reaction quickly. The only thing worrying me by the time I spread my legs over Giselle's face is I may drown her in my wetness. I bend over and focus on her upside-down pussy in front of me. I suck her clit between my lips and nibble it softly. Giselle's hands are on my buttocks, spreading them apart and her breath caresses my pussy lips.

The sensory overload is almost too much. Giselle's clit throbs under my nose as my own is inches away from her tongue. I lower myself some more and lick up and down her lips. I curl an arm over her hip until my fingers reach her wet entrance. I lose focus again when I feel her tongue licking and entering me. All I hear is the sound of mouths feasting on juices and tongues lapping at wetness, interspersed with soft groans. I alternately suck her lips and clit in my mouth while my fingers graze the rim of her pussy.

I inch a finger up her and as soon as I'm in, Giselle mirrors my movement. I have her inside me again and, instinctively, my body leans backwards because it wants more. But I need to concentrate on my own task before allowing myself to give in to Giselle again and shift forward to allow my fingers better access. I use two now to explore the inner sanctum of Giselle's pussy. I flick my tongue over her clit from left to right and bury my fingers inside her as deep as possible. Giselle responds by adding a second finger as well and the tip of her tongue circles around my clit. The angle at which she comes at me from behind seems to awaken several untouched nerve-endings inside me. Before I have a chance to consider how unfair it is that she has better access, I come again with my nose buried in her lips and my fingers inside her. I can't keep my elbows flexed and buckle down on top of her pelvis.

"I'm sorry," I whisper to her glinting unsatisfied pussy.

Giselle gently coaxes me off her and slips from underneath my trembling legs. She crawls up towards my face and smiles. "Don't worry. We'll work on your stamina."

I kiss her and taste myself on her lips. I push her down and resume my position between her legs. Obviously making me come has turned her on. Wetness oozes out of her pussy and this time I leave no room for hesitation. I gorge on her juices and lap at her pussy until her hands are in my hair again, only this time they push my head down instead of pulling it up. I nibble on her lips and let my tongue slide between her folds. I focus on her clit and lather it with tongue and lips and saliva. I don't bother easing one finger in and start with two immediately, coaxing a husky groan from her. She thrusts up to meet my strokes and the rim of her pussy is tight around my knuckles. Her inner walls contract around my fingers and suck me in.

"Yes," she hisses.

I increase my pace while spreading my fingers. One rubs the soft ceiling inside of her and the other goes deep until her pussy clenches my knuckles together and I can barely move my fingers.

"Oh fuck," she screams.

I nudge her clit with my tongue and she shivers beneath me. Her hands lift up my head and I search for her eyes.

"Who has no stamina now?" I ask as I ease my fingers out and pull myself up until we're face to face.

She smirks and cups my chin with both hands. "A for effort."

It's gone completely dark outside and I stretch myself

against Giselle's warm body. I rest my head on her shoulder and listen to her slow deep breaths. The air around us smells dense and lush and the only sound comes from the occasional car hissing past outside.

"Wanna go to Berghain tonight?" she asks. I don't see her face and I can't make out ironic inflections in her voice yet, but I presume she's joking.

"You've exhausted me."

Giselle runs her hand through my hair and stops to twirl a strand around her finger. "I've been having a certain fantasy of us in the dark room since I saw you exit last week."

I pull my mouth into a smile against her naked skin. "Such inappropriate thoughts for a teacher."

"Doesn't everyone secretly want to fuck the teacher?"

"I can only speak for myself." I lift myself up and turn my head. "And I sincerely hope inviting all your students up for a glass of wine is not some quirky habit you have."

"Only the lesbians." Her eyes glisten and mischief tugs at the corners of her mouth.

I know she's toying with me but doubt gnaws at me. "I can see the headlines already: 'Predatory private teacher shunned after wining and dining too many lesbian pupils.'"

"You forgot the sixty-nining."

"No I haven't." I shuffle upwards on my elbows. "I'll never forget that."

"Let's go to Berghain tomorrow." She pulls my face close and leans in for a kiss. "I have some more teaching to do tonight."

The Honeymoon

"Time for a fresh layer of sunscreen, babe," Anna said. "Come on, I'm offering my services." Roz opened her eyes to slits and was blinded by the reflection of the midday sun on the ocean. Everything around her was blue, except for the waves when they crashed to shore with white frothy heads, loud and wild. She turned sideways to look at her wife whose skin was always the colour of lightly milked coffee. Grains of sand dotted Anna's long legs and Roz felt them drizzle on the back of her thighs as she straddled her from behind.

"This place is paradise," Roz said and let her forehead fall back onto the deck chair. The lotion was cool on her hot skin and the touch of Anna's fingers sent a small shiver up her spine. They'd arrived three days ago and had divided their time between sun tanning on the beach and sipping mango daiquiris by the hotel pool.

"It's not a bad life," Anna agreed. "I could get used to it."

This trip was their honeymoon. They'd flown into Bangkok Airport from New York a week ago and this stop in Phuket was what Roz had been looking forward to the most.

173

"Maybe we should change careers. I'm sure Phuket needs lawyers." Anna's fingers still lingered on Roz' back. When her wife didn't immediately reply, Roz pulled one eye open and, before turning to face Anna, peered into the indigo sea. "Try to keep your eyes in your head, babe."

They'd first noticed the woman two days ago when she dined at a table next to them at the beach club, just her and a copy of Jeanette Winterson's 'Why Be Happy When You Could Be Normal?'

"Hardly a beach read," Anna had said.

"Maybe." Roz had leaned over the table. "But it does give us some vital information about its reader."

They had both appraised the Asian woman in their own way.

"What a shoulder line," Anna, the more sporty and health-aware person in their relationship, had said. "You don't get muscles like that just by sitting around reading books."

"You should know." Roz had admired Anna's toned biceps and pronounced collarbone and vowed to take more body pump classes when they got back. Anna's gym attendance was regular like clockwork while Roz practiced a more slacking regime. She'd turned her attention back to the woman. "A white tank top on exotic skin should be declared one of the great wonders of the world."

The woman had briefly looked up and Anna and Roz had quickly averted their gaze, realising they must have come across as lusty teenagers. Of course, only Roz' cheeks had turned pinkish—the curse of being Irish and having the sensitive skin that comes with that particular heritage. The woman had smiled briefly and when they'd returned to their room half an hour later Roz had practically jumped Anna's bones.

"You're one to talk," Anna teased. "Every time we see

her you can't get in my pants quickly enough." Anna tied a knot into Roz' bikini top, pushed herself up and sat down next to her wife.

"Some women just beg to be ogled. Look at her, she oozes sensuality." Newlyweds or not, Roz had been together with Anna long enough for remarks like this to be considered harmless. The woman dipped her toes into the water, both her hands resting just above her buttocks. She stood sideways and Roz feasted her eyes on the copper-skinned profile a few feet away. She wasn't tall like Anna, probably about an inch shorter than Roz even, but her breasts nearly spilled out of her floral-themed bikini. "Curves in all the right places," Roz murmured and, for an instant, forgot where she was.

The woman turned on her heels and walked away from the sea. Backed by the sun she seemed more like a magical apparition, or a naughty wedding gift, Roz thought. She shot them both a sly smile and Roz, who'd already been melting because of the heat, expected to find herself reduced to a mere puddle of wetness when she could finally pull her gaze away.

"Room. Now," Anna whispered in her ear and Roz could only be grateful that, by and large, they had the same taste in women.

———

As soon as they set foot in their hotel room, Anna slammed Roz against the door and thrust her tongue deep into her mouth while peeling off her bikini top. Anna was usually a patient lover, someone who revelled in postponing her partner's climax long enough for it to leave them ruined and breathless in bed after. This woman must have quite the effect on her. Roz wasn't complaining though. After seven years together, they still had a more than satisfactory sex life.

Who cared if it involved lusting after strangers and transporting the spark into the privacy of their bedroom? It only added to the intimacy between them. They didn't stray, didn't feel the need to open up the relationship. They just made it work. Of course, with Anna being as fit as she was, with her long brown limbs and big dark eyes, Roz would have to be blind and very stupid not to take regular advantage of what was on offer.

Anna rolled a finger over Roz' left nipple, gently at first but soon she was tugging at it, almost pinching, and Roz cried out with pleasure. She caught Anna's glance and the feverish glint shining in it. Roz braced herself for a rough quick ride. Anna caressed Roz' lips with her thumb before inserting it into her mouth. Roz tasted sand and salt and sunscreen on her tongue. The door was cold against her slightly burned skin and goosebumps spread across her body. Roz yanked the cups of Anna's bikini top down and was floored again by the majestic curve of her breasts. As much as she loved Anna's never-ending legs and toned arms, the bronze complexion of her skin and the tautness of her abs, her breasts were the real masterpiece of her body. Drops of sweat cascaded down from them, curving around the nipples and resting there. Roz cupped them in her hands and ran her thumbs over Anna's erect nipples. She wanted to lean in and suck them, but she knew Anna was in charge and she was ready to follow her lead.

Anna's right hand trailed down from Roz' throat to her collar bone, stopping for one last squeeze at a nipple before shooting straight down to her bikini bottom. With one finger she traced a path between Roz legs, tantalising her and sending rush after rush of pure desire through her blood.

"Let's see how wet you are," Anna said, flashing her a dangerous smile. Anna slipped a finger between the fabric of Roz' bikini and the softness of her wife's touch made Roz' head spin. Roz pulled Anna closer and kissed her ferociously. She bit her lips and sucked her tongue while Anna ripped the fabric off her and let it drop to the floor. Instinctively, Roz spread her legs wider. Anna's index finger rubbed her clit and Roz' pussy lips throbbed and slithered beneath it. She was more than adequately wet.

Roz' knees buckled slightly when Anna inserted the first finger. Anna's mouth was at her ear now and she breathed heavily onto the sensitive skin of Roz' neck. Anna quickly added another finger and, with the thumb of her other hand, kept stroking her clit. Roz caught her reflection in the wall mirror. She was pushed into the door by Anna, naked and shivering, her eyes on fire and her legs spread wide.

The sight of herself on the brink of orgasm aroused her even more and she brought one hand to her breast. She watched herself as she pinched her nipple and gasped at the obvious effect it had on her body. Anna's dark skin, contrasting with the milkiness of her own, stretched tautly over her muscles as she worked on Roz, fucking her with three fingers now, filling her while manipulating her clit. Roz wouldn't be able to hold it much longer. She let her finger dwell on her nipple and, with one final tug, came all over her wife's hand. It was quick and messy but highly satisfactory. Roz let Anna hold her up and kiss her, too spent to rely on her own muscle power.

"You were dripping wet, babe," Anna said, a smidgen of irony tainting her voice. "Yellow fever?"

Roz caught her breath and made her way to the bed. She pushed Anna down onto the stark white sheets and towered over her.

"It seems to be spreading these days," she hissed into Anna's ear, undoing her half torn-down bikini top. "I'm sure you won't last longer than five minutes either." Roz kissed

Anna right next to her lips and felt her mouth stretch into a smile.

"Only because of your expert tongue." She planted her hands in Roz' hair and nudged her head down. Roz delayed briefly at Anna's chest, dividing her attention between the two perfectly rounded domes. Anna's nipples were so tiny and perfect, the way they reached up all perky and creased. Roz enjoyed their stiffness on her tongue and the testament they were to how her wife still longed for her—and the mysterious Asian woman.

Roz manoeuvred Anna out of her bikini bottom and savoured the tangy sweet smell of her pussy. It glistened and shone with wetness and Roz licked it up and down, her tongue only sparsely disappearing into the folds. Roz let her hands roam over Anna's belly, her fingers travelling daintily over her hot skin. Anna's head was already thrown back into the pillows, a soft sheen of sweat covering every inch of her. Roz delved deeper with her tongue and gave Anna's clit a nudge along the way. A soft moan escaped Anna's mouth, spurring Roz on to finish what they had started. This wasn't a sexy lazy honeymoon afternoon. This was about getting off and going out there again, in search of the stranger who brought it on.

Roz rubbed Anna's clit between her lips and allowed her tongue to slip down occasionally until she felt Anna squirm underneath her. She shoved her tongue as far into Anna as possible and tasted her salty stickiness.

"Yes, there, babe," Anna groaned and Roz intensified her movements. She positioned one thumb right above Anna's clit and focused all she had on licking her wife. She pouted her lips and applied pressure on Anna's outer lips while her tongue kept penetrating, stopping every few seconds to let it swirl around the rim of her pussy. Anna pushed her body up, brushing against Roz' thumb and Roz noticed her breasts shaking to the joint rhythm of their movements.

"Oh God. Oh yes." Anna started shuddering underneath Roz' mouth, short uncontrollable movements Roz was so familiar with. Hair next, Roz thought, and sure enough, a moment later Anna's hands gripped her hair, pulling at it and pressing Roz' mouth into her. The trembling stopped and Anna released the pressure on Roz's head.

Roz straightened herself and covered Anna's sizzling skin with her cool limbs. Anna kissed her full on the mouth, lapping at the juices that still clung to Roz' lips.

"Great honeymoon so far, babe," she said. "And we haven't even gotten to the toys yet."

Roz smiled as she remembered the velvet-lined handcuffs they'd packed—and the double-headed dildo. Without warning, another thought entered her mind. Oh, how she'd love to tie the Asian woman to the bed, strip off her top and tease her nipples. The idea of two pairs of perfectly shaped breasts at her disposal made her a little dizzy. Would it be wrong to make this kind of suggestion on their honeymoon? Judging by how opulently the juices were oozing from her wife earlier, Roz figured it would be more like a wedding present to each other.

"Here's a crazy idea," she started.

"A shower followed by some poolside drinks?" Anna guessed. Her words were innocent enough, but Roz noticed the naughty glimmer in her eyes.

"Something like that." She casually ran her thumb over Anna's nipple again. "And maybe we can have a little something extra for dessert."

"You're insatiable." Anna giggled and grabbed Roz' hand. She isolated Roz' index finger and brought it to her mouth, letting it slide over her tongue and lips.

Roz stared deep into Anna's eyes. "Are you thinking what I'm thinking?"

"If you're thinking that I want to fuck you in the shower, then yes." The prospect sent a pang of lust through Roz' core. The hotel bathrooms were about the size of their entire Manhattan apartment and the shower was a huge walk-in affair with two different kinds of nozzles and variable pressure speeds. They had yet to test its full potential. Roz ignored the distracting thoughts swarming her brain and focused at the task at hand. She knew it wasn't a question of convincing Anna, more a matter of making her agree to it out loud.

"Sounds good, but——" Roz searched for the right words. "Why don't we save ourselves for later? That shower can easily fit three."

Anna played with Roz' fingers, a sign of either excitement or nerves. Roz guessed it was a mixture of both. "You have a dirty mind, Mrs Parker-Ellis."

"Not dirtier than yours." Roz ran a fingertip over Anna's cheek. "Which is why we're so good together."

"What's our plan of action?"

Roz felt the excitement grow in her belly now that Anna had as good as verbally agreed—as good as she ever would, anyway. "Hope she's having dinner at the beach club again tonight, for starters."

"By herself, with only some lesbian literature as company."

"We can do it old-school. Send her a drink."

"Or maybe one of us should approach her alone."

"But she already knows we're together." Roz believed they should go through every stage of seduction together.

"Let's not plan it," Anna said. "Let's order a bottle of champagne and see how it goes."

"And if it doesn't work out, we'll still have each other."

———

"She's not here," Roz said as she gulped greedily from her glass.

Anna fixed her calm dark eyes on her. "We're quite early. It's not even dark yet."

The sun hung just above the horizon, its orange glow setting the ocean on fire. Roz kicked off her flip-flops and found Anna's ankle with her toes. As far as romantic moments went, this one was pretty perfect. It didn't really matter if the woman showed up or not.

"This is gorgeous." A profound sense of fulfilment spread through Roz. It wouldn't matter at all. With one eye on Anna and one eye on the sea, she witnessed how the sun dipped behind the water, coating the evening in a magical multi-coloured sheen. Roz saw a smile build on Anna's face.

"Look behind you." Anna nodded once.

Roz didn't even have to turn her head because, sure enough, an instant later the woman appeared in her field of vision. She'd pinned a few strands of hair together on the top of her head and the rest of it cascaded down her neck, all black and sleek. She wore a short white see-through dress over a black bikini and brown leather sandals. She sat down two tables away from them.

"Best spot in the house," Roz grinned.

"Give her time to eat first. She'll need the energy." An excited giggle escaped Anna.

The champagne started going to Roz' head and she plunged her fork into a fish cake. Tipsy would do tonight, she concluded. There's no use in engaging in a threesome if you can't hold on to the memory afterwards. A nervous buzz tingled in Roz' blood. Would they really do this? Never mind the outcome, she realised, it was this part of the game she had missed most. The early stages, the anticipation, the sweet thrill of seduction, and the complete unpredictability of it all.

They finished the rest of their bottle and nibbled on small snacks, their stomachs too jittery for a big meal, and cast covert glances at the woman. She'd ordered a green curry and washed it down with San Miguel Light while staring into the blackness of the ocean.

"No book tonight," Anna stated the obvious. "Maybe she's expecting company."

"Shall we buy her a beer?" Roz didn't wait for Anna's response and waved over a waiter. Anna shuffled restlessly in her chair. Their eyes followed the waiter as he padded to the bar and put in the order. It wasn't busy so it didn't take long for a bottle of beer to emerge, a wedge of lime squeezed into its neck. Roz' heart raced as the waiter transported the drink to the woman and nodded in their direction when he presented it to her. She prepared her sexiest smile and tried to hold on to it when the woman looked at them.

"Cheers," the woman said, a gold bracelet around her wrist catching the moonlight as she lifted her bottle to thank them.

"Enjoy," Anna said.

"Feel free to join us." Roz took the lead. "If you'd like some company."

The woman got up and strutted towards them as if she were walking a catwalk. "Don't mind if I do." She spoke with a posh British accent, which, truth be told, surprised Roz. It didn't temper her acute case of yellow fever though.

"We've seen you around," Roz said clumsily, suddenly feeling very self-aware. She'd been out of the game a long time.

"I always try to catch a few days here when I need to come to Asia for business. It's so beautiful and peaceful." She sipped from her bottle. "Unfortunately, I'm leaving tomorrow."

"I'm Anna and this is my wife Roz. Very nice to meet you." Anna extended her hand and Roz noticed how her thumb lingered longer than necessary on the woman's when she shook it.

"Violet," the woman said. "Thanks for the beer."

"Our pleasure." Anna exchanged a strange look with Roz, one Roz had never seen on her in the years they'd been together.

"What brings you to this lovely island?" Violet sipped from her bottle while waiting for a reply and Roz wondered if she could possibly do it in a more sensual manner.

"We're on our honeymoon, hence the fancy drinks." Anna clinked her glass against Roz' as if they were having the most casual of conversations.

"Congratulations." Violet peered at her bottle. "Excuse my more vulgar tastes." She shifted her glance from the beer to Anna's and then Roz' face. "Any special plans for your special holiday?"

Roz swallowed hard and let Anna take care of the small talk. She'd play a more active role later, when it was time to strap on.

"Maybe." Anna batted her eyelids suggestively. "If the right person crosses our path."

"I have a pool villa." Violet drained the last of her beer. "If you ladies care for some night swimming as a special honeymoon treat."

The villa was a duplex boasting two bathrooms, a large dining room, twenty-four hour butler service and a private, discreetly lit swimming pool.

"Drink?" Violet asked and swung the mini-bar open. "I've been waiting for the right occasion to open this." She pointed at a bottle of champagne and reached for the flutes hanging overhead. "Something tells me tonight's the night."

Roz looked at Anna but she seemed too caught up in the sheer lavishness of the place.

"Let's try to get an upgrade next time, babe," she said.

"You both certainly have the looks for it," Violet said and handed Roz a glass of sparkling champagne. "To charm the staff at reception, I mean." Roz wondered who was doing the seducing now. Violet opened the sliding door to the patio and put her glass on the wooden deck floor. With one hand she loosened the string holding up her dress around her neck and let it slip down. She wore a simple black bikini, which came as no surprise to Roz since she'd been eyeing it through the translucent fabric of the dress all night. Violet sat down and dangled her legs into the water. "Are you joining me?" she asked.

Anna, who seemed to be dealing with the situation like a well-seasoned swinger, had already unbuttoned her shorts and was pulling her tank top over her head, exposing a bright green and blue bikini. Roz could kick herself for not putting on swimwear but she hadn't allowed room for swimming in her grand scheme for tonight. Not that the course the evening had taken wasn't already exceeding her plans far and beyond. She had, however, hoped to have access to the bag of goodies waiting in their room.

Anna walked down the steps into the water and positioned herself next to Violet, an elbow leaning on the marble next to her and a glass of champagne in her hand.

"Come on, babe." She fixed her eyes on Roz. "Show us your sexy red boy shorts." Her smile was soft and teasing. Anna knew well enough Roz wasn't wearing a bra. Roz decided this was no time for shyness and slid out of her jeans

184

shorts. She dived into the pool headfirst with her faded black Blondie t-shirt still on and re-emerged with it clinging to her skin. Violet handed Roz her glass of champagne and all three of them stood scarcely dressed while sipping bubbles in the hot Asian woman's private swimming pool. Things could be worse, Roz pondered.

"You'll get cold if you don't take off that wet t-shirt," Violet said. "Unless your wife keeps you warm." Roz gulped down the champagne, mainly in order to switch off the self-conscious thoughts racing through her head. Should someone take the lead? What are the rules? Are there rules to begin with? She padded over to the side of the pool and topped up her glass.

"Gladly," Roz said and started peeling the wet t-shirt off her chest, "but surely you won't let me stand here topless all by myself."

Violet shot her a sexy grin. "Most certainly not." She brought her hands behind her back to untie the string of her bikini top. "In fact, I'll raise you." Roz' mouth went dry as Violet lowered herself into the pool. "And challenge you to a skinny dip." Her arms disappeared under water and, when they re-emerged, triumphantly held up a wet black piece of clothing. Without breaking eye contact Violet slung it behind her and it landed with a soppy thud on the marble edge of the pool. Violet dipped under and sliced through the water, her body mere inches away from Roz.

Roz pinned her eyes on Anna, who looked just as mesmerised by Violet's words and actions. She turned her wife around and planted a single kiss on her back before proceeding to undo her bikini top.

"My pool, my rules, girls," Violet grinned beside them, her hair slicked back and drops of water trickling down her exotic skin. Roz felt a hand tugging at her undies. "Off. Now." Suddenly, it was pretty clear who was in charge. When

Roz slithered out of her shorts she could feel the heat of her pussy radiate through the cool water. Anna followed suit and a wet plop announced the landing of her soaking bikini bottom on the teak floor boards next to the pool's marble lining.

"Three women naked in a pool," Anna said, her voice low and hoarse. "I wonder what will happen next."

"We swim, of course," Violet added, and buried her head under water for a split second, only to have it rise up again coated in a fresh layer of drops cascading down her naked chest. Roz had trouble keeping her eyes off Violet's breasts and she couldn't wait to taste her nipples.

"You call that swimming?" Anna asked. She dived under and writhed her body between Violet and Roz, her skin brushing against theirs.

"What gave me away, anyway?" Violet asked, looking amused at Anna's continuing pool antics—she was somersaulting now. "What made you buy me that beer?"

"Pure lesbian instinct," Roz lied. "You looked in dire need of some entertainment."

Violet leaned over, her wet shoulder gliding against Roz. "Let the show begin then," she whispered in her ear. Anna gushed out of the water next to them and sprayed them with a fresh layer of wetness. Roz found Anna's firm buttocks under water and started stroking them with one hand. Her other hand searched for Violet's belly and a shudder of lust swarmed through her as she touched both women at the same time. She watched as Anna leaned in to kiss Violet and the heat inside her tummy exploded.

Roz slowly inched her fingers towards Violet's breast. She stroked it with the back of her hand first, letting the nipple graze the gaps between her fingers. Her other hand cupped Anna's breast and soon she was pinching both their nipples and the sight of them kissing right in front of her, despite the cooling pool water, set her skin on fire.

Anna broke the lip lock with Violet and trailed her tongue along Roz' neck, stopping at the earlobe and nibbling it briefly. Violet's hand touched Roz' breast and squeezed. Roz let her hands roam freely between both Anna's and Violet's breasts and cupped and massaged and stroked them more frantically as the seconds ticked away. Anna kissed her, her moist tongue dancing inside Roz' mouth.

"The pool was a good warm-up," Violet groaned, "time to get serious." She placed her hand on top of Roz' and gently yanked at it, leading her out of the pool. Roz gave Anna's nipple one final pinch and dragged her out by the wrist. It was the first time Roz saw Violet completely naked and the vision of her standing next to her own naked wife, ready for a night filled with pleasure she couldn't yet imagine, made her knees go weak. Violet handed Roz and Anna a towel from one of the deck chairs and Roz wiped herself dry as fast as she could before the uncontrollable urge to touch both women's naked flesh seized her again.

"I have some toys in the bedroom upstairs," Violet half-grunted. She walked into the living room, her nipples perking up again under the chill of the AC. Roz couldn't climb the stairs quickly enough and waited for the other two awkwardly standing around in the bedroom. Violet had snagged the half-empty bottle of champagne from downstairs and let it dangle loosely in one hand while the other curled itself around Anna's fingers. Their skin tone seemed to be only a shade apart, making Roz feel very pale. Anna towered over Violet with her tall frame, but not for long because Violet, after draining the remainder of the champagne straight from the bottle, pushed her onto the bed. Anna took Roz by the hand and dragged her onto the bed with her. Violet hopped between them and Roz crawled backwards to get a better look at things.

"Hi," Violet said cheekily, reaching for a remote on the nightstand and dimming the lights. "Welcome to my boudoir."

Anna caressed Violet's neck, her body pressing against Violet's back. Roz noticed the raw lust in her eyes, a bold glimmer laying her desire bare and stripping Roz of any inhibitions. Roz intertwined her fingers with Anna's on Violet's neck and together they explored her skin. Roz pushed Violet onto her back and kissed her deeply, her tongue discovering every corner of her mouth. Anna's hands were in her hair now, slowly travelling lower and soon all of their hands were lost in a caressing frenzy of hot burning body parts. Roz groaned as her nipples were pinched and another hand brushed against her lower belly. She didn't know whose fingers travelled up her inner thighs and whose lips kissed her belly button. She had no idea how she had become the focus of the action and she couldn't care less. The lips travelled lower, below her mound of carefully trimmed pubic hair—this was their honeymoon after all— and just as she felt the tip of a tongue brush her clit, Anna's face was suddenly close, her mouth whispering, "Enjoy, babe." Roz felt Anna's smile stretch against her ear and revelled in the tongue bath Violet was giving her pussy.

Roz felt the wetness ooze out of her as Violet covered her pussy with her mouth. Anna fondled Roz' breasts, pinching and releasing her nipples the way she knew drove her crazy. Roz already felt it build, like an unstoppable force bursting inside of her. Anna's lips nuzzled her neck and her fingers worked her breasts while Violet let her tongue slip in and out of her pussy, straying at just the right times to her throbbing clit.

"Oh yes," Roz moaned, the sign for Anna to kiss her full

on the lips. Violet's hands clasped her buttocks as she tried to drive her tongue as deep as possible into the folds of Roz' pussy, alternated with long strokes along the length of it. "Oh god." Roz' groans were absorbed by Anna's mouth as they grew louder and heavier. Her nipples felt electrified and so hard, as if a current ran through them. Violet focused on her clit now, flicking the sensitive bud back and forth with her tongue. The fire in Roz' belly intensified and seemed to form a straight line from her nipples to her pussy until it erupted into a million explosions, gushing juices all over Violet's face.

"Hold on," Anna hissed into her ear, her voice almost a growl. She manoeuvred herself down and exchanged a wicked smile with Violet. "She likes to get fucked after she comes." Anna's fingers already brushed the edge of Roz' pussy. Violet took Anna's place at the top of the bed and, without hesitation, slipped her tongue inside Roz' mouth. Roz smelled herself on Violet, a sweet and pungent perfume mixed with hints of chlorine from the swimming pool.

Anna penetrated her with one finger. "You're so wet, babe," she said, and, as if she had to prove that point, inserted another one. Roz realised that in seven years she hadn't kissed another woman, let alone had someone else touch her like that. Anna soon fucked any coherent thoughts she still had out of her though as she found a steady rhythm and had a third finger join the party. Roz loved the full feeling of being penetrated after a climax and she let the sensation rip through her. Violet's lips had trailed off towards her breasts and spread balmy saliva on her nipples. Roz' breasts bounced against Violet's mouth as her wife fingered her with that delicate but firm touch she had. Roz felt a different kind of orgasm build now, a more animalistic one, making her shudder all over. The walls of her pussy clenched around Anna's fingers and she felt the cool air of the AC rush over her wet hard nipples as her breasts shook back and forth. She lost control and surrendered to the abundance of touch that was bestowed upon her.

A fresh ripple of electricity tore through her and Anna's fingers kept filling her and Violet's mouth was everywhere and then there was the first wave, tentative but already transforming into something much stronger, something so irresistible she had to catch her breath again and again.

"Oh fuck," she said and repeated it. "Oh fuck, oh fuck, oh fuck." Her blood sparkled and her limbs tingled and her pussy blasted juices over Anna's fingers. Drained, Roz relaxed her muscles and let the softness of the mattress envelop her. And this was only round one, she thought.

As she lay there spent, Roz watched Violet get up from the bed and rummage through a suitcase. She produced a shiny purple dildo and a black leather harness.

"Meet Lily," Violet said lovingly, "who outlasts all my relationships." She grinned and ducked back down to grab a bottle of lube. "I take her with me wherever I go."

Roz instinctively grabbed Lily and the sight of the toy filled her with a fresh burst of energy. She vowed Violet wouldn't forget her last night in Phuket easily.

"Allow me," Roz said and let the supple leather of the harness slide between her fingers. She caught the twinkle in Anna's eye and was forced to face the real dilemma of the night: who to fuck with it first?

Violet tightened the straps around Roz' buttocks with soft hands and Roz suddenly felt very powerful. Anna was already nibbling on her ear, her breath hot and her words quiet and dirty.

"Fuck me, babe," she hissed and put her hand between her legs. "No need for that lube. I'm so wet for you." Anna grabbed Roz' hand and guided it to her slithering pussy. Meanwhile Violet pressed her hot body against Roz' back, her nipples rock hard and her lips trailing a moist path along the back of her neck. Roz had been having the fantasy ever since the notion of a threesome had started budding. She was going to fuck them both at the same time.

Roz kissed Anna and lowered her onto the bed. She turned around and looked straight into Violet's face. "Come here," she said and curled her fingers around Violet's wrist. "I need you in front of me." Roz slipped her tongue briefly into Violet's mouth, still smelling her own juices on her lips. She gently coaxed her down and positioned her next to Anna. The pair of them laid out in front of her, ready for the taking, their skin touching and their legs spread wide, made Roz' head spin. This honeymoon was already a dream come true, but this night topped every expectation she could ever have had.

Roz felt in control now. In her mind and in that moment, whoever carried the goods was in charge. She was about to encourage Anna and Violet to kiss but they'd already found each other's lips, their heads turning towards each other and their hands drifting across each other's bodies. Roz' clit throbbed beneath the leather of the harness, but it was her turn to give. She crouched down and let her hands snake up the two women's thighs—left for Anna and right for Violet. The strap-on dangled between her legs, powerful and full of promise. Both Anna's and Violet's breath quickened as Roz' fingers inched closer to their pussies.

Still on her knees, Roz manoeuvred forward to give her fingers better access. Simultaneously, she slipped one finger into both women's heat, causing a fresh wave of juice to gulp out of her, smothering the harness. If finger-fucking one woman was already so mind-blowing, doing it to two at the same time was spectacular. Lily swung between Roz' legs as she increased the intensity of her movements. Anna was right, not a whole lot of lube would be required. Just to be on the safe side, Roz slowly retracted her fingers and grabbed the bottle from behind her. She applied the lube generously until the purple of the toy glistened just as much as what it was about to enter.

Violet and Anna played frantically with each other's nipples, their mouths unwilling to break contact. Roz repositioned herself between Anna's legs and slowly trailed the tip of the dildo along her wife's pussy. Despite its respectable girth, the toy slid in easily and a short gasp escaped Anna as Roz inched it in farther. Anna, visibly too wrapped up in her own pleasure, stopped kissing Violet and threw her head back on the pillow. Her breasts bounced up and down to the rhythm of Roz' movements and Roz could have come there and then, just by thrusting her clit into the soft leather of the harness every time she buried the dildo deeper into Anna.

Violet's hands crept towards her clit and she started touching herself. She spread her pussy lips wide with one hand and rubbed the index finger of the other over her clit.

"Don't come," Roz groaned at her, "you're next." She treated Anna to a few more strokes and pulled out.

"Touch yourself, babe," Roz said to Anna, "I'll be right back." She shuffled towards the opening of Violet's spread legs and shot her a cocky grin.

"Your turn." Roz repeated the actions she had earlier performed on Anna. She started slowly, but gradually amped up the pace until the dildo disappeared into Violet's pussy in a steady back-and-forth rhythm.

"Kiss me," Violet moaned and yanked at Anna's hand. Roz caught Anna's hungry gaze and it shot an electric pang of desire straight up her spine. Her clit was rock hard and the constant feed of tantalising live images in front of her wasn't helping. Anna cupped Violet's breasts and let them slam against her palms as she flicked her tongue in and out of her mouth and nibbled on her lips. Anna's mouth stifled Violet's high-pitched groans only up to a certain point. Roz didn't want Violet to come yet—she wanted to drive her crazy first. She pulled out and locked eyes with Anna who fell on her back and spread wide. The wet pink of her pussy glistened and Roz didn't bother with penetrating slowly this time. She dug in deep, burying the dildo into Anna's pussy until she cried out with pleasure.

"Oh yes," she started moaning and Roz judged it too cruel to pull out again. It was Anna's first release of the night and there should be plenty more to come. Roz bent forward, over her wife's trembling body, her knees digging deep into the mattress to support the feverish rhythm of her thrusts. She tried to find Anna's eyes but her head was thrown back again, little currents of sweat trickling down her long neck.

"Oh god," Anna continued and dug her nails into the sheet. She thrust her pelvis upwards to receive as much as possible from the dildo and Roz couldn't suppress a gasp when she noticed a copper-skinned hand sneak towards her wife's clit.

"Let's make it one she never forgets," Violet said and pushed Roz' body upwards so she could get her head—and tongue—close enough to Anna's clit.

Roz watched Violet's tongue slip back and forth over Anna's clit while she drove the dildo into her pussy. Roz felt her own climax build but she had to focus on her wife first. Anna's hands tore feverishly at Violet's long black hair, pushing her mouth onto her clit. A long loud groan announced the arrival of Anna's orgasm. It beamed through the room and made the hair on Roz' neck stand up. Violet licked her lips when she lifted up her head and shot Roz a triumphant smile. Roz pulled out and slipped her body next to Anna's so she could kiss her. Anna lay there as if in a trance, her eyes screwed shut and her body still trembling. Roz planted a gentle kiss on her forehead and felt her own juices seep down between her legs.

"My turn, I believe," Violet said while tapping Roz on the shoulder. "No need to get up." Violet straddled Roz and pushed her down by the shoulders. She lowered herself onto the dildo and started bopping up and down. After the first few thrusts Roz knew she wouldn't be able to stop it this time. The leather, moisturised by her own juices, rubbed against her clit every time Violet pressed down. Anna still lay recovering next to her, her hot skin rubbing against Roz' arms every time she moved to meet Violet.

Violet stretched herself out over Roz's body and Roz grabbed her heaving breasts, her thumbs stroking the erect nipples. As if she was manipulating her own clit, Roz intensified the movement of her thumb over Violet's nipple the more aroused she got, which seemed to spur on Violet's excitement as well. Violet's mouth opened wider and wider as her moans got louder and soon Roz was mixing in her own yelps of pleasure.

She searched for Anna's hand next to her and found it just in time to squeeze it as she came, shuddering and panting under Violet and the harness. Violet's eyes were reduced to slits while she rode herself to ecstasy. Roz, wiped out by the succession of orgasms and the strapping on, still had a few thrusts inside of her and swayed her hips to the beat of Violet's body. Roz needed her to come quickly because her clit had become ultra-sensitive and was getting desperate for some fresh air. It didn't take long before Violet sighed her own prolonged sigh of relief, shivering on top of Roz.

"Blimey," Violet said as she dismounted. "Lily never lets me down." Roz couldn't wait to get out of the harness and Violet helped her undo the leather straps. "The woman wielding it was not so bad either," she whispered in Roz' ear as she lovingly put Lily to the side. "How's the wife?"

"Still catching her breath," Anna said. "That was so damn hot."

"We may need to cool off in the pool," Violet remarked. "I'm flying back to London tomorrow and god knows when I'll get to skinny-dip again."

"Something tells me it won't be that long," Roz said, wondering about this mysterious woman and the lifestyle she led at home.

"If you're ever in New York…" Anna said, a lazy grin plastered across her face.

"Time for some more night swimming, ladies." Violet, looking surprisingly energetic after the orgasm she just had, hopped off the bed and raced down the stairs.

Roz' legs trembled when she tried to get up, but then again, she had the largest climax count of the night so far.

"Are you all right, babe?" Anna asked.

Roz grabbed her wife's hand—it smelled of sex and pussy—and planted a firm kiss on her palm. "I love you." They descended the stairs together and found Violet with her hands in her hair, her magnificent chest pushed forward, while she showered under the cascading water fountain in the corner of the pool. "The night's not over yet."

Head first and unrestrained by clothing this time, Roz dived into the pool. The water flowed sensually around her skin. She swam towards the thrilling image of Violet's naked breasts, water spilling over her pert nipples. Maybe it was anatomically impossible, but Roz felt her pussy lips throb again. It was clearly a case of mind over matter. Roz cradled Violet's breasts with both her hands and pushed them together, letting her tongue travel between the brown buds of her nipples.

"Save some for me," Anna said behind her back and soon they were each feasting on one of Violet's breasts, sucking and fondling them as if they were the world's greatest treasure. Violet leaned backwards until her body found the support of the fountain wall and she stood there, like some Asian Goddess descended from the heavens, sent especially to make their honeymoon a trip worth remembering forever.

The water rained down Roz' back in a soothing stream, washing her clean of the earlier produced juices and firing her up for the next round. Anna kissed Violet against the wall and her hands trailed lower and lower. Roz could see her wife's fingers approach the pitch black mound of Violet's pubes and, rather than any kind of jealousy, it sent wave after wave of raw lust through her bones. They were just bodies now, bodies looking for pleasure and release. Roz joined the party just in time to hear Anna say, "I want to lick your pussy." Violet's eyes shone wildly under the faint outdoor lighting.

"That can be arranged." Violet moved a few inches to the corner of the pool. She climbed the two steps and grabbed a towel from the deck chair, bunched it up and planted her behind on it, her legs already starting to spread. Anna kneeled on the pool stairs and started kissing Violet's inner thighs. Roz, never one to have idle hands, positioned herself behind her wife and caressed her buttocks. Anna's pussy bobbed in and out of the pool while she moved her face up and down over Violet.

Roz concluded she had the best seat in the house again and proceeded to fondle her wife's butt, zoning in on the pinkness of her sometimes exposed pussy. She watched as Anna slipped two fingers inside Violet and decided it would be a good time to do the same. Anna was so wet and bucked down so hard on Roz' fingers that she was soon going at her with three, contemplating a fourth. She watched Anna's tongue slip and slide over Violet's glistening clit while her fingers slammed in and out. Roz let Anna set the pace and moved her other hand under water in search of Anna's clit.

On the other side, Violet's grunts grew hoarser and when Roz looked up she saw how Violet dug her nails into the soft fabric of the towel. Drops of water shimmered on Violet's body as Anna fucked and licked her to another orgasm. The sight of her own fingers disappearing inside Anna's pussy caused a tingle to creep up Roz' spine every time she pushed forward. Her other hand manipulated Anna's clit under water and Roz marvelled at the sight of so much pleasure. Anna had let her forehead fall onto the towel and she rode Roz' fingers hard. Her body made sloshing sounds in the water and they mixed with the slapping sound of Roz' fingers in her pussy. Roz continued fingering her until Anna's back was so arched and her muscles shook so hard, Roz feared an orgasm-induced seizure.

Anna let herself fall on top of Violet, her head landing on her pillowy chest. "Fuck," she said, "all this swimming has exhausted me."

"It is a very high-energy activity," Violet said with her eyes closed.

Roz took in her surroundings, maybe for the first time since entering the villa. A green palm tree leaf hung over the wooden fence next to the pool, rustling in the faint breeze. The night was quiet around them—this was not a party hotel. The only sound was the steady drum of the fountain water splashing into the pool. Roz hoped the nearest villas were far enough away for their cries of pleasure to get lost in the wind. Most beautiful of all was Anna's head rising up and down on Violet's chest. Her wet hair was draped over Violet's nipples and her hand rested almost innocently on her belly.

Maybe paradise is not a place where you watch your wife

lick another woman's pussy, she thought, but it can't be far off.

————

Roz woke to the sound of water drumming against glass. Anna lay next to her with her head resting on Roz' arm and her body still gently heaving with the slow breath of sleep. They weren't in their room and this wasn't their bed.

"Morning," Violet said as she emerged from the bathroom, a white towel slung across her lower body. "I don't mean to be rude, but I have to dash."

Still dizzy with sleep, Roz took in the sight of Violet's naked breasts one last time before she fished a bra out of her suitcase and covered them. "No worries," she said with a dry mouth.

"No need to wake the wife." Violet grinned. "We're all a little tired this morning." She jammed some more stuff into her suitcase, and then faced Roz again. "I've arranged an upgrade with the butler." She flashed Roz a glamorous smile. "The villa's yours for the rest of your stay. It is your honeymoon after all." She slipped into a pair of white linen pants and topped it with a tight navy t-shirt. "Enjoy."

"But—" Roz started to protest. "That's not—"

"I know it's not necessary." Violet walked over to the bed. She smelled clean and fresh and of a million flowers. "But seeing as we've already shared so much." She pecked Roz on the cheek and shot her a quick wink. "Give my best to Anna." A few minutes later she was out of the door and out of their lives.

Piano Lessons

"Your heart's not in it, Ruby. I can tell." Jill scolds me for the umpteenth time.

I reposition my fingers and put them in motion, starting on "Für Elise" again. My movements stall, my fingers unwilling to move further. Why am I still coming here, anyway? It was never entirely my own idea to take piano lessons. It was Amber who spurred me on. And Amber is long gone.

"What's the matter?" Jill—I haven't been allowed to call her Mrs. Banks since my first class with her—perches on the edge of the bench I'm sitting on. "Amber?"

At times, my lessons with Jill resemble therapy sessions more than anything else. She charges less than a shrink, so I'll take it.

"Her Facebook relationship status went from 'single' to 'it's complicated'. It's been eating at me. What does it mean? Is she seeing someone?" I'm not really looking at Jill. It's not as if she has the answers, or can tell me anything I don't know.

"It's been what? Four months now?" I always like it when

Jill squats next to me on the bench. It feels nice and cozy. Less lonely. "Maybe it's time you started distracting yourself as well. And stop checking her Facebook thing or whatever that is."

"Play four-handed with me?" I turn my face toward Jill. Seeing her fingers travel gracefully over the ivory keys always lifts my spirits.

"I'll tell you what. I'll play you a tune if, afterwards, you'll come up and have a gin and tonic with Charlotte and me. Maybe it will give you some liquid courage, and you'll actually drag yourself out of the house tonight. It's Saturday, dear. There must be someone out there for you, if only for a rebound one-night stand."

"Why Miss Banks." I feign indignation. It's not the first time she's said something like this. "You really shouldn't talk to your students like that."

"I wouldn't if they didn't need me to."

It's no coincidence that Jill became my piano teacher. After Amber bought me the keyboard and basically instructed me to 'take some lessons already' because she 'didn't want to be with someone who suffered from unfulfilled wishes', I scoured the internet for piano teachers in town. Jill's website displayed a picture of her, and her biography openly quoted her long-term relationship with ex-ballerina Charlotte Carpenter. It was a no-brainer. I was surprised I got in so easily, but Jill—Mrs. Banks at the time—told me I was lucky. One of her regulars had just moved away and a spot had unexpectedly opened up.

That was two years ago. I've become a much better piano player since then, but Amber is no longer around to hear me play.

"Nothing turns me on more than pianist fingers," she used to say, and for a while, at least, she seemed to be speaking the truth.

"Fine," I say to Jill. "But only because Charlotte is always so nice to me."

"I told you. That's because she has the hots for you." Jill swings her legs over to the other side. "Now move over."

I wouldn't call it flirting, these presumptuous words we exchange. It's just the way we've come to interact with each other. I was shocked the first time Jill said something to me I considered untoward—during our first lesson together, when she alluded to the various benefits of possessing long, strong fingers—but I soon learned it's all part of her liberal, free-thinking teaching methods.

Jill is not your typical piano teacher. Her posture is regal and could imply her being stern, but when she smiles, and the skin around her eyes crinkles, I always only see warmth. It's not the first time I've been invited to hers and Charlotte's living room either. A cozy den with pictures of Charlotte, her body all sinew and muscle, at the height of her career, flanked by one single picture of Jill playing at Carnegie Hall. Together, they make a striking silver-haired couple.

Jill positions her fingers where mine were earlier, and delivers a deeply emotional, slightly show-off-y rendition of "Für Elise".

As always, I'm enthralled by the swift grace of her fingers on the keys. By the sweeping, wide way with which they lift and land.

When she's finished, while I'm still catching my breath, she turns to me, a bit of a smile on her face, and says, "That's how it's done, Ruby. At your service."

Ostentatiously, I clap for her, and she gives me a tiny bow.

"Come on," she gets up from the bench. "Your lesson's over for today. But don't come back here until you've prac-ticed that into perfection." She straightens the crisp white blouse she always—always—wears for teaching. "I'll pay you back the five minutes you have left of your class today with a glass of truly exceptional gin."

"Hey, I'm not complaining." I always think that just being around Jill Banks, just being near her and breathing the same air she does, already makes me a better pianist.

She heads to the door of the practice room and holds it open for me. I grab my affairs and quickly follow her, after which she switches off the light and closes the door behind us.

"Char," Jill shouts as soon as we've climbed the stairs. "I hope you're decent because I've brought a guest."

Instantly, Charlotte appears in the living room.

"Oh, what a treat. It's the lovely Ruby." She sends me a half-coy half-seductive smile.

"Told you," Jill says. "I'm sure Charlotte will make you feel very welcome while I fix us some drinks. Hendricks for you, babe?" Jill quickly kisses Charlotte on the cheek. I've heard them call each other babe before. It astounded me then, and it still does now.

"Come on, dear." While Jill's teaching methods definitely have a flirty edge, it's not the same kind of boisterous, out-in-the-open style of flirting Charlotte applies. When Jill injects some innuendo in what she says, my mind—apart, perhaps, from that very first time—doesn't even go there. When Charlotte, like now, invades my personal space, and her perfume wafts up my nostrils, the vibe is totally different. She puts a hand on the small of my back and coaxes me toward the couch. I don't object. Quite the contrary. I never was one to reject the obvious admiration of another lady, and certainly not of a class act like Charlotte. Also, given the emotional state I'm in, I more than welcome the lavish attention bestowed on me.

"I take it you still need cheering up?" Amber dumped me on a Friday night and, after I called Jill to cancel my weekly

Saturday afternoon class, she sussed me out and told me to come over anyway. I sat sobbing in this very couch for hours, trying to make sense of it all.

"Please don't tell me there are plenty more fish in the sea." I say it with a half-smile pulling at my lips. What if, one day, I decide to flirt back? The thought flits through my brain the way a neon sign pulses. On. Off. On. Off.

"Well, it depends what you're looking for, Ruby, really." Charlotte slings one leg over the other. She was always tall for a ballerina, but it never impacted her grace. She's dressed in hip-hugging jeans and a loose shirt and still manages to ooze elegance. "If you're looking to take your mind off things, I'm sure I can help."

I give a chuckle. "Oh yeah?" I challenge. "And how would you do that?"

Charlotte hitches up her eyebrows, visibly surprised by my come back. I'm usually much more demure. Perhaps I am starting to get over Amber. "Well, you know, Jill and I are here for you, of course." She tilts her head to the left a fraction, baring the still taut muscles of her neck. "In more ways than one."

"But what does that mean, Charlotte?" I play along. "Can you be a bit more specific, please?"

She sinks her teeth into her bottom lip. "I can if you let me." She shuffles closer, and lets her hand hover over my knee. We both eye it simultaneously, as though it's a foreign object that may well decide our future.

When I find her gaze again, apparently the look in my eyes is enough encouragement for her. Slowly, her hand lands on my knee. Just then, Jill walks in carrying a tray with three glasses.

Charlotte doesn't retract her hand. It stays there as we both watch how Jill deposits the tray and stands taking in the scene in silence for a moment.

"Well," Jill says, in her teacher voice. "Glad we've gotten that far."

I don't consider myself particularly naive, but I didn't really see that one coming. The atmosphere is quickly changing from playful to charged.

When Charlotte shifts her body to take reception of the gin and tonic her partner is holding out to her, her hand slips off my knee, but is quickly replaced by her other.

"Thanks, babe," she says, exchanging a knowing glance with Jill.

As I take my drink from Jill, Charlotte's hand still firmly planted on my knee—even gripping a bit now—as a clear declaration of intent, I wonder if I should address this or just go with the flow.

Jill sits down in the one-seater on the other side of the coffee table. At least I've spent enough time with her to know she won't give me a straight answer.

"I told Ruby we could help her forget about her nasty break-up for a while," Charlotte says to Jill, while digging her nails further into my jeans.

"And what does Ruby have to say about that?" Jill eyes me with those pale grey-blue eyes of hers—a stare that shoots right through me.

"Ruby is still here," I say, referring to myself in the third person in a ridiculous manner. "So I guess she's willing to give it a shot."

Perhaps I can't use the pronoun 'I' because I need to distance myself from the person speaking those words. Yet, I have no desire to question my motives for being here. The past four months, all I've done is process. Tore my personality apart, listing the many flaws that drove Amber away. Looked deep into my soul and wondered who I was now, without her. But I'm still Ruby Cliff. Web designer and piano enthusiast. More life weary than before. And, perhaps for a while, more careful about romance, but this situation is as far removed from romance as can be.

And yes, I'm looking for a good time. For that moment of pure oblivion, where nothing else exists but my body in tune with my mind. I also quite like what I see in front of and next to me. Jill and Charlotte may be significantly older than me, but I'm not someone who needs to look past a laughter line to see a beauty that once was. I see it as it is right in front of me. They're both beautiful because of the life they've lived already. Their amassed experience, inherent wisdom, and the sly, sexy intelligence with which they play me, arouse me much more than a smooth patch of skin ever can.

"As long as it doesn't jeopardize my piano lessons," I say, to lighten the mood a little.

Jill shakes her head. "It's time we put some new life in those fingers of yours, Ruby. Surely they have other talents than producing code and melodies."

My attention is drawn to Jill's fingers now. Oh, what those dexterous digits could do to me. This isn't even about Amber—she's just a pretext now. This is about that sudden drum of excitement in my blood. That pulse of lust I lost months before Amber left. I know Charlotte and Jill have been together for more than twenty-five years. The dreaded bedroom drought must have come knocking on their door once or twice during that time. But this is no time to ask that question. Besides, the passion between them now fills the room. They wouldn't be propositioning me—and I wouldn't be so receptive to it—if it weren't.

All this talk of fingers while Charlotte's nails dig ever deeper into my knee. I clearly feel them through the thick fabric of my jeans. She's making the effort, and it's working.

In response, I sip from my gin. It's very smooth, and the tonic is not overpowering like when you drink it at an ordinary bar.

"Hm," I say, and, instantly, Charlotte's hand travels upward.

"I guarantee you'll play better," Jill pauses for effect, "after."

Charlotte drains half of her glass and bends over to put it on the coffee table and then, both hands free, turns to me. "Jill knows her stuff, Ruby. You can trust her."

I look into Charlotte's dark brown eyes. Did she instigate this? Did she start the conversation with her partner that led to this moment? Do they do this often? I have many questions, but they all get pushed to the back of my mind as soon as Charlotte slants her torso toward me and finds that delicate patch of skin just below my earlobe with her lips. Between them, they have a century of experience. The possibility that my mind is about to be blown increases the pulse between my legs.

"Let's take this into the bedroom," Jill says. "Much more comfortable."

"Best do what she says," Charlotte whispers in my ear. Perhaps it was Jill's idea after all. She releases her grip on me and pushes herself out of the couch, extending her hand.

"Come on, Ruby." Charlotte's voice has dipped into a lower register already.

Eagerly, I take her hand and get up. Only half an hour ago I was taking my regular weekly piano lesson. Now I'm being led into the bedroom by two women. Earlier, when I rang the bell to this house, my head was filled to the brim with Amber and who the complication in her life was. Now she's barely still a blip on my radar.

Charlotte is in front of me and Jill behind me. They're both close enough for me to sense their body heat. A blush creeps up my neck, and even more so when I feel two fingers there, gripping me tightly. Instinctively, I turn my face toward Jill.

"Before I kiss you, know this. If, at any time, for whatever reason, you want this to stop, say so. This needs to be fun for everyone. You are not a prize for us, Ruby. We want to make you feel good." Jill's words are delivered with such passion and assurance that they connect with something in my gut. I never realized, until that moment, how much I've wanted to kiss her.

"Understood?" Jill is adamant that I reply.

"Yes." I nod vigorously. Charlotte curls her fingers around my hand more tightly.

"Good." Jill's bedroom voice doesn't differ that much from her classroom voice, yet there's a subtle, but surprising difference. In the bedroom, her tone is much more insistent.

She leans in. Her lips are painted the lightest of off-red. Almost the natural color of lips, but not quite, giving the impression that, under every circumstance, she's willing to make the effort. As our mouths connect, Charlotte moves in behind me, pressing her body into mine. They seem so attuned to one another—seem to know exactly what they're doing.

When Jill's tongue enters my mouth, a crash of lust thunders through my flesh. Behind me, Charlotte's hands travel up my sides. A thick, slow pulse takes over my heartbeat. Already, I can feel myself transforming. Not having my attention focused on one person makes everything feel different. More physical, perhaps, but also more intense. Not as emotional as when making love to my girlfriend, and, maybe, requiring a higher level of abandon.

But to be in the center of this, to be standing between Jill and Charlotte, one of them kissing me, pulling me close with those strong fingers of hers, while the other pushes her ex-ballerina's body into my back, effortlessly takes me to that higher plain of letting go. I always thought I would be too self-conscious, too caught up in questions such as 'does she not mind that I caress her wife there?' When Amber briefly touched on the topic of a threesome once, I didn't speak to her for the rest of the day, so put off was I by the thought of another woman's hands on *my* lover.

When my piano teacher and I break for air, her partner starts hoisting up my sweater. Her breath comes quickly, and I can feel it meeting the skin of my neck in hot, short gusts. As Jill puts her hands over Charlotte's, and they lift up my sweater together, the intimacy of that moment sends a fresh burst of lust into my bloodstream. I lift my arms above my head and, seconds later, I stand between them in my bra.

Jill takes the time to run a finger over the edge of my bra cups, making my skin break out in goosebumps. Charlotte is already unfastening the clasp behind me and soon Jill's fingers dip down as my bra slips off me. Somehow, in that moment, it still feels inappropriate to make my own move toward the buttons of Jill's blouse. There's two of them and one of me, and they are very much in charge. State of undress included.

While Jill looks at my naked chest with an appreciative grin on her lips, she starts undoing the buttons of her blouse. Underneath, she wears a pale blue bra, and her skin is frail and white, like the thinnest of porcelain. From behind me I hear more rustling sounds, indicating that Jill and I are not the only ones getting naked.

Before I know it, a pair of pert nipples presses into the flesh of my back and, from behind, a hand comes for the button of my jeans. Charlotte opens it and then leaves Jill in charge of disposing of my trousers. And then, I stand there in just my panties. If I had known, I would have worn something a bit more exotic than this red pair of well-worn boy briefs, but then again, I don't suspect it still matters a whole lot this late in the game.

Jill slants her head though, as if pondering my choice of underwear.

"Very retro," she says, in that commanding voice of hers.

Behind me, I feel hands on my ass, cupping my cheeks over the fabric of my briefs.

Jill starts getting rid of her own trousers and, boldly, takes off her underwear in the process.

I gasp for air as she stands before me in all her glory. Although there's a new vulnerability about her, stripped of that starched white blouse I always see her in, she still comes across as utterly confident and strong. It's the mixture of the two—the frailness and the power emanating from her—that makes me catch my breath.

There's nothing more alluring than a woman who isn't afraid to show herself like that. No qualms, just desire glinting in her eyes. Desire for me.

The hands on my bum travel upward and fingers hook under the waistband of my knickers. Jill watches me as Charlotte tugs down my panties, and we stand in front of each other, both of us naked.

I have no idea when exactly Charlotte disposed of her garments, but she must be an expert, because the next thing I know, she glues her naked body against the back of mine.

"Come on." Jill reaches for my hand and pulls me toward the bed.

Before I can move, I feel Charlotte's teeth scrape gently against the back of my neck. I'm eager to see her naked. Eager to see what I've already felt against me.

Charlotte gently pushes me and a few seconds later, I'm on my knees on the bed. When Charlotte slides into my field of vision, I can't take my eyes off her wiry, thin body. She has a Wikipedia page stating her date of birth. I checked it when I first started taking lessons with Jill. But whatever that number says, it's not what I see with my very own eyes today.

Her muscles flex under her skin as she comes for me on the bed. She displays a different kind of eagerness than Jill. More to the point. Less time for foreplay. She grabs me by the back of the neck, her nipples connecting with my own, and kisses me while pushing me down. It's clear where Charlotte Carpenter wants me. On my back, for her. And Jill.

Charlotte lets herself half-fall on top of me as I surrender to the pillows beneath me, and to her touch. Jill clearly wasn't lying when she said Charlotte had the hots for me.

Her hands are in my hair and her knee is already driving itself between my legs as she appears to lose control for an instant. But then, she pulls back, gazes into my eyes, and lets herself slip off me, flanking my left side.

"You're so hot," she whispers as a few of her fingers travel from my collarbone to my nipple. She traces a wide circle around it, making it reach up as if under the spell of an upward-tugging force field. To my right, I feel Jill move in, her body glueing itself to me.

And there I lay, in between them, blood racing in my veins, my body exposed to them. Jill mirrors Charlotte's movements with her own hand, and repeats the process on my other nipple. I glare at their fingers while they caress me. Over my breasts their hands find each other and their fingers interlace. Charlotte lifts Jill's hand from my rib cage and brings two of her fingers to her mouth. I watch how she sucks in Jill's fingers, deep and with lush smacking sounds, then lets them drop from her lips to push the hand down to my crotch.

Oh jesus. Those fingers. There.

"Spread your legs," Charlotte says, her voice a throaty groan. With her own free hand, she tugs at my upper thigh a little, just to be sure I've understood. But how could I possibly misunderstand? "Jill is going to fuck you first," she says, "and then I will join her."

What does she mean? I'm confused. But confusion soon makes way for obliterating excitement as I feel Jill's fingers in my pubes, then traveling lower, skating through the wetness that has already accumulated there.

"She's so wet," she says to Charlotte and the fact that she doesn't address me—almost takes me out of the equation— sends a fresh rush of lust tumbling through my flesh.

"Fuck her," Charlotte replies, and then Jill does.

Her fingers easily find my slick opening, and she slides two of them inside of me. Watching Charlotte watch her adds to my arousal and my muscles tremble as Jill goes deep with those pianist fingers of hers. I feel it in every cell of my body when she starts stroking me inside and I wish I could see what Jill and Charlotte are seeing. Their glance on me instantly takes me to a place I haven't visited for the longest time. That moment of tipping into a different kind of consciousness, where the body takes over. Although what they're doing to me is as much a mind game as anything.

When Jill looks away from my pussy and her eyes find mine—those kind, warm eyes—I feel her warmth traveling through me. There's something else on display in her glance. A tender recklessness, an echo of the abandon she sometimes displays in class, when she plays me a tune.

I watch Jill watch me and, as I do, I see how Charlotte watches Jill. She takes in her face and her fingers and what they're doing to me, and her expression changes in the process. There's pure need in her eyes now, and something devilish as well. When Jill briefly looks away from me, I see something pass between them. Their connection is what turns me on the most. To be witness to what they have together while Jill pistons her fingers inside of me turns my insides into molten lava. Underneath my skin, it's all heat and starbursts and lust jittering through me. I'm about to lose it already.

But then, they both turn their attention to what's going on between my legs again—oh how I wish I could just catch a glimpse of Jill's fingers disappearing between my thick, swollen lips—and Charlotte brings a hand between my thighs as well.

Make the change quick, I think, because my muscles are contracted to the maximum already; they're ready to let go, ready to surrender. But maybe that's what the change of hands is all about. Stall. Draw it out for me. Maybe I should have told them that I have no issue coming multiple times, that there's no need to delay my climax. But it's not really a topic one works easily into conversation.

But Jill's fingers stay inside of me. There's no breach of contact between fingers and cunt. Not for a split second. Still, I'm spread wider, the rim of my pussy opening more for them. I see both of their arms move, as though in unison and engaging in the same action.

Charlotte has a finger inside of me as well. They're both fucking me simultaneously. That's what she meant earlier. As soon as this realization registers, I can't hold back. It's too much. The sight of them. The thought of their hands touching down there. Of their joint effort to make me feel good. Of being invited into this act of intimacy between them.

"She's coming," I hear Charlotte say, and it's exactly those two words that send me over the edge. Just like that, I topple over. The walls of my pussy clenching hard around their fingers, intensifying the sensation of having them both inside of me.

It's Jill's eyes I find when I climax. Those kind, knowing eyes with all that boundless understanding in them. This too, she understood.

A wave of something hot and unstoppable washes over me. It bounces back between the spot where I feel their fingers the most, and every extremity of my body. I've only been in bed with them ten minutes and already they've given me an earth-shattering orgasm. If this was foreplay, I wonder what will be next.

"Oh jesus," I moan, when I fall back on to the mattress, my body relaxing as I feel their fingers retreat.

"We thought we'd take the edge off, Ruby," Charlotte, definitely the more talkative of the two in this setting, says when she crashes down next to me.

I shake my head, a big smile plastered on my lips. "Jesus christ," I mutter, staring into her face. Her eyes have gone darker, although there's a lightness in her grin. A bit of smugness as well, which I, again, don't fail to find highly arousing. The orgasm has temporarily exhausted me, but just looking at Charlotte's lean body fires me up quickly again. I trace a finger along her belly, and am surprised by how hard the flesh is that I meet there.

A surprise that seems to register with her as she says, "Yoga and Pilates, Ruby. All I need."

"Not all." Jill sits chuckling on my other side.

Charlotte looks up at Jill, then back to me. "She's right. The juice of a threesome virgin has also been known to keep me in excellent shape."

"Hey. How do you know I'm new at this?" I ask, my finger trailing upward, finding her nipple.

"Oh please." Charlotte shoots me a wink that feels more like a tug at my clit, the way it darts through me with red hot speed.

"Ruby." Jill's voice has gone all serious. "Do you mind if I tie your hands to the bed?"

"What?" My eyes go wide. Jill bends over to the night stand and produces a scarf from one of its drawers. It's bright red and looks soft as silk.

I can't say I didn't have other things in mind at this point

—like delving my tongue between my piano teacher's thighs —but this is not my show.

"Time for you to watch," Charlotte says and holds out her hand to Jill, who passes her the scarf.

"I don't mind," I say, loud enough for Jill to acknowledge I mean it.

"I knew you wouldn't." Charlotte is such a smart ass. Doesn't mean she's wrong, though. "You can watch, but you can't touch," she says as she lets the edge of the scarf slide along my body. "Bring your hands up and make sure you're comfortable." She drags the scarf all the way up to my neck, letting it skate along my nipples.

I lift my arms and grip my hands around the railing of the bed.

"Good girl," Charlotte says, and I already feel the fabric tightening around my wrists. She ties me up with a secure knot and then sits back to admire her work.

"Show time," she says, but doesn't move for a few seconds. I lay there, on display for them, my blood beating in hot pulses for them—but I remain untouched.

"You've felt them," Jill says, "but I know you would also like to see what my fingers can do." Her words alone are enough to send a jolt of electricity up my spine. Involuntarily, I stare at her fingers. Already, I want them inside of me again.

Charlotte, who has suddenly gained the ability to read my mind, says, "You're going to have to wait for those a bit longer, honey. It's my turn now."

My pussy contracts at the mention of those words. Charlotte shuffles to the furthest side of the bed, and positions herself on her knees where I can clearly see her. Jill inches closer to her partner and, long fingers curling deliciously, pulls her toward her by the neck. They kiss passionately, not shy about showing tongue, eyes closed, fully engaged. I can see how their bodies respond, how their bellies glue closer together, how their patches of neatly trimmed pubic hair connect.

To have to watch them like that, tied up and completely unable to touch myself, is pure torture. My clit throbs wildly between my legs, and I feel wetness coat my inner thighs again. My skin feels as though it's on fire and I find myself tugging at my restraints, so great is the need to bring a finger to my clit.

But I can't. I can't look away either. This show on display for me is a once-in-a-lifetime opportunity, I know that much. I try to commit as much of it to memory as I can. I'm fully aware of the misery sex tapes can cause, but of this specific encounter, I wouldn't mind owning one. I wouldn't even mind looking at myself—wouldn't mind seeing their fingers disappear into my pussy.

Jill's hands wander down now, making Charlotte moan already. She tilts her head back and Jill nips at her neck, her lips traveling lower as well. I can see her trace a circle around Charlotte's clit as she wraps her lips around one of her nipples. I strain my neck so as not to miss any details of this performance, although I know it's much more than a performance. If I was touched earlier by their intimacy and their invitation to witness it, I'm floored now by what they're doing for me. They're giving me their most private selves, showing themselves at the height of abandon.

Jill shifts her body away from Charlotte's a bit, and I know she does it for me. She wants me to see. She wants me to see how her fingers work—the way they did on me earlier. She breaks contact even more and pins her eyes on me while parting Charlotte's swollen lips.

Did you get a good look? Her glance seems to ask of me, but all I can do is lie there swallowing the lust out of my throat.

The sexual energy in the room is going through the roof. My clit is trembling as though it's being touched by an expert hand. I'm so incredibly aroused by what I see that I think I might just come hands-free. And then, the tips of two of Jill's fingers slide in, through Charlotte's glistening wetness, into her cunt. Charlotte drapes an arm over Jill's shoulder, holding on, her legs spread wide, her knees pointed at me. And I know that, as long as I live, I will never forget this image.

Jill's fingers pick up pace quickly and as much as I want to take a look at Charlotte's face, at the ecstasy shown in the lines of it, I can't tear my gaze away from her cunt. When Jill adds another finger, opening up Charlotte wider, I can't take it anymore. It's as though I'm right there with Charlotte. On the verge. Ready to come again.

"Come for me, babe," Jill whispers in Charlotte's ear, but I hear it loud and clear too, and she might as well be saying the words to me.

The climax that rips through me isn't as powerful as the previous one, and it shocks me more than anything, but it's there in the tremor of my muscles, in the halting of my breath. I see the sensations of my own body reflected in Charlotte's as she tips her head back even further, her fingertips now digging deep into the flesh of Jill's shoulder, as she comes for Jill—and me.

"Oh fuck," Charlotte groans as her head bobs back. She pulls Jill in for a kiss and I believe that, this time, she does forget I'm there. Jill brings the hand she fucked Charlotte to climax with to her partner's chest and spreads the sticky juices over her nipples.

When they break from the kiss, Jill looks from me to Charlotte. "We have one frisky student on our hands here, babe."

Charlotte's eyes connect with mine, and they've gone

even darker. There's nothing but lust brimming in the shadows there. She may have just come, but she's nowhere near ready yet. I watch how her gaze meanders from my bound wrists to my still-pulsing pussy lips.

"Did she come too?" Charlotte asks without taking her eyes off me.

All I can do is lie there, mute, biting my bottom lip.

"Oh yes," Jill says. How can she be so certain?

"That wasn't the plan." Charlotte paints a wicked smirk on her face. "But let me see what I can do." With that she lets her behind fall onto the back of her legs, and brings her face between my legs. Meanwhile, Jill gets up from the bed and opens the drawer from which she retrieved the scarf earlier. I want to look, but I can feel Charlotte's breath warming up my clit—as if it wasn't hot enough yet.

I don't need to turn my head though, because Jill presents me with a black dildo, and the sight of it sets my blood on fire again. If I could, I'd pinch myself, to make sure I wasn't in the middle of a feverish, endless sex dream.

While Charlotte's tongue connects with my clit, her hands firmly buried underneath my behind, Jill trails the tip of the dildo over my nipples. My clit, although untouched before, is sensitive from the two orgasms I've had already, so I flinch under the touch of Charlotte's tongue. She's gentle though, not applying too much pressure, following the cues my body gives her. She licks me with light, broad strokes, giving me time to recover, while making clear that I shouldn't take too much time either.

My eyes, meanwhile, are glued to Jill's fingers wrapped around the silicone cock. The tip of it is still busy with my nipples and the impersonal touch of the silicone sends a different kind of shiver up my spine. I grip the railing tightly, holding on as Charlotte's tongue strokes are getting more insistent. The pulse in my groin picks up, deepening, moving through me with slow, thick beats, spreading warmth underneath my skin. I can't remember a time in my life when I was more aroused than in this moment. When I add up what came before, the vision of Jill's fingers fucking Charlotte still fresh in my mind, and what I can logically conclude will happen within the next few minutes, heat takes me again. It's all I am. Rising heat and bated breath. My flesh but an instrument of lust, a place where their and my intentions meet.

I wish I could step out of my body and see myself, tied up and completely at their mercy. The fact that I'm subject to their will is not solely due to my restraints though. It's much more present in how they play me so expertly, so in tandem, like a well-practiced double act. I may be a threesome virgin, but it's obvious that Jill and Charlotte are anything but.

Charlotte trills her tongue over my clit before dragging it all the way down, across my opening, lapping up the copious juices that have gathered there. She does this with so much gusto I'm beginning to believe what she said earlier is more than a joke. Maybe my wetness does procure her with something undefined but exhilarating.

Jill's eyes are on me when she presents the dildo to me in a different fashion. She holds it in front of my lips suggestively.

"Open up," she says and her voice has nothing teacher-like in it anymore. This is the voice of a woman who is ready to completely surrender to lust as well.

I part my lips and let her slide in the dildo. She doesn't push it deep, but I'm fully aware that I have to trust her. I have no hands at my disposal to defend myself. I twirl my tongue around the end, coating it in saliva. Jill slips and slides the toy in and out of my mouth, and I see her pupils dilate a bit. This is turning her on more than anything that came before. The abandon in her eyes excites me beyond belief in return as well.

Between my legs, Charlotte's tongue now seems to have become a part of my body, the way she's been welding it to my most intimate, sensitive organ. She twirls and drags it up and down my split and I can feel it building inside of me again. Charlotte can feel it too, because she stops the motion of her tongue and breaks contact, looking up at me. Her chin glistens and her eyes are wild.

"Don't you dare come again," she says, but there's no threat in her tone, only amusement and, perhaps, a little bit of pride.

Jill slips the dildo from my lips, leaving my mouth agape. "Move over, babe," she says to Charlotte, as she shuffles to the end of the bed. Charlotte shifts a bit, but not too much, so her mouth still has access to my clit when she bends over. I can't see what's going on down there, my vision is blocked by the back of Charlotte's head as she slants over me from above, which makes the sensation increase even more. She parts my swollen lips, exposing my clit to the air, while I feel the head of the dildo prod at my entrance.

"Fuck her with it," I hear Charlotte say. "Give it to her."

With one hand on my inner thigh for balance, Jill slides the dildo inside of me slowly. A totally different sensation than being fucked by their joint fingers earlier. The dildo isn't huge, but big enough to fill me, to touch my flesh from the inside in a way that makes me give in even more. My clit is only exposed to air, which is a good thing, because Charlotte hasn't given me permission to come yet. The instant she touches it again, I'm gone.

"Gorgeous," Charlotte says, and although I wish—again —that I could see it for myself, the sensation of being filled to the brim, of being taken by them once again, is too over-whelming to have many other wishes left. Jill fucks me slowly but deep, spreading me wide, opening me up for them. My pelvis starts getting lost in a repeated upward motion, meeting Jill's thrusts. How can I ever take a piano lesson with her again now that she has seen me like this?

Jill adjusts her rhythm to the bucking of my pelvis and, together, we gradually increase the pace.

"Oh god," I moan, as the dildo starts hitting that sweet spot inside of me, and it's as though Charlotte was waiting for me to give her that sign—that first throaty, involuntary moan. My outer lips still parted by her fingers, my clitoris still on full display, she leans over and coats it with her warm mouth. I just feel liquid heat covering my distended nub, while Jill is now pistoning the dildo in and out of me at great speed. But then Charlotte lets her tongue come down as well and, quickly, everything turns to black in my mind. My pelvis takes on a life of its own, creating a wave that both Jill and Charlotte expertly ride. One fucking me, the other licking.

Behind my closed eyelids, I see darkness interspersed with rainbows and stars, colors colliding as my pleasure mounts. It all adds up to this. Charlotte was right. If she hadn't 'taken the edge off' earlier, I wouldn't have reached these heights now. This climax would have arrived too quickly, robbing me of the exquisite build-up and anticipation that intensifies this very moment of starburst and ultimate surrender.

I whimper out some moans as my muscles go rigid then limp, as I come down from that peak they drove me to. Two pairs of hands did that to me. I can barely feel my wrists and I happily ignore that short jolt of pain in my shoulders as I crash onto the bed, my body so spent I could possibly fall asleep within seconds. But I'm also fired up, ready for another round—but not with me as the centre of attention this time.

Jill slides the dildo out of me and chucks it behind her on the bed. My cunt feels as open and wide as she left my mouth earlier. My clit is so tender, anything coming within a radius of an inch to it, would make me recoil. Charlotte shuffles to the top of the bed, a big grin on her face.

"Let's get this off you," she says, and motions toward the scarf. It did its job brilliantly, immobilizing me in moments where, if I had not been restrained, I surely would have fought for control. To have it taken away added to the shattering climax I just had, of which the aftershocks still tremble in my muscles now.

As soon as she has loosened the scarf, Charlotte grabs my wrists and takes them in her hands, massaging them and printing kisses where the fabric left dents in my skin.

"God, you're a treat," she says, as she finds my eyes. "Now let's show Jill what you're made of." Music to my ears, I think, chuckling inwardly at the musical reference. "She doesn't like to be tied up, but we can make do without." From that moment on, from the instant Charlotte gives me permission to go to town on Jill, I only have one wish. I want to spread her legs and lick her pussy. Through all the hours we've sat together behind the piano, the thought has never crossed my mind, but something has been unleashed in me, and now it's all I want.

I glance at Jill, who has given me so much pleasure already.

"Come here," she says, and beckons me with those fingers of her.

"I'm going to sit this one out and watch," Charlotte says with anything but a resigned expression on her face. On her knees, she crawls to the end of the bed, rests her back against the railing there, legs spread. "I'm ready for my show." She exchanges a quick glance with Jill who shoots her a wink. I'm flabbergasted by this pair, by their devilish horniness and the ease with which they play, by how they've invited me into their bed without any other agenda but pure pleasure.

Do I have Jill all to myself? Is my short-lived dream about to come true? I think so, because Jill's hand is in my hair already, dragging me close. Before she kisses me, she looks into my eyes, her glance full of kind lust. "Let's show her," she says, before pressing her lips to mine.

And then I kiss my piano teacher. This woman who has seen me walk through her door almost every Saturday afternoon for the past two years, and I'm hit by a sudden wave of understanding. By being the person that she is—calm, witty, forthright and warm—she has helped me through my break-up more than anything. Jill is no longer just my teacher, she's my friend. Lines have been blurred and I'm ready to blur some more.

Perhaps, in the back of my brain, I'd like to submit to her again—over and over again—but Charlotte instructed me to show Jill what I'm made of. Four months ago, after Amber had just left, I was made of pain and self-pity. An obliterating hurt originating in the pit of my stomach, preventing me from eating, sleeping and other basic functions. Now, many piano lessons later, I'm made of a brand new resilience, a new awareness of love in the world, and liquefied lust replaces the blood in my veins.

I start pushing Jill down onto the bed. When we break from our kiss I stare into her eyes, into the bottomless warmth of them, and just by looking at her, I can feel some of her kindness spread through my flesh.

"Fuck me, Ruby," she says then, a hitch in her voice, and her desire for me lifts me up even higher. My body may be worn out from the three climaxes they've given me, but Jill's demand is all I need to refuel my energy. If Jill Banks asks me to fuck her, I will.

I glue my body to hers, finding her lips again, and kiss her with renewed abandon. I'm aware of Charlotte's eyes on my back, and the raggedness of her breath. I wish I could position Jill so I could glance at Charlotte from time to time, but I don't want to obstruct Charlotte's field of vision.

My lips slide down to Jill's long neck, tracing a wet path downward, occasionally nipping at her skin with my teeth. I taste saltiness on her skin, and when I reach the exquisite hollow between her collarbones, I get a distant whiff of perfume. That scent I know so well because it always lingers in her classroom. The smell that hits my nose as soon as I walk in. I take in her small breasts before tasting them. They're pale and delicate, demanding a sort of respect I'm not used to giving. With Amber, it was all youthful energy in bed, taking what we could get, until that faded, and we were unable to replace it with something else.

I approach Jill's nipples with unprecedented reverence, savoring the moment they meet my lips. I don't go too easy on them though, and clamp down with my teeth briefly, gauging her reaction.

"Harder," she says, her voice shot to pieces, connecting instantly with my throbbing clit.

I sink my teeth into the same nipple again, pulling it upward a little, while gazing into her eyes.

"Fuck, Ruby," Jill says on an exhale of breath and shakes her head a little. She's so close already, which is no wonder after all the pleasure she's given me and Charlotte. She's had her fingers inside of me and Charlotte, and has fucked me with a dildo. Yet, I can't imagine the blood in her veins running more riot than mine. I feel as though, for tonight only, my body has been blessed with an unlimited supply of sexual stamina and renewable energy. Lust crackles underneath my skin again, and I can't imagine the fire in my belly diminishing after what I'm about to do next.

I move on to Jill's other nipple and repeat the process of biting down on it, of alternatively taking it between my teeth and letting my tongue lap over it. Jill's breasts couldn't be more different from Amber's—the only ones I touched during the five years of our relationship. Amber's were high and big—always in the way, she claimed—while I can take most of Jill's breast all the way into my mouth.

"Come on, Ruby," she spurs me on, starting to push me down by the shoulders. I'd already gathered she has a bossy streak in bed, and it's rearing its head again now. Although it could also be sheer impatience. My poor, tortured piano teacher has waited long enough.

I also want to give her what she gave me, although I can never return the words of wisdom she bestowed upon me when I was deep in despair. But I can give her this.

I kiss my way down to her belly button, but don't dwell. So drawn am I by the trimmed triangle of her pubic hair, that I let my lips and tongue travel straight down. I pause a moment to take in the scene, to etch this image into my memory: me between my piano teacher's legs.

"Fuck her," Charlotte's voice whispers from behind me. "I need to see." I'd been so wrapped up in planting kisses over Jill's body I had momentarily forgotten about Charlotte.

I move to the side a little so Charlotte has a better view of her partner's soaking wet pussy. And then I move in. I bend at the waist and let my lips come down on Jill's swollen cunt, pressing a light, introductory kiss to them first.

"Ah jesus, don't tease me, just lick me already," Jill groans. I guess, when engaging in threesomes, you have to be articulate about your wishes. Another lesson learned.

I drag my tongue all the way up her crease, delving the tip between her lips slightly, ending with a teasing flick at her clit. Jill's body tenses the instant I touch her blood-shot clit.

"Go easy on her clit," Charlotte instructs. "Make her wait for it." If the circumstances were any different, I imagine I wouldn't be too pleased with getting instructions at a delicate time like this, but to hear Charlotte say the word 'clit' and having it refer to Jill's sparks another riot in my blood. I take my tongue away from her clit and focus its efforts on her lips, digging in between, teasing her opening. In between sucking her lips into my mouth and drawing wide, careful circles around Jill's clit, I start to change my position, sitting up a bit more so I can get a clear look at her face. I need to see her eyes for the next part.

I move my face away from Jill's pussy, her juices clinging to my chin and nose, and lock my gaze on hers.

"Oh god yes," Charlotte groans behind me. I can't see her but I can clearly hear the sucking sound her fingers produce while fretting over her clit. I can't look away from Jill now, though. Her eyes look as though they're on the verge of shedding tears.

While staring into her face, I let two fingers run along the length of her pussy. Once, twice, until it feels as though her pussy is literally sucking them inside. Then, I enter her. Slowly, like she did to me before. Her heat envelops my fingers, her moist flesh wrapping itself around them.

"Oh Ruby," Jill says, while shoving herself onto my fingers with wild, thrusting gestures. God, she's such a top. Charlotte appears to be quite the dominant type in the bedroom as well. They must have interesting fights for top. I'd kill to see them in action—not like before when they made me watch, but to be an invisible fly on the wall while they share true intimacy.

"Oh damn," Charlotte says behind me. "Oooh." Her prolonged moan makes me believe she came, and I can hardly hold that against her. I may have my eyes on Jill's face, but from the corner of them I see my fingers disappear into Jill's cunt and the sight makes my own pussy contract around nothing.

I'm on my knees, fucking Jill, my ass sticking out behind me. After Charlotte's orgasmic series of groans, I'm so enthralled by Jill's face, the way her eyes remain locked on mine—as though she needs that connection—while I stroke her deep on the inside. I'm so caught up that I don't register Charlotte coming up behind me until she starts caressing my behind.

"Go on. Don't stop," she whispers, but it's hard to keep focus with her hand already delving south of my crack.

A bit thrown off guard, I decide it's a good time to add another finger. The sound that withdrawing my two fingers makes, instigates another contraction of my pussy walls, but the fireworks in my flesh really stir when I focus on Jill's cunt as I push three fingers inside of her. She's wide for me, eager, and ready. Between my own legs, Charlotte's finger is finding my clit.

"You'd better not come before Jill does," she commands, and makes her finger retreat. Instead, it finds my entrance, and probes gently through my wetness there. The nails of Charlotte's other hand dig deep into the flesh of my behind, and don't fail to add to my growing arousal. But, I've had 'my edge taken off'. I want to focus all my attention on Jill now.

I push deep with my fingers, and she pushes back. Judging from her body language, she'd appreciate a quickening of the pace, so I drive up my rhythm, filling her with all I have—not just three fingers, but all my intentions and energy behind them. Then, I bend down again, lifting my ass higher into the air and, no doubt, giving Charlotte better access. I feel a rush of hot air travel over my pussy lips: Charlotte's breath.

I'm trapped between licking and fucking Jill, and Charlotte's lips hovering over my own pussy lips. Charlotte's ask of a few moments ago suddenly seems like a very tall order. I try to block out what she's doing to me outside of my field of vision, the sensation of her fingers and, now, also her tongue, enhanced by not being able to see what's going on.

But it has to be all Jill for me now, who is twitching and writhing underneath me. I need to rise above my own need to climax again, and put hers first. Jill digs her nails deep into my shoulders—while Charlotte's still do the same to my left butt cheek. I'm caught between them, caught in this frenzy of lust and approaching orgasms. Jill's moans grow more high-pitched, uttered as if expressing disbelief. I can't quite believe it either. And then, she surrenders. Jill Banks gives herself up to me. My vision is impaired because I have my mouth on her clit and my nose in her pubes, but I can clearly feel it in the clench and release of her pussy around my fingers, and the trembling of her lower belly against my forehead.

"Oh good god," she says, releasing her hold on my shoulder, and I revel in this moment of satisfaction, of having her come at my fingers, of her smell all over my face, and the slight cramp in my neck and her fingers in my hair now, caressing gently, lovingly. And the thought of those fingers, and the ones entering me from behind now, at an angle I'm not used to, takes the last ounce of resistance I still had and destroys it. My cheek on Jill's belly, her hands in my hair, the smell of her pussy in my nose, I come, again. Liquid heat travels through me, reaching every extremity of my body, flooding it with dizzying warmth.

This orgasm feels as though it has been demanded of me by the curl of Charlotte's strong fingers, and therefore, it's different. It feels more communal as well because it followed Jill's climax so closely, and Charlotte had her own party only moments before. This scene, me doubled over on Jill, Charlotte's fingers now slowing down inside of me, feels like the ultimate climax of our threesome.

When Charlotte's fingers have left me and she gives me a

playful tap on my right butt cheek, I let my lower body sink down, my cheek still glued to Jill's belly. I'm shattered, and I want to lie like that forever. I don't know what else they have in store, but whatever it is, it will have to wait.

"I think she's done now," I hear Jill say to Charlotte over my head. She pats the back of my head lightly, but I couldn't move if I wanted to. Jill trails her fingers over my spine lightly, making my flesh break out in goosebumps. I don't want to leave this room. I don't want it to be over, although I have nothing left to give.

"Hey, Ruby," Jill's voice is all warmth again. "Why don't you take a little nap, sweetie. Come here." She tugs lightly at my upper arm, hoisting me up.

I let her drag me up, only helping a little, my muscles too spent to cooperate much, until my face is almost level with hers.

"Mission accomplished?" she asks, a crooked grin on her lips.

Slowly, I nod, blinking my eyes shut. I nestle my head in the crook of her shoulder and enjoy the cozy heat of her body, the after burn, and the hot glow somersaulting through my flesh. Any thought I have of Amber now is instantly eclipsed by the memories I made today. By Jill and Charlotte's tenderness and openness. By their invitation and the avalanche of physical thrills they have unleashed. I drift off with nothing but sweet, exhilarating thoughts occupying my mind. For the first time since entering their bedroom, I allow my body to relax and replenish, my face pressed heavily into the safety of Jill's body.

———

I wake up I don't know how much later. I have no indication of the time, but I quickly realize where I am because, when I open my eyes, I instantly recognize Jill's pianist fingers stroking the skin of my belly. I'm no longer lodged on top of her, and she smells clean and fresh.

"Hey," she says, her voice soft.

Instinctively, I look around for any signs of Charlotte.

"She's in the shower." Jill can now also read my mind, but I guess it's an easy assumption to make. "This was a sticky and wet affair." Her smile is mesmerizing, her eyes glowing with kindness. A tingle manifests itself in the pit of my stomach. It's another beginning of lust, for sure, but it's not all. It's more.

"I should probably join her." I'm fully aware of the musky smell of sex still emanating from my body, starkly contrasting with Jill's clean, flowery scent.

"I'm sure she'd like that." There's no urgency in Jill's voice and she doesn't stop tracing her fingertip over my skin, meandering a bit higher up now, toward the curve of my breast.

Because of Jill's determined calmness, I don't move. I just lie there, her eyes roaming across my naked flesh, her finger dangerously close to my left nipple. And I feel that tug again, that desire for her fingers inside of me. As of now, every time she plays something for me on the piano, I will always think of her fingers inside of me.

And I realize that, during this late afternoon, I've fallen in love with her a little bit. The seeds of infatuation sit at the ready in the pit of my stomach. It's her infinite kindness that does it more than anything. And how she looked at me while her fingers spread Charlotte so wide. Because Jill is what connects me to Charlotte—that one degree of separation—I can't be as equally fond of Charlotte. Jill made this happen. She enquired about Amber, invited me up, and let Charlotte do her thing.

But this is not a jealous sort of infatuation. I have no

desire to come between them, or to nestle myself into their bed on a more permanent basis—although I wouldn't be entirely opposed to the occasional repeat performance. I revel in this feeling shooting through me, in the knowledge that this wasn't mere carnal pleasure. It's friendship taken to a higher, kinkier level. Not just fingers in openings and endless climaxes.

Because of that, because of how I can luxuriate in Jill's solo touch guilt-free, I let my body surrender once more as her finger draws smaller circles around my nipple, until it reaches all the way up, and my pussy lips throb again as though they haven't been touched in ages. I revel when her lips close around my nipple, the furthest one removed from her, so I feel her own nipples pressing into my side.

"Would you like me to fuck you again, Ruby?" Jill says after she lets go. She doesn't wait for my reply. Her finger is already on its way down, making my skin tremble again, and my pussy wet for her. I can hardly protest. All I want is her fingers inside of me again. And, perhaps, if I'm so lucky, her tongue on my clit.

Her tongue is still busy with my nipple. She laps gently. This moment is far removed from the earlier frenzy we found ourselves in. It's more sedate, perhaps more thoughtful.

"Wait for me," I hear Charlotte say. Totally naked, she leans against the bedroom's doorframe, no obvious signs of envy displayed on her face.

Jill looks up at her partner. "We have all night. I don't think Ruby has any other plans."

I don't? I guess not. What better way to spend a Saturday night. I also like how Jill makes the decision for me.

Charlotte stands there in silence for a few seconds, nods, and straightens her posture. "Okay," she says, sends us both a quick wink, and leaves me alone in their bedroom with Jill. Such enlightenment, I think, but not for long, because Jill is tugging at my nipple with her teeth now, and I'm starting to be completely beside myself again. Now that it's just Jill and me in bed, the level of intimacy changes immediately.

"Is this"—I hesitate—"is this okay?"

"It's fine, Ruby." The look Jill sends me leaves no room for doubt. "As long as this is still what you want." She tilts her head a little bit, but there's nothing quizzical about her expression. She knows how much I want this by now. She bends over and finds my ear. "Charlotte and I have been together a long time. We have arrangements in place. Nothing for you to worry about."

For a split second, the thought of Amber fucking someone in our bedroom while I casually lounge in the living room runs through my head. I can only catalogue it as complete madness, but perhaps this sort of freedom, this setting of looser boundaries, comes with age. And anyway, Amber is gone. Jill is very much present, her finger trailing across my belly again, her breath on my neck.

"Do you mind if I turn you over?" she whispers, and I need to take a moment to let her question sink in. Because of how gently she roused me from sleep with the slow caress of her finger, I believed this was going to be a slow, luxurious fuck, Jill gazing deep into my eyes. But apparently she has other things in mind.

"Not if you kiss me first," I reply, my blood beating heavily in my veins. And then she does. She stares into my eyes for a few seconds, and it's that look that will make me do anything for her, even surrender my backside—not something I have done often, or very successfully, in the past.

When she kisses me, my body relaxes. If she'd asked me earlier, I'm not sure I would have declined the offer, but I would never have been so quick to agree. In the space of a few hours, Jill and Charlotte have given me so much pleasure, have reset a part of my brain in dire need of it—have given me a clean slate. In this bed, under her touch, I'm re-inventing myself as well. If my piano teacher wants my ass, she'll get it.

Jill's tongue probes deep into my mouth—a lover's kiss. And in that moment, I am her lover. There's only the two of us in that bed and in that room. Charlotte's spirit lingers, but she's not part of this. Although, in a faraway corner of my brain, the thought rises that, if she were watching, it would probably arouse me even more. Maybe next time.

"Turn around," Jill commands when we break from the kiss. She uses her stern teacher's voice, the one I've hardly ever encountered. She tried it in our first few classes a couple of times, but I could always tell she wasn't that kind of teacher. The kindness in her eyes always betrayed her, and I soon found out she was just gauging me, trying to find out to which teaching methods I responded best.

I'm responding now, though. She unglues her body from mine to give me room to flip onto my belly.

"Relax." Jill's hand is in my hair, then on my still-straining neck. I take the hint and let my head fall into the pillow—is it hers or Charlotte's? "Good girl." Her words heat up my blood even more, but it might also be the lone finger Jill traces down my spine. She paints an intricate pattern on my butt cheeks, raising all the hairs she comes across in her finger's journey. Then, her finger slides down my side, her entire hand nestling itself underneath my belly, while I feel her lips touch down on my bum. She kisses me gently first, but soon her teeth scrape along my skin, and the fingers under my belly make an upward motion.

"Lift up your ass," she says, and to hear her say 'ass' is like hearing a magical word that sparks more fireworks in my blood. I drag myself to my knees, my face still buried in the pillow, my position reminiscent of the one just before I fell asleep, when I was licking Jill and Charlotte stroked me to

In the Mood for Love

another orgasm. The memory of being caught between them fires me up more.

If only I could see, I think, how Jill is shuffling to that spot behind me, positioning herself between my spread legs, my ass—and the rest of me—ready for her. But I only hear, and I can only imagine, and feel, of course, how her lips reconnect with the delicate skin there. She kisses a path down while two of her fingers rub along my cunt. My lips are swollen from all the action earlier, but the nap has done me a world of good. Fresh energy fizzes through my flesh as Jill's kisses travel inward, her tongue flicking along the upmost tip of my crack.

Oh jesus, she's really going to do this. Her tongue is hot and wet as it dips lower and traces a moist line along my hole. I react instantly, my muscles contracting, my clit throbbing wildly. Jill pushes her fingers up to my clit, encircling it, revving up my engine. Her tongue doesn't wait, as she laps it up and down my crack, spreading moisture and blissful heat. Then, the tip of her tongue enters me, and a bolt of lightning races up my spine. My thighs are starting to tremble, my body losing control already. The circles around my clit tighten and I feel the tip of her thumb on my pussy lips, slipping through the wetness there. Jill is all over me, and all I see is darkness, until the stars unveil themselves again. Her tongue is stiff as it penetrates deeper and sets something off in me that has remained untouched until now.

On the back of my eyelids, I can clearly see Jill's long fingers and how they zone in on my swollen clit, her strong thumb rubbing my entrance, adding tension there. Her tongue flicks in and out and I want to come, but I also want more. I'm lubricated enough everywhere. I want one of her fingers.

I slide onto my forehead, looking at her between my legs. She senses my shift in posture and finds my eyes.

"More," I whimper.

All she gives me is a slight nod but I know she has understood. Before I let my head sink into the pillow again, I catch a last glimpse of Jill's fingers and in the pit of my stomach, something turns to liquid. First, Jill slides two fingers into my pulsing cunt, deep and high, just like Charlotte did earlier. But Jill's fingers feel different, perhaps because I've observed them flying over the piano keys so many times, they hold a different meaning, bring a higher degree of intimacy. But nothing is more intimate than the finger of her other hand pressing at my other entrance, negotiating access. The tip slips in easily, but spreads me wide nonetheless. It's an altogether new sensation, but I got what I wanted. Jill's fingers everywhere. She finds a slow rhythm, in between my pussy lips, gently, ever so slowly, out from between my butt cheeks.

Deep inside of me, the fire ignites. The sparks have been glowing for a while, but now the flames are alive. I feel them burn through my stomach, licking at my flesh.

My poor clit feels neglected though—and, again, I wish Charlotte were here—so I shift on one shoulder, finding my balance again, and bring one hand between my legs. I only need to touch a finger to my clit a few times to send myself over that edge again, my mind free-falling, my body controlled by Jill's fingers—like a puppet controlled by strings. Another climax roars through me, this one quite different from the previous ones because of the interconnectedness of most of my erogenous zones, and Jill's finger probing into my most intimate opening.

White heat in my brain and a new awareness in my body. Stars exploding on the back of my eyelids and the image of Jill's fingers imprinted in my brain forever. Spent, I sink down, pushing Jill's fingers out of my cunt and ass in the process. What the hell did she do to me? I wonder, as our bodies lose contact for a brief moment.

Then, she glues herself to me, her lips finding my ears again. "You're magnificent, Ruby," she whispers. "Jesus christ."

We lie there for a while, Jill on top of me—how fitting—until my breath comes slower again, and the last tingle has disappeared from my muscles. Will she tell Charlotte about this later? Will they get aroused at the memory of me in their bed? Am I really spending the night here?

When Jill slips off me and I turn around, I feel like a different person. As though what she just did to me, altered me somehow. When I leave Mrs. Banks's house later, it will not be as the same Ruby Cliff who entered. Not because of Amber, and how they wanted to take my mind off her, but because of what they've given me. Because of how, when they let me step into their bed, they allowed me to step out of my tortured, one-track mind. On top of that, the passion I shared with these two women, tells me—once and for all—that what Amber and I had between us, was never enough to go the distance. Not if my piano teacher can make me feel like this.

"Are you okay?" Jill asks, caressing my cheek with the back of her hand.

"I'm not sure okay is the right word." I giggle and shuffle closer toward her because I can't get enough of her warmth. "But definitely much better than before our lesson."

"I'm glad." I can't believe this same, sweet person, just minutes ago, claimed my ass. On the pillow, she brings her face closer to mine and presses a kiss on the tip of my nose. "How about a nice hot bath?"

"That would be lovely." As appealing as it sounds, I want to stay in bed with Jill a little while longer though. But then there's a knock on the open door and Charlotte appears in the doorframe. How long has she been there? Was she watching all this time? The thought sparks up a fresh pulse in my clit, reverberating all the way to my rear entrance.

"Hey." Charlotte's voice is soft. "Shall I order pizza?"

The question sounds so extremely silly to me in that moment, I burst out into a chuckle. This sudden display of domesticity sucks a good part of the sexual energy straight from the room. Will we all be hunched around the TV in thirty minutes, munching pepperoni?

"What do you say?" Jill looks at me expectantly. I can leave at any moment, but I get the distinct impression neither one of them wants me to.

"Pepperoni for me, please."

"I ran you a bath, Ruby," Charlotte says, leaving me with the idea that this is a well-practiced Saturday evening routine of theirs. "Hop in now and the pizza will be here when you come out."

I can't help but shake my head. "Thanks," I say, as I start to slip out of their bed.

A few instants later, when I sink into the spacious bath tub, my exhausted muscles thankful to be enveloped by hot water, I'm still chuckling at the strangeness of the situation, but mostly, I'm just happy because of how good I feel inside and, wordlessly, I thank Amber for urging me to take piano lessons.

About the Author

Harper Bliss is the author of the *Pink Bean* series, the *High Rise* series, the *French Kissing* serial and many other lesbian romance titles. She is the co-founder of Ladylit Publishing and My LesFic weekly newsletter.

Harper loves hearing from readers and you can reach her at the email address below.

www.harperbliss.com
harper@harperbliss.com

Made in the USA
Monee, IL
22 September 2022

14431427R00142